Other Titles by Susie Bright

Three the Hard Way (editor)

*Mommy's Little Girl: Susie Bright on Sex, Motherhood,
Porn, and Cherry Pie*

The Best American Erotica, 1993–2005 (editor)

How to Write a Dirty Story

Full Exposure

The Sexual State of the Union

Nothing But the Girl (with Jill Posener)

Herotica, 1, 2, and 3 (editor)

Sexwise

Susie Bright's Sexual Reality: A Virtual Sex World Reader

Susie Sexpert's Lesbian Sex World

http://www.susiebright.com

The
Best
American
Erotica
2005

EDITED BY

Susie Bright

A TOUCHSTONE BOOK
Published by Simon & Schuster
New York   London   Toronto   Sydney

Touchstone
Rockefeller Center
1230 Avenue of the Americas
New York, NY 10020

Manufactured in the United States of America

ISBN 0-7394-5106-5

Dedicated
to
Ronald Sukenik
1932–2004

CONTENTS

INTRODUCTION

Every February, I have a crisis of erotic conscience. This is the month in which I must cull the best of my favorite erotic stories from the past year. I make cruel decisions among dozens of perfectly excellent candidates I've savored the past year. I sit there, reading the pages again and again, asking myself, "Is *this* the story that no one will be able to resist?"

In the middle of this year's meltdown, I got a phone call from a saucy men's magazine. It's one of those newer "laddie" mags you hear so much about, where girl celebrities in their underwear taunt readers but never quite take it all off. As a child raised on *Playboy*'s centerfold formula, I am mystified. But laddie magazines don't offer that kind of third act. They specialize in an endless loop of second-base titillation.

The reporter began his interview with me by asking how young men can employ erotic lit as foreplay, to lubricate their female dates and get them to acquiesce to intercourse. "Isn't it easier to just pop in an X-rated DVD?" he asked.

I imagined my hand inserting a disk into a woman's vagina and then programming her to my will.

I didn't tell him that. I actually had no idea what he was talking about. I've never been on a date where my beau seduced me with a porn movie. I'm usually as interested in having sex as my companion, so no tricks are necessary.

Of course, I'm a pretty odd porn watcher. In my heyday, I watched more XXX videos than any other woman I know, and most men for that matter—because I reviewed them professionally. I'm in the X-Rated Hall of Fame for porn criticism. I would load up dozens of tapes in front of my screen and watch them as fast as possible with my reporter's notebook in my lap. Sure, I had to relent and masturbate every once in a while, but even that was at breakneck speed. I was completely alone, except for occasional friends who would walk in and make fun of me. They left when they realized my dedication to deadlines was devout. I wouldn't have dreamed of subjecting a lover to my bizarre work ethic.

Clearly, in order to answer this laddie interview, I needed to speak to some ordinary young people to see if porn DVDs and videos are part of their customary foreplay. Furthermore, what was so "easy" about it?

My first informant was rather cynical. "If 'easy' is what you're interested in," he said, "then you ply your date with liquor until she's helpless. It doesn't matter whether you screen Barney or Paris Hilton. Your only task is to maintain enough alertness to take advantage of her."

"That's raping, not dating," I protested.

He cut me off: "What do you think these stupid magazines are promoting? They're incapable of considering women's sexual self-interest."

Harsh? Yes, but I heard similar disdain from others. The most innocent response I got was from a college student who said that it was just another twist on 1950s drive-in nostalgia. "When you go out with someone, you like an excuse to get it on. You watch a dumb movie, and you start getting busy, 'cause neither of you cares what's on the screen."

It's the American Puritan Reflex again: two people who pretend they're not going to have sex even though that's exactly where they're heading. It's not easy, it's contrived.

It certainly is more challenging to tell your date an erotic story, or hand her some provocative pages to read. *Sharing is caring,* but where to begin? The hard part is that such disclosures are so intimate—you're showing her something private. It's the beginning of mutual rapport, and it's also taking a risk, the ultimate aphrodisiac.

I did talk to some couples who watch porn for fun . . . but they weren't exactly the laddie crowd. These were longtime couples way past the dating phase. Porn night is part of their familiarity.

The most popular porn-watching *group* activity I found occurs at parties. Someone throws a kegger and keeps a sleazy porn tape on the tube for the whole night's activities—the more ridiculous the better. Fat actors, inflatable sheep, corncobs. Everyone who walks into the room mocks the action. Bets are placed on the prospects of the most unattractive characters. Butt blemishes are tallied.

But the producers of the disdained video should not feel insulted. Unconsciously, they're still working their magic. Even though all the partygoers make fun of the movie, they're influenced by the images of naked sex. They don't want to be fat or pimply, but they do want to be hard and wet. People who went to such parties confided to me that even though the videos were stupid, they later found themselves in compromising positions, even if they were all alone.

Would this have happened if they had gone to an erotic reading/performance or had sat down to write their own erotic stories? Sure, it would've been even *more* exciting, but such acts require active intentions!

The thing about watching TV is that it's more inert than reading or any kind of self-expression. You walk by it and you get a whiff of whatever. If you're tense or unhappy with sex, if you wish you were dating someone else, the porno will make you even more uncomfortable. The TV isn't a good enough magician to change that . . . its hallmark is its passivity. It sits there and grates on whatever is already under your skin. In its ultimate mind-vise trick, it puts you to sleep.

How would I advise an enterprising young man to "use" a book like *Best American Erotica*? Well, first he'd have to read it, which might be an adventure in itself. He might read it over and over, savoring each illumination. This is all before the "date" even happens.

The night of the big event, he should put the book out in some prominent place, perhaps in the doorway, so the young woman is forced to trip on it. What could be more simple?

The idea is to make her yelp "You're reading this???" or at least to raise an eyebrow. A better response might be, "Ohmigod, can I borrow it?" So much can be gained by these first impressions.

At this point, the boy could feign surprise or humor: "Can you believe it? My mom left this in my car!" Or he could be the suave playboy who whispers, "This is one of my favorites."

Whatever the case, his date will be wondering what it is he likes so much in this provocative edition. Now it's his move to uncloak himself. He must flip to the opening page of a story and make a nonchalant comment: "This is pretty good."

The spell has now been cast. If the young woman replies, "Oh, no, the next story was so much hotter," then what can I say? You really have hit Easy Street.

Susie Bright
February 2005

Slippy for President

Steve Almond

My first year in college was a total dud, sexually. What was I doing? Nada. Hanging out with a bunch of jerk-offs in Foss Seven. The big event of the week was "someone rented *Deep Throat.*" Friday night and these guys are marching up and down the hall, screaming, "Who wants to watch *Deep Throat*?" All that bad skin. Those rotten teeth. How did I end up on that hall? I have no idea.

But something miraculous happened my second year: I moved into a house off-campus with a group of beautiful blonds, three of them seniors. A total fluke. One of them, Dana, had split up with her boyfriend over the summer and he'd withdrawn from the house and the slot had gone to the next loser on the list, which was me. These girls were so far out of my league. I'd catch sight of one of them coming out of the shower, maybe Liza, with the towel tucked tight around her chest and shampoo fumes coming off her, and I'd run the other direction.

As it turned out, this was just the right move. Of the twenty thousand male undergrads at our school, at least five thousand of them hit on one of the blonds—and that's not counting grad students or professors. So the last thing they wanted at home was some mouth breather like me panting all over them. But, see, what the blonds missed was this more friendly male energy. Before long, they started joking with me, kind of hassling me to get a rise. One Sunday, the three of them went to an afternoon concert, some kind of reggae thing, and they got blitzed. I could hear them downstairs, laughing, yelling. When I came down I found Dana and Julie hunched over a bucket of fried chicken. They had wide bands of grease around their mouths.

"Hey, Josh," Julie said. "You hungry? You want a drumstick?"

Dana said, "Come on now, Jules. You know Joshie Boy doesn't eat dark meat."

Then, from the bathroom, Liza screamed, "Does that include pussy, Joshie? Is pussy considered dark meat?"

"Cool it," Julie said. "You're going to scare the poor boy."

"Oh please," Dana said. "Are you kidding me? A little pussy-eating fool like Joshie? He ain't scared. He just acts scared."

She got up from the table and walked over to me and kind of pinned me against the wall with her long body. She put her face in front of mine. I could smell the fried chicken on her breath. "You're not scared of a little pussy," she said. "Are you?"

It was one of those moments, I could tell, where I'd either prove interesting as a plaything or sink into the background.

So I straightened up into this soldier pose and said, "Not a little one, sergeant!" Kind of barked it out, actually.

They liked that.

So after that they called me Sergeant Little Pussy, which was shortened to SLP, then Slip, then Slippery Rock, then just Slippy. That's what they called me, these crazy chicks. Slippy. *Where's Slippy? Slippy, did you eat my fucking grapes?* They kind of adopted me. Or actually, it was more like I was a cat or something. Because part of what they dug about me was the fact that I didn't suck up to them, sort of kept to myself, went off to my lab classes (I was a biochem major), and hung with my lab buddies and did my chores, nothing more. I don't know how I pulled this off. Honestly, it was like God was acting through me.

I came into the kitchen one day to get a Coke. Dana and Liza were in the TV room, with a box of mint chocolate chip ice cream on the table between them. It was the strangest thing. These girls ate like horses, but they never gained a pound.

Liza looked up and started laughing. "Ask him, Dana."

"Ask me what?"

"We made a little wager," Dana said.

"What kind of wager?"

"Liza thinks you're a square."

"Shut up!" Liza said. "That's not what I said."

"She thinks you've never gotten high," Dana said.

"That's the bet?"

"I didn't say you were a square, Slippy."

Liza sunk her spoon into the box of ice cream and flung it at Dana. A gob hit her cheek. Dana tilted her head and let the ice cream slide toward her mouth. She stuck out her tongue and licked the ice cream off her cheek. It was clear the two of them were stoned.

"So the question is whether I've gotten high?"

"Right," Liza said. "Smoked pot."

"Marijuana," Dana said. "Cannabis."

"I don't think that's any of your business," I said.

"See," Liza shouted. "I told you."

I went to the fridge and grabbed my Coke.

"He didn't say no. He said it was none of our business."

"That means no."

"Why do you assume Slippy is such a wussball? The guy's playing you. Can't you see that, Liza? Slippy's one clever son of a bitch." She looked at me and grinned. The green spot on her cheek was glowing a little. "Answer the question, Slippy. I don't want to have to use my interrogation tactics."

"I've got to hit the books," I said. "Big exam tomorrow."

I hurried out of the room and up the stairs. Down below, I could hear them squealing with indignation.

The truth was so utterly boring, compared to their fantasies. But here's the thing: I did know something about drugs. I knew about the chemistry of them, how they affected the nervous system and the brain. I'd studied this stuff. Also, as it happened, I was the lab assistant to a grad student named Mike Sherman, whose unofficial specialty was synthetic amphetamines.

Sherman was a first-class head case. There were rumors that

he often went several days without sleeping. He tramped around the lab with bloodshot eyes and a wrinkled orange windbreaker, and his body gave off a peculiar, sulfurous odor. At the same time, he could be a very persuasive guy.

One night I was working late at the lab, grinding through a set of spectral refractions, when Sherman came by my cubicle.

"Take five, Igor," he said. (He called me Igor.) "I want to show you something."

He led me back to his office and took a tiny key out of his pocket and reached into his desk drawer and pulled out a small lockbox. He opened the lockbox and took out a bottle of pills and poured a few onto the desk between us. They were about the size of aspirin, bright yellow, with smiley faces on both sides.

"Any idea what these are?" Sherman said.

I shook my head.

He held a pill up to his mouth and pretended it was speaking. "Hello, Igor! My name is methylenedioxymethamphetamine, or MDMA. But my friends call me Ecstasy!"

"Okay," I said.

"Don't you want to know about me? Is that a yes? Okay. I'm what's known as an empathogen-entactogen, not to be confused with your standard-issue amphetamine, Igor. No no no. I activate the neurotransmitter serotonin, along with various components of the midbrain dopamine systems. I have the power to make little boys like you very very happy. Would you like to be happy, Igor?"

"I'm pretty happy as it is," I said.

Sherman set the pill down and gazed at me. "No, you're not," he said. "You're a pathetic little ball of inhibitions. This is not your fault. It's just the natural human response to stress. You flinch. You put on the body armor. We can put an end to all that, though. Six hours of bliss, yours for the taking."

"No, thanks," I said.

"Now now, Igor. I'm really a little disappointed. I'm offering you quite an opportunity here." Sherman reached down and grabbed a bottle of water from the mini-fridge beneath his desk.

He picked up a pill and gulped it down. "You shouldn't be afraid of Dr. Sherman, Igor. He wouldn't prescribe anything that might hurt you. You think about this, Igor. Just between us, okay? Think about it."

I should mention that everything I'm telling you about took place in 1981. Ecstasy wasn't even a blip on the radar yet. It would take another couple of years before the college dealers got hold of the stuff. The only reason Sherman knew about the drug was he'd done some lab work at UC Berkeley, where he met a biochemist named Alexander Shulgin, who later became the high priest of the Ecstasy movement.

An hour later, Sherman stopped by my cubicle. He smiled at me. "Listen," he said gently, "I didn't mean to give you the hard sell before, okay? It's just, you know, sometimes I worry about you a little bit. You work hard. I respect that. But you've got to learn to enjoy yourself, too. You deserve that. Seriously. You're an amazing kid, Igor. You should let the rest of the world see that." Sherman set his hand on my shoulder and smiled at me again. It sounds a little creepy as I describe it, but it really was the sweetest moment. Sherman had this expression on his face like he was a monk floating around in a giant pool of nirvana.

He tossed a tiny Ziploc bag onto my desk. "Just in case," he said.

Now, you probably think I hatched some clever plan. But it didn't even occur to me to tell the blonds about Sherman's gift. I stuffed the Ziploc into my pocket and brought it home and forgot all about it.

A couple of weeks later, I came home from a late night at the lab. It was a Friday, so I expected the blonds to be out at one of their A-list parties, breaking hearts in unison. But all three of them were in the kitchen. They were dressed for bed, ratty pajamas, T-shirts and sweats, clothing that should have made them look frumpy but that somehow made them look even hotter. I was too tired to look at all that hotness. I just wanted to go to my room and whack off and go to sleep. I waved to Liza. " 'Night," I said.

Halfway up the stairs, Dana called out, "Oh, Slippy!"

"Yeah?"

"Could you come here for a second?"

I came back down. "What's up?"

All three of them were looking at me.

"You remember when Jules and me were arguing about your drug use?"

"Not really."

"And you wouldn't answer us?"

I shrugged.

Dana reached into the pocket of her pajamas and drew out the Ziploc bag. "Slippy," she said. "You've been a naughty, naughty boy."

"Where'd you get—"

"Now now, Slippy. Don't get upset. Nobody's been snooping. You gave Liza your pants for the wash. She just checked the pockets."

"Family habit," Liza said. "My brothers were always leaving interesting things in their pockets."

"Interesting," Julie said. She took the Ziploc from Dana and removed one of the pills. "What are these?"

"Sugar pills," I said.

"Sugar pills?" Dana said. She took one and handed one to Liza. "So we could just take these and they wouldn't have any effect, right?" Dana put the pill between her front teeth and held it there.

"Listen," I said. "Okay, listen. Those are something I've been working on, a thing for the lab. They're not sugar pills. Please don't take that, Dana. That's medicine, a blood pressure medicine. It's very strong stuff and it has serious side effects."

"That must be why they put a smiley face on them," Julie said. "Because of all the serious side effects."

Dana removed the pill. "Are you going to tell us the truth, Slippy?"

The blonds were sitting there in all their unattainable beauty and I was suddenly very tired. I thought about Sherman. I'd seen him take a pill and he'd been just fine. Better than fine, actually.

The blonds were each holding a tiny pill in their palms, waiting for me to say something. So I told them everything Sherman had told me.

Dana looked at Julie and Liza. Then she put the pill on her tongue and took a swig of Diet Sprite and the other two, after a second, followed suit. Down the hatch.

"You shouldn't have done that," I said. "This isn't a joke."

"You told us your friend was fine," Dana said.

"Yeah, but he's sort of like a professional drug taker."

She smiled. "Slippy, you need to lighten up."

"Seriously," Liza said. "Take a chill pill."

She got up. They all got up, all three of them. Liza handed me a pill and Julie got me a glass of water and Dana leaned in close to whisper in my ear. I could feel one of her boobs brush my arm. "Take that pill, Slippy. Or bad things will happen to your soul."

I took the pill.

"Now what?" Julie said.

"We wait," I said.

That's what we did. We went into the TV room and turned on the set and waited. After a few minutes Julie said, "I feel funny."

"What kind of funny?" I said.

"Like, queasy."

"Me too," Liza said.

I felt the same thing, something like motion sickness. And I was sweating. For a moment, it occurred to me that I was in big, big trouble. I'd just ingested a pill of unknown origin, given to me by a guy who considered Hunter S. Thompson his spiritual mentor. I had supplied the same pill to my gorgeous housemates, one of whom (Julie) was walking unsteadily toward the bathroom. What was that? Accidental manslaughter? Dana followed her. Liza glanced at me. "This friend of yours," she said. "He's a doctor, right?"

"Not really," I said.

"Shit," she said.

We both sat there, not saying anything. Then Liza got up and went to the bathroom. I sat and tried to focus on the TV. It was a talk show of some kind. The guest was an actress I didn't quite recognize. Her laugh sounded like a broken squeezebox. After a while, the actress left and a man in khaki shorts brought out a monkey.

I could hear the water in the bathroom being turned on and off. I went to check on Julie. I pushed the door open, but it took me a second to process what I was seeing. Julie was seated on the edge of the bathtub. She had taken off her sweatpants, so she was just in her panties. She was letting water run down her calves and across her feet. Dana was sitting on the toilet (the lid was down) and running her hands through Liza's hair. Liza was moaning with pleasure.

Dana turned to me. She was smiling and her eyes were closed. "Slippy," she said. "Oh, Slippy. This is very good medicine."

"I wanted to check on Julie," I said.

"Good," Julie said. "The water feels so nice."

I stood in the doorway, looking at the blonds, and suddenly the queasiness faded and everything gathered a bright intensity, the bodies of these girls, the sweet smell of them, the sound of the water and Liza's moaning. It was like my sensory receptors went into overdrive. At the same time, I felt this great weight lifted from my shoulders, which was basically the weight of the doubt I carried around with me all over the place. So I also felt very light, but not light-headed, more just an internal floaty sensation, like a gentle breeze rippling through my body.

"Come here," Julie said. "Feel this."

I went and sat next to her on the rim of the bathtub.

Julie reached down and took off my shoes and socks. She brought my feet under the spigot. "Wow," I said. Warm water washed over the skin of my feet and made them tingle. I stared at the water and at Julie's legs and then I was stroking Julie's legs, her smooth brown calves and the shiny skin behind her knees.

"Mmmmm," she said. "That feels good, Slippy."

"Your legs are so killer," I said. "They're, like, the perfect size."

"You should see her tits," Dana said.

"My tits," Julie said. "Yeah."

"Seriously," Dana said. "Those are some outstanding mammaries."

Julie smiled. She had these square, little teeth. "I like your tits, too."

"Big and bouncy," Dana said.

"I like my tits," Liza said, "even though they're kind of small. What do you think, Slippy?"

"I like breasts," I said. "I haven't felt that many of them, but they've always struck me as very comforting."

"That's so sweet," Dana said. She reached up and stroked my cheek.

"Boys love tits so much," Julie said. "I don't blame them. Breast-feeding and all that. But it really doesn't feel that good to have them touched. I mean, it's all right, better than nothing. But it's nothing like a good scalp massage."

"The scalp," Liza said. "God, yes."

"Would you like one?" I said to Julie.

She nodded.

I slipped my hands into her hair, which was very fine, and ran my fingertips over her skull. It was so much smaller than I'd thought, and covered with delicate bumps and knobs.

"Pull my hair a little," Julie murmured. "Not too much, just a little."

All this should have been very fucking weird. It should have been weird that we were all in the bathroom talking tits, that Julie was sitting on the rim of the tub in her panties, that I was softly yanking at her hair. But this was the miracle of Ecstasy. It had wiped away all our inhibitions and left us to pursue our natural affections.

"I want to lie down," Liza said. "On, like, a bed."

"Jules's bed," Dana said. "She has the best mattress."

So we tromped to her bedroom. I'd never been inside any of their bedrooms. It smelled so good I wanted to swoon, like some kind of fruity perfume, with maybe a little talc underneath. Julie had a queen-size bed and we all piled on and lay there stroking one another.

"This feels so amazing," Liza said. "Good work, Slippy."

"Slippy rules!" Dana said.

"Slippy for President," Julie said.

"Dana's the one," I said. "I was scared to take them." I flipped over so I could look at Dana. She had these big green eyes, cat's eyes, set kind of far apart, and a plump red mouth. "You're so brave, Dana. How do you do that?"

"Older brothers," she said. "They used to whale on me. But they also looked out for me. So maybe the combination of those two things, like, taking a beating but knowing I was protected, something sick like that. Plus, I was always chasing around after them. It makes you do crazy stuff just for the attention."

"Didn't you jump off your roof?" Julie said.

"It was the low part," Dana said, "over the garage. But it was still pretty fucking stupid. Broke my ankle. I've still got the scar." She pulled up her pajama pant leg and I ran my finger over the scar. Liza gave it a little kiss.

"I wish I was brave," I said.

"What are you afraid of?" Dana said.

"You name it. Loneliness. Failure. Girls."

"Oh, Slippy," Julie said, "that's so sad."

And it was sort of sad. But the thing about Ecstasy, it allows you to recognize the sadness of something without that heavy, blue feeling. It's more like a math problem, something you examine, hope to figure out.

"You shouldn't be afraid," Dana said. "I've been watching you, Slip. You've got empathy. It doesn't matter what you look like. That's just the way men think. Girls don't care so much about that crap. And they care less and less the older they get. What they want is a guy who listens, who connects emotionally. Chicks are going to dig your biscuit, Slip. Look at us. You've got three of the most desirable women in America eating out of your palm."

Julie crawled over and started kissing my neck, and Dana ran her hands through my hair. I reached out and felt something round, which was Liza's hip, and ran my hands along the smooth curve. There were all these smells and textures to absorb: perfume, deodorant, sweat, baby oil, silk pajamas, skin, tongues, breath. I wanted to freeze each moment, break it all down, Dana's fingers massaging my scalp, Julie's lips on my Adam's apple, my hands caressing Liza.

I know how all this sounds, like some kind of soft-core porn situation. But I wasn't that sexually excited. I mean, I was a little. But mostly I just wanted the sensual contact, like to communicate how much I liked these girls, how grateful I was for their kind of taking me in and paying attention to me.

"It's so nice to be touched," Liza said. "I swear, I could give up sex altogether if I found a guy who knew how to touch."

"I couldn't," Dana said. "I love it too much, the old in-and-out."

"That's because it's always a bit of a fight," Julie said.

"Maybe so. But I also just like how it feels to have a cock inside me."

"How does it feel?" I said.

"There's like this pressure, but a good pressure, against the walls inside, you know, and then there are these places, like hot spots, that feel so good when they get rubbed you want to jump out of your skin. And there's the rhythm of the thing, too. It's like you're dancing with someone, figuring out how to move your body with his. And hopefully there are other things going on, too. The guy should be touching you, kissing you, telling you things."

"They never get that," Julie said.

"Some of them do," Liza said. "But not many."

"You have to tell them," Dana said. It sounded as if she'd gone over this before. "You're responsible for your own orgasm, sisters."

"I do tell them," Julie said softly. "They just don't listen."

"It's true," I said. "We're not great at listening."

"You boys," Dana said. "Always in such a hurry." She reached for my crotch and roughed it up a little. "Just be patient. Follow the signs. Really, most girls know what they need."

"What do you mean, 'need'?" I said.

"Need. Need. Like, Liza needs a lot of pressure right on her clit, but only once she's excited enough."

"Correct," Liza said.

"Jules likes it when guys just sort of butterfly around. Full labial coverage. I'm partial to both." She paused. "But what gets me is if a guy touches my ass. I don't think I'd want to have anal sex just yet. But I like a guy who's not afraid to touch me there. And the skin in between, that little patch of skin between. It's so sensitive."

Julie lifted her head from my chest, where she'd laid it. She looked at me tenderly. "Slippy," she said, "you wouldn't tell anybody this stuff, would you? Like guys who might take it the wrong way."

Dana laughed. "Slippy knows, Jules. Come on, he's not some kind of frat pig."

"I would never." I was almost breathless with goodwill. "Really, you guys, you're like my pals. I mean, I know we just live in the same house, but I have so much admiration for all of you. There are some girls, like, really beautiful girls, who would look at a guy like me and just keep walking. But you guys are different. I mean, you've really been kind to me."

Julie was still looking at me. She had tears in her eyes. "You remind me of my little brother," she said.

"He doesn't want to hear that," Dana said. "He wants to hear us talk about sex."

"That's not true," I said.

"Cock sucking," Dana said. "Pro or con."

"Pro," Liza said. "Pro pro pro."

"It depends," Dana said. "Some of these guys, they've got no idea how to behave. They're pushing your head down, feeding you these lines."

"Then they don't tell you when they're going to come," Julie said.

"Just total scumbags," Dana said. She had a wicked grin on her face.

"How should men behave?" I said.

"Grateful," Liza said. "Extremely grateful. And here's a hint, Slippy: Make sure you go down on a girl. Act like you can't get enough of her stuff."

"And let the girl make the move," Dana said. "The whole turn-on for us is the chance to have a little control."

"How does it feel for the girl?" I said. "I've always wondered that."

"Go suck on a banána," Dana said. "And then imagine the banana can move on its own and that you can't let your teeth touch the banana and that you have some paw on your neck, forcing you to take bigger and bigger bites."

"For me," Julie said, "it's like sucking a giant jewel. It's just, like, this thing that men are so proud of, like their secret treasure."

"And you get to see it up close, all shiny and eager. The veins all defined. That part is a turn-on," Liza said. She swung around and my hand slipped around to her belly. I could feel her ribs, too, beneath the soft flesh. "I love sucking on balls, too. I know it's a little kooky. But they're so vulnerable in that little sac. And they never get much attention. It's like you're doing charity work down there."

All this talk should have made me absolutely out-of-my-mind horny. It was the kind of thing I'd fantasized about constantly. But now that I was actually here, in the midst of the blonds, I found myself snagged on the emotions of the thing.

Finally, Liza said she was hungry and Dana decided we should walk down to Chickee's, which was this all-night place where they served broasted chicken. Broasting was a special process where they breaded the pieces and steamed them at, like, a million degrees, the result being that the chicken was crispy on the outside and so totally moist on the inside that the juice ran down your arms when you took a bite. Holy God! That chicken! We ate it like we'd been starving, stuffed into a booth and gasping.

And then we walked home through wisps of early-morning fog. It was one of those March days when the first warm rains wake up the tar and the flowers go crazy. We couldn't get over how sweet the air smelled, how beautiful the sun looked rising over Hope Hill, how supremely cool it was just to be alive to appreciate these things.

When we got home, I remember that we listened to some music, Dead Can Dance, OMD, all that trippy ambient stuff. At one point, Dana whispered something to Liza and they grabbed Julie and pulled off her sweatshirt. It almost made me cry to see those breasts.

Then Dana unbuttoned her shirt and Liza took off her shirt, too, and Dana screamed, "Tit smother!" and all three of the blonds descended on me and slithered their boobs all over my face and chest. I didn't know what to do. There was simply too much boob to deal with. It's not a problem I ever thought I'd face. I had a nipple in my mouth and one in my eye and a third grazing the soft hairs of my armpit.

Later on, we'd make a big breakfast and sleep for the rest of the day. The blonds would eventually graduate and head off to conquer the world. I'd return to the grim precincts of my lab work. Mike Sherman would eventually get himself kicked out of school, allegedly for producing synthetic heroin. And Ecstasy itself, just a few years later, would become the scourge of the anti-drug zealots. At their behest, the dopes in the media would portray Ecstasy as some kind of zombie pill designed to anesthetize ravers. The beauty of the drug, the ways in which it connected people, would be lost.

But all that was still to come. The moment I'm talking about, the greatest single moment of my life, was still happening. The blonds were rubbing themselves on me, all that round warm flesh, and giggling and running their hands across my body. It was like having all the mothers in the world embracing me at once and loving me just for being me and there was no awkwardness afterwards, no shameful looking away, because, after all, we'd only been telling each other the truth.

View from the Fourteenth Floor

Greta Christina

"HUMILIATE ME"

If you've ever wanted to humiliate another woman, here's your chance. Bring what you need on our first date—if we click, I'll want to do it right away. One-night stands only.

Dana read the ad on Thursday. She masturbated furiously and then called the number. They made a date, and she spent most of Saturday making arrangements.

They met in a bar on Sunday evening. Dana arrived on time, and found Elizabeth already sitting in a corner booth. She was a blonde, with an expensive haircut, dressed in a crisp white blouse and a single strand of pearls. She already had a drink in front of her. Dana settled into the booth. "So how long have you lived in New York?" she asked.

"Six days," Elizabeth said. "Look. Here are my limits. I don't like extreme physical pain, but keep it reasonable and we'll be fine. Psychologically you can do almost anything. My safeword is *safeword*. And I mean it about the one-night stand. After tonight, we're done." She took a sip of her drink. "You?"

Dana bit her lip. Elizabeth's tone offended her, made her want to slap the woman down. She noticed her clit thumping, and wondered for a moment if she was being played, if the girl was pissing her off on purpose. She stared rudely at Elizabeth's tits, and decided it didn't matter. "Your limits are fine," she said. "And mine aren't relevant to you. Do you want to do it?"

Elizabeth looked at Dana like she was appraising china. Finally she gave a small nod. "Yes. Let's do it."

"Good," Dana said. "That's the last word I want to hear from you until . . . well, ever, I guess." She strode out the door, leaving her drink untouched, and whistled for a cab. Elizabeth followed, eyeing her suspiciously as they got into the taxi. "Lester Hotel," Dana told the cabbie. "The one in midtown." She stayed silent all the way to the hotel, where she led Elizabeth to the fourteenth floor and pulled a key from her pocket.

Elizabeth looked around as the door closed behind her. The room looked untouched, except for an armchair set at an odd angle in the dressing nook off the bedroom. The decor was elegant and unpretentious, with tall windows that took up most of the outside wall. Dana switched on all the lights, switched off the one in the dressing nook, settled into the armchair, and began to speak.

"Did you know that every week, dozens of telescopes are sold in the city of New York? Hundreds even, on a busy week. Interesting statistic. Nobody seriously thinks all those people are stargazing in Connecticut on weekends. Everyone knows exactly what all those New Yorkers are doing with all those telescopes. And yet everyone goes on with their lives, in front of their open windows, as if they actually had privacy.

"Open the curtains."

She could see Elizabeth flinch before she obeyed. Good, she thought. This could work.

"It's Sunday night," Dana continued, "so a lot of people are home. And bored, and looking for something to do. When I scoped out the room earlier, I estimated about five thousand windows with a direct view of this one. Probably about fifty have telescopes. More if you count binoculars. So I'm guessing we've got anywhere from ten to thirty people in the audience tonight. Maybe more.

"Now take off your blouse and wander around the room. Act like you're a normal human being who's just changing for dinner, but keep turning to face the window."

Elizabeth stopped in her tracks. She turned from the window and looked Dana in the face, dismayed, her arrogance slipping off like a discreet partygoer escaping a bad soiree.

"Don't look at me," Dana snapped. "Face the window again. Now." Elizabeth complied, her shoulders slumping, and Dana went on, calmer. "See, I placed this chair very carefully. I can see you, and your reflection in the window, but people outside probably can't see me. So don't look at me again. I don't want our audience to know I'm here. I want them to think you're doing this on your own.

"I was going to build this up nice and slow, give you some time to get used to it. But now I don't think I'm going to. Strip down to your bra and panties, and start doing jumping jacks."

This was good, Dana thought as she crossed her legs. She could see Elizabeth squeeze her eyes shut as she wriggled out of her skirt and stripped off her shoes and pantyhose; she could see the reflection of the woman's blushing face as she tentatively began to jump up and down. She could see Elizabeth's butt jiggling through her panties, her breasts bouncing in her white bra, like a jiggle girl in a music video. She cleared her throat.

"Right about now," she said, "your audience should be figuring out that something's up. They're realizing that you haven't just forgotten about the curtains. By now they know you're doing this on purpose.

"Open the bedside drawer."

Elizabeth complied. She looked inside and cringed, arrogant revulsion arguing on her face with shame and disgrace. Dana hadn't picked the toys to be tacky on purpose: She just hadn't wanted to mess with condoms and stuff, so she'd picked up a few cheap things she could throw away. But now the choice seemed serendipitous. Inspired, even. She loved the thought of making this arrogant bitch put these sleazy things into her body in full view of midtown Manhattan.

"So let's get started," she said. "Lay the toys out on the bed. Take off your bra and panties. Then lie on the bed with your cunt facing the window. Put the pillows under your head so people can see your face, and spread your legs."

She could see Elizabeth breathing hard. The woman was obeying, but she was doing it slowly, hesitantly, and Dana wasn't sure if she was genuinely scared or drawing things out on purpose. Either way was fine with Dana. She pressed her thighs together as she watched Elizabeth display her new toys and spread herself out.

"So we've shown them you're an exhibitionist," Dana said. "Now let's show them that you're a pervert. Put the ball gag in your mouth. Stick the buttplug in your asshole. And then spread your cunt lips apart with your fingers. Don't touch your clit. Not yet."

Elizabeth stared fiercely at the wall as she bit down on the pink rubber ball and fiddled behind her head to buckle the straps. She turned over to insert the buttplug, but Dana snapped her fingers. "No," she barked. "Stay on your back. I know it's awkward. That's what I want." She felt a warm glow in her stomach as she watched Elizabeth struggle, groping for her asshole with her feet in the air. She could see Elizabeth fighting to regain some dignity as she settled back into place; she could see that dignity slip away again as the girl remembered her instructions, put her fingers on her pussy lips, and slowly spread them apart. Dana paused for a moment to enjoy the view: the city lights, the wall of highrise windows shining in the night sky, with Elizabeth's debased reflection superimposed over it all. She let Elizabeth lie quietly for a minute, let her exposure sink in. Then she spoke again.

"I notice you keep your eyes away from the window. You keep focusing on something else, or else you close your eyes. So look out the window now. Think of the people watching you, and look them in the eye."

Dana waited patiently as Elizabeth squeezed her eyes shut, shuddered, and reluctantly turned to face her reflection. She caught Elizabeth's eye and saw her whimper; her pussy clenched, and she pressed on. "Now take the dildo in one hand," she said, "and the ruler in the other. Stick the dildo in your cunt and fuck yourself. Every few strokes, pull the dildo out and smack your pussy a few times with the ruler. Then do it all again. And keep your eyes on the people watching you.

"Here's the picture they're getting. They see a woman who goes into a hotel room and puts on a free sex show. They see a woman who opens her curtains, strips, jumps up and down to get their attention, then opens her legs, puts a gag in her mouth and a plug in her asshole, and spanks herself on the pussy while she fucks herself. All for them to see. And they're looking you in the eye. You can't hide from them. They know who you are."

The dildo was a squishy plastic one, a lurid pinky-tan with prominent veins. She could see Elizabeth cringe as she slid it into her visibly wet pussy; she watched her flinch as she pulled it out, gripped the ruler, and gave her clit a few hesitant smacks. It was all gone now, the arrogance, the composure, the sense of entitlement. She had stripped the woman down to a trashy slut giving a free sex show to strangers with nasty toys from a corner porn shop. Dana took a deep breath and delivered the final blow.

"I'm leaving now," she said. "I have another hotel room across the street, with my own telescope. I expect you to keep up the show for another hour. You can do any nasty degrading thing to yourself that you like, but keep the ball gag in, and keep your eyes on the window. If I don't like what I see, I'm coming back, and you won't be happy about that." She paused. "If I do like what I see, I won't be back. In an hour you can shut the curtain and do what you want. The room's paid up for the night. Checkout's at noon. It's been lovely."

Dana dropped the room key on the floor and left Elizabeth on the bed, violating herself, alarmed, shivering, near tears. She whistled quietly as she shut the door and rode the elevator to the lobby. She caught a cab in front of the hotel and told the driver to take her home.

The Ugly Cock Dance

Mary Gaitskill

Mitchell and Michelle were a good-looking, middle-aged couple who were getting hairy in the wrong places and going to fat. Michelle was approaching menopause, which meant she couldn't sleep, couldn't remember things, meant that her face broke out, that she was moody, meant her pussy felt sort of dry a lot of the time.

She would wake at five-thirty in the morning and sit next to Mitchell, staring out the window at their beautiful yard thinking hateful, despairing thoughts for hours. Either that or she would giddily leap up and go downstairs and clean the house, thinking, "I am coming into my power!" which would've been good except she couldn't think straight enough to do anything with it. After she finished cleaning she'd sit and stare and feel broad, wordless feelings surge through her body. Sun, air, furniture, paper, dust; it all became monstrously corporeal and dense. She felt the molecular heaviness of it pressing in upon her while the force of her own blood and organs pressed out, mashing her between them. It used to be that when she felt between her legs, her pussy felt alert and full of energy, unfurled like a hairy, sensate flower. When she checked it out now, it felt tentative, weak and blind, like the moles her cat used to drag in.

Today was Sunday, which meant she didn't have to go to work—Michelle was a senior editor for an online magazine—on no sleep. Instead she went out in the garden in her underwear, weeding and thinking about her past. She had been something of a hippie and a bon vivant in her youth, which somehow over time had gotten translated into "slut." Sometimes that was okay, sometimes not. Sometimes it was okay that she hadn't had a child, sometimes it wasn't. Sometimes thousands of voices would be arguing about it inside her. Today, a particularly loud voice was yelling, "Ugly cunt." Well, let it yell. Virtuously, she weeded. It was hot and muggy. It hadn't rained for days, and the dirt was too dry. Bugs and beetles crawled around, making everything seem complex and full of holes. She had arugula, lettuce, chard, garlic, and basil. Soon she would have tomatoes. Suddenly, it was unbearably heavy to her, all those things with their roots digging down. She got up and dragged the sprinkler out, stuck it in the dry center of the garden. She turned it on, and it threw a bright, festive arc of water that slapped her ankle as she went back inside.

Upstairs in the bedroom, Mitchell was having his own problems. He was realizing that while he would continue to make a good living doing portraits and weddings—selling his work in stores and galleries as well as the occasional magazine—he would never be a famous photographer. He was realizing he would never be as strong as he used to be: When he lifted too much weight at the gym, his back hurt. If he ate late at night, his stomach got gassy and gross. He could sleep, but when he woke up his wife was sitting there staring like a zombie, sometimes intoning weird, depressing things about moles. She hardly ever wanted to have sex anymore, which hurt his feelings. It used to be she always wanted to have sex. She would wake him up sucking his dick with nice slurping noises; she'd climb on top of him and sit on his penis, bracing herself with her hands on his chest and using her legs energetically. She liked it with him on top, too, frontward and from the back. She liked it when he grabbed her legs and pushed them over her head so he went as deep as he could go. Once when he did that, she raised her head and chest and spread her arms wide like he was spreading her legs, popped open her eyes, and stuck her tongue all the way out like a sex demon while he fucked her.

Given this history, it was hard not to take her sudden withdrawal personally. They had been married only five years, and Mitchell was still romantic about Michelle. He was the kind of guy who was actually sort of excited by domesticity—just the phrase "my wife's asshole" was enough to get him going sometimes. He thought guys who lusted after younger women were an embarrassment, and when he fantasized, he almost always thought about doing something really dirty with Michelle. His imagination had room for enjoyable sidebars about faceless sluts or the girl at the store with the big ass, but basically he was outrageously faithful. And because of this, Michelle's stark, staring asexuality made him feel especially uncertain and self-questioning. It made him look in the mirror and think awful things.

That's what he was doing that morning when Michelle walked in on him. Standing barefoot in his shorts, sucking in his stomach, thrusting out his chest, and tilting his head back with his hands on his waist in a hopeful parody of arrogant pride, he was actually thinking, "I'm fat." Michelle threw him a sarcastic glance.

"Stop being silly," she said, "you know it doesn't matter if men put on weight." She had that bristling, coming-into-her-power look, which, on the whole, he liked better than the ugly cunt/mole thing. She opened the closet and stood in her panties and bra, scanning its contents. Dirt from the garden was on her feet and her butt, and she was a little sweaty. Her stomach was bloated in that way it tended to be these days; it gave her otherwise pert figure an extra-nasty look that he rather liked. He did not feel the same way about his love handles, which, as far as he was concerned, did too matter.

"It's horrible out," she said. "Humid and hot."

"Once," said Mitchell wistfully, "a woman looked at me and said, 'That's a nice piece of steak!' She said it loud enough for me to hear her."

"That's sort of nice," she said absently, and it was; his voice conveyed the woman's affable relish, the joyous animal feeling of pouncing and eating in the refined form of a horny, good-natured woman. Wonderful to be the cantering zebra that aroused this leonine roar—wonderful to roll that feeling of eating and being eaten back and forth between you until it didn't matter who was doing which. She remembered it very well.

He dropped his hands and relaxed his stomach, letting it hang out. "I used to be a lithe young man," he said softly.

"And I used to be a pristine girl." Her tone was light, a little impatient. "Where's my fucking sundress?" She closed the closet and turned to face him. Frontally, her small waist gave her hips and thighs a blunt, slightly ursine look. He felt a burst of animal warmth pass between them and thought, "Maybe—"

"Even when I was a pristine girl, I was probably an ugly cunt. Even then." She turned away and began going through her drawers.

"Oh, goddammit," he thought. But what he said was, "So? I was an ugly cock then, too. Stuffing it down every throat, up every cunt and ass."

She chuckled mildly and continued to paw through her drawer.

"Ugly cock," he thought. Weirdly, a little strain of music rose up around the words in his head, a sort of oafish, optimistic theme song, like something dwarves would dance to. He could just see them, marching single file, full of dirty purpose. Suddenly, it popped out of his mouth, three crude, happy syllables on an upswing: "Nah nah NAH!"

Still bent over, Michelle turned and regarded her husband, a matted curtain of bed hair hanging in her face. "What?"

"I think I need to do an ugly cock dance."

"A *what*?"

"Nah nah nah nah nah NAH!" He squatted slightly, put his hands in front of his crotch like he was jerking off a tree, and stumped around thrusting his hips, grunting tunefully.

She turned around and stood with her mouth open. Her husband was grimacing like a lewd troll! He was letting his stomach hang all the way out! He was cavorting like ... like ...

An ugly cunt dance: What would it look like?

Now Mitchell was standing sideways to her, sensually peeling his lips back to show his teeth as he rotated his hips like he was fucking a hippopotamus. "Nah nah nah!" he asserted.

It was like watching a member of a primitive tribe do a rain dance. It made no sense, it had nothing to do with your life, and it was stupid-looking—yet something in you would rise in response. Without even knowing what it was, Michelle felt the ugly cunt dance coming on. As Mitchell locomoted across the room—thrusting his hips and bossily shaking them—she pulled her panties down to midthigh and reached down to daintily part her labia.

"La la la la la LA!" She sang the same tune, only instead of grunting, her noise was high and pungent as a glandular odor, foul and pretty as a little cat with a mole in its jaws. Mitchell turned to see her prancing across the room on her tiptoes, shoulders back, chin up, legs together, and cunt lips open as she prissily twitched her hips and la la-ed, her little red tongue gaily hitting the ridged roof of her mouth. He gave a bellow—"ahhh!"—a sound of animal rightness, even probity.

"Nah nah nah!" His syllables got blurry and focused at the same time, like somebody honing in on a bright, flashing target and letting everything else fall away. He strutted around behind her.

"La la LA!" She reached back to lift and spread her butt with both hands so he could see her pussy between her closed thighs plus her eggplant-colored asshole. "La!" That one little sound, so ladylike and dirty and smug! Still on her toes, she pranced ahead of him, into the middle of the room. Here was her youth, she thought, high-pitched and self-involved, parading itself as if it were special, not knowing it was everything ordinary in a fresh envelope. Ridiculous and beautiful in spite of itself.

She turned and there was Mitchell. There was his youth,

clumsy and buoyant, all gross enthusiastic want, everything about him hanging out, his b.o. flying like a flag. He put both hands on his belly and rubbed, and suddenly, there was his middle age—the crude happiness of an animal with a comfortable stomach, rooting, snuffling, hairy belly wagging as he padded through the forest on his rough paws. Still on tiptoes, she spread her legs and squatted slightly, bringing her hands up front and moving them like she was stirring a pot. What was in the pot? Her voice got deep, guttural. All the sun and air and dirt. All the vegetables in her garden, the bugs and fungi eating leaves and flesh, the worms tunneling underground. The mournful earthen smells, musty and fresh at the same time. Slowness, heaviness, tenderness, wordlessness. She dropped down off her toes and danced in place with a humble flat-footed plod. This was her middle age. The dark pit opened, and inside it, all the slow heavy things of the earth seemed to move with sickening velocity: boulders, babies, skeletons, strings of intestines, heads of lettuce, the wicked witch on her bicycle. Bloody hearts cannonballed past; there was a storm of ovaries. Outside, thunder rumbled. Michelle laughed. This was her old age. Outside, it began to rain. Michelle put her hands over her eyes and laughed, standing still with her panties down and her bush sticking out.

Mitchell went to grab her—but before he could, she sank down on the bed and began to cry. Both of them were sweating slightly, and their skin stuck together as they embraced. He unfolded her and laid her down. She stopped crying and looked at him with young-girl eyes. She pulled the cups of her bra down so she could feel his hairy chest on her breasts. He unzipped his pants and breathed with little grunts as he worked them down, his weight on her for an awkward moment. The sound of the rain pulled her attention out the window; she had a feeling of dissolving, like she was breaking up into sparkling gray dots and scattering. Then Mitchell pushed into her, bringing her back with the solid *ka-chunk!* of dick in cunt. And then they were in the dark flesh pit, flying along with everything else.

When they were finished, they lay together on their sides, Mitchell embracing her from behind. He was not sleeping. He was deeply resting in his feelings of love and pleasure. Michelle was resting in her feelings, too. She was also listening to the rain. She imagined it hitting her garden, making rich mud and running rivulets. She imagined it pouring through her, breaking her up like a clod of earth. She imagined opening a door in the rain, stepping inside it and vanishing. She closed her eyes and slept.

My Puritan Reader

Bert Hart

In the Yeare of Our Lord 1692, when I was but a maiden, Satan sent a greatt Plague of Witches unto us here in Salem Village. By the end, many had confessed to riding through the air on poles, to casting Sicknesse upon the People, and e'en to loathsome Carnal Knowledge of Satan himself. Those that confessed and repented were Saved. But some nineteen persons, whom we had thought to be Godly, woulde not confess. And so despite the Lamentations of their Families, they were Hanged, and so they dyed outside the mercy of Our Lord Jesus Christ. Somme few charged as Witches were found to be Innocent.

At eventide on a day in May during this troubled time I was ahome with Family when there came a knock upon the door. We womenfolk made haste to don our Bonnets. Upon opening the door, I was pleased to see John Smythe, a lusty and Godfearing man of twenty-one, as yet unmarried. He was faire of face and sturdy of body and of diligent providence in his carpenter's trade. I smiled. But today he didde not return my smile, for his face was stern. He didde shew my Father a Warrent for my arrest, that I must goe with John, for I had been named as a Witch. My Mother and young Brother didde crye out at this, and my Father was grave of face, so to spare them I spoke lightly.

Knowing my Innocence, said I, I woulde gladly goe with John and answer who might question me, and the Truth should make me free. Therefore I repaired with John to his cabin, whych he hadde made himself, and fairly donne it was.

Then setting me down on a bench before the large fyreplace, John spake to me most gently, that he must ask me somme questions that he might know whether I be a Witch or no. And then he tooke a metal Cross and put it in my Palm, pressing my fingers about it. And he bade me recite the Lord's Prayer, for it be known that none in Satan's Power can do so without error. And I spake it clearly without mistake, nor was my Palm burnt where I had grasped the Holy Cross. And then he brought forth the Holy Bible, and placing my right Hand upon it, he bade me state whether or no I had lain foully and carnally with Satan. And I said I hadde not, nor with any man.

Then John said that there must be a further test, whych would cause me somme distresse. But as I knew him to be a kindly, Godly, and judicious man, and as I was sure of my Innocence, I answered him plainly that I woulde do whatever he desired. And he said that a Witch may be found out by two certaine tests. Primus, that a Woman who gyves herself carnally to Satan will be marked about the Breasts and Body by his fearsome Claws, and that though she may heale, still fainte Marks may be seen. And Secundus, that Satan places a smalle Mark upon the body of all his Servants. And that this Mark be well hidden about the Privy Parts.

And therefore, said John, ye must needs cast off your cloathes, that I might espy whether or no thou hast these Marks. I hadde not the wit to speake, but I gave him my legge, and he drew off my shoe and then my stocking, and so on the other legge. Whych caused me much distresse, for he saw my Ankles all bare, and no man had seen them thus, nor is it fitting for a man to see such, for even as Godly a man as John may be moved to Lust by such a sight. And then he reached up and took off my Bonnet, and undid the Ribbon holding back my Haire, letting it fall about my shoulders, whych was most unseemly. And then he went behind, and with nimble Fingers he didde undoe the laces of my Bodice, wherewith I gave a small crie. And then going about my front, he didde pulle forward my Bodice and bade me take my Arms from the sleeves, and so it fell about my Waiste. And now my Breasts were only covered by my thinne linen shirte. My skirte now being undone about the Waiste, it and the Bodice now fell upon the floor.

My two Petticoats also being unclasp'd, they and all the cloathes upon the floor were taken away, and there I stood in my Shirte alone. Then most gently didde John reach up and undoe the Ribbons about the Sleeves of my Shirte and at the neck. And then he bade me take the hemme of my Shirte in my Hands and raise it up and over my Head and off, and I didde. And there I stood, ablush to stand before this man as Naked as Eve, nor didde I try to cover my Nakedness with my Hands, for I knew I must stand for examination. But I sorely wished I hadde more Haire about my Privy Parts, whych would have afforded me less Shame.

Now didde John goe about my Back and touched me there most lightly, and then he went lower about my Fundament, and taking each roundnesse in a Hand, he pulled them apart and brought his Face close by, that he might see the Secret Mark, if there be one. But there was nonne. Then turning me about before the fyre, John placed his Hands upon my Breasts and stroked them as lightly as does a hummingbird to a flow'r, to see if there were healed Marks of the Claw. And though my mind desired my Nipples not to rise, my Native Nature o'ercame me, and they rose unto his Palms as readily as if he were a Baby, and his Fingers a suckling Mouth.

Againne finding no Marks, his Hand descended slowly unto my Nether Regions, and once againne he brought his Head cloase, that he might fairly see. And he beganne to stroke my Privy Place, whych caused me much Shame, for againne my Body didde act against my Will, and caused in me a greatt lubriciousness. And John must have known of this, for there are so many Folds and Secret Passages about a woman that it took John somme tyme to complete his Holy Task. As his Fingers worked here and there about my Privy Place, I could not lay still, but pushed myself forward unto his Hands.

And I do not know the names for all the Parts he touched, but of themme all there is one I call my Button, whych causeth me to smile, for many a maiden whose Button is touched indeed becomes undone. And when John touched my Button, I lost all thought, but only wyshed that he might doe it more, and with greatt Force. And my Body cried out that he might continue to Please me with his Fingers, but soon he was sure there was no Mark, and he took his Hands away. And his Fingers glistened in the fyrelight.

And thenne some tyme passing while I recovered my Wits, and as I stood still Naked before the fyre, I spake plainly to John that I hadde need of the Chamber Pot, whych he brought me. And I asked that he might turn away, but he said that he woulde nott, for he wyshed to see how a Woman didde use one. And so my need being greatte, I didde use it before his eyen, and I didde blushe. Then he spake, saying that he too hadde need, and so to my surprise he cast off his breeches and indeed all his cloathes and stood before me as Naked as Adam. And he was faire to mine eyen about the Shoulders and Cheste, but in especiall I lyked his Privy Part, whych was as straight and hard as a Fence Post, and poynted straight up towards Heav'n.

I knew not whether a Man in that state could Make Water. But he sat upon the bench before the fyre and took the Pot in both hands between his Legges, and bade me take hold of his Privy Part and pulle it down until it poynte into the Pot, whych I didde. And then he made copious Water, whych mingled lascivi-ously with that whych I hadde made.

And I lyked to feel his Privy Part, for to my Palm it was as soft as silk, but underneath, an Iron Bar.

Then he gyved a greatt Groane, and said the Lord hath filled him fulle of Seede, and that he must spill it forth or suffre greatly. And seeing him in greatt distresse, and being fulle of Christian Charity, I said that I woulde help him. And that I knew not of such matters, but I woulde take his Privy Part in my Hands and touch it in such divers ways as he might direct until he might Spill his Seede. And then he Groaned again, and said that he had a Covenant with the Lord that he not ever be no Onanist and Spill his Seede upon the ground. And that though he had broken that Covenant many a time, it be when he was abed, and that no Man may be accountable for what might happen while asleep. So I said that I knew not how I might help him yet not break the Covenant. Then he said that if I took his Privy Part into my Mouth and didde place my Tongue about it and do other divers things as he might ask, I coulde thenne swallow his Seede, and the Covenant woulde not be broken.

And that I shoulde not be with childe didde I do so, according to the Promise of the Lord. And so I didde do as he asked, accepting his instruction as one with little Experience but assiduous in my Task until his copious Seede came forth and I didde swallow. And once more he Groaned, but methinks a Groane of Pleasure, for he said he saw the Face of God.

And thenne I thought againne of my Button, and I didde ask John could I also see the Face of God. As so I laide me down upon his bedde and said that he woulde do to me what I had donne to him, and in that way I woulde not be with childe, but that I must direct him in his Task even as he had directed me. And he asked me to speake plainly as to whych of the Parts about my Secret I wyshed him to tongue. And so I put aside all Shame and I shewed him my Button and bade him place his Face upon it and then I coulde not speake more, for he waited not for advice, but went to worke. And I put my Hands about his Head and pressed him to me and brought my Legges about and Groaned and Groaned and saw the Face of God.

And then, falling back, I seemed to float about the room. And then for some greatt sweete tyme we lay in each other's Arms, each praising the other for the Christian Service that was donne. Yet I knew that somme would calle what we had donne the Sinne of Sodomy. But it seemeth to me that what gyves a Man and Woman such Pleasure must come from God, and not be a Sinne.

Then gathering up our cloathes, we dressed each other tenderly. And John took me back to my Family, and said I was no

Witch, so there was much rejoicing. And then John asked of my Father would he gyve permission for John to court me. And my Father said he must ask me two questions.

Was I still a maiden? Didde I wish John to court me? To whych I answered Yes, and Yes, and Yes, Yes, Yes!

And so it was from that day forth, John didde court me, and we woulde goe into darke thickets or dismall swamps and there he would open his Breeches or lift my Petticoats and we woulde both see the Face of God againne. And when Winter came, my Father said that we might Bundle. And whenne the candle flickered out and the Family about us fell asleep, we woulde undoe the wrappings about us and take away the board between us, but hadde to learne a hard lesson, not no more to Groane.

And never againne didde John break the Covenant. And when I turned seventeen, we were married, and never was I so happy. And the proof that God smiled upon us is my two daughters, Abigail and Chastity. And now I am againne with childe and hope that it may be a boy.

As I write this, I know that it is not fitting for a Christian to read. Yet I cannot put it into the fyre, for the things I write here are dear to my heart. So I place it within the Secret Compartment of my desk, that somme may find it long after I moulder, and marvel. And perhaps somme day all the world might know of my love for John.

Signed and sealed, this day of Oct. 12, in the Yeare of Our Lord 1698. Humility Smythe.

Bottle

Martha Garvey

It was my dad, not Evan, who taught me how to drink: you did it to the sound of jazz, in the middle of a cloud of smoke.

I taught my own damn self how to be a drunk.

And I learned how to stop being a drunk the usual way: with a group of fellow drunks hip to my bullshit. As I was hip to theirs.

But it was Evan who taught me something else, about myself, about love, maybe, and finally, about grief and about the bottle.

My dad and I were always close. My mother called us the co-conspirators. So it wasn't so strange one day when I walked into an AA meeting, there he was: my hipster daddy, hanging with the sober sisters and brothers, porkpie hat cocked back, trying not to drink.

He waved at me. If I'd been the sentimental type, I would have cried, but that's not how my father raised me.

"Want a ride?" he said.

"I guess so," I said.

So we hung in, my dad in Pittsburgh, me in New York, miraculously contradicting our Irish-American DNA by not doing the thing we were so fucking talented at doing. One day at a time.

When we were in the same city, we would go to meetings but not sit together, then go to a jazz club where we'd drink seltzer water and lime and Dad would tell me how many times he'd seen Charlie Parker fall off the stage. Dad had wanted to be a musician, but he was smart enough to know he wasn't good enough. So he settled for being a fabulous audience. It was his great gift. AA was the full flowering of that gift. Every night, he got to hear a new story.

The last time we were truly together, Dad and I went to a new Brooklyn club, where, in return for listening to some awful jazz, they gave us a small sapphire-blue bottle of gin shaped like a mermaid. Dad shook his head when they plopped it on our table, and the smooth waiter shrugged: "So save it for your lady friend."

"She's not," Dad said, but the waiter was gone. And so my father shrugged, too, and handed it to me, and said, "Don't say I never gave you anything."

I kept the bottle, but I didn't open it. It was waiting for Evan—though, of course, I didn't know it. I still served booze in my house. I was still someone who liked to watch others soften and blur under the influence of alcohol. I kept the mermaid on my night table. I imagined opening the little blue fishwoman and my next boyfriend giving me a gin-tinged kiss.

Besides, it became a kind of code between my father and me. We were far too cool to discuss our sobriety openly, but each time I talked to my father on the phone, he'd ask, "How's the mermaid?"

And I'd say, "Completely full."

"Good enough," he'd say.

"And you?"

"Oh, still completely full . . . of shit!" Dad would say, and laugh.

And then the doctors found a big lump in Dad's big brain, and there was no way to get it out. I knew the end of that story.

In the meetings, they told me to be grateful for something about the brain cancer, and this is what I came up with:

Gratitude part one: It wasn't a heart attack, so I got to see him a few more times before he slipped into a coma—which, if you're interested in knowing, looks nothing like the ones on TV. In real life, comas are noisy and smelly and expensive. Know this before you decide to slide into one.

Part two of my gratitude: It wasn't Alzheimer's, which meant that the forgetting and drooling he experienced while he wasn't in the coma wouldn't go on forever.

Part three was Evan: At the tail end of the worst year of my life so far, I found a man at the food co-op, right by the dried apricots. I liked this, I liked this Evan, this massage-energy-balancing guy who does not talk like a New Age twit because he is from a part of Brooklyn that still has not, and may never become, chic. Built like he should be hauling meat, not realigning "chi." Downybodied, red-haired, with skin lit from within. A ripe peach who talks like a longshoreman. Evan has a reputation as a massage therapist: he has the kind of hands that can make anyone cry. In a good way. Under Evan's touch, people release their grief, while Evan watches over them, detached. This doesn't happen when he massages me; I am, he says, "one tough customer."

Evan is into detachment in our relationship, except about one thing. Evan thinks keeping the bottle is sick. I tell him I'll throw the bottle away when he can promise me that he will never look up La Bitchface Unforgettable Girlfriend on the Internet when I'm asleep.

The bottle stays on the night table. Once it was lonely, now it has company: an amber glass bottle of Evan's massage oil, bergamot and coriander, oranges and spice. Sometimes Evan rubs me down before sex until I nearly pass out. And sometimes, after we have sex, Evan gets up and borrows my computer and types a hundred words a minute into the ether to another woman who doesn't want to touch him. The bottle, the bitchface: if we thought this thing was going to last, we'd give each other a hard time. But we don't. At least, I don't.

My father dies one cold Pittsburgh morning, and by the end of the evening, I'm packed in Brooklyn, all black clothes and Big Book and positive tapes and phone numbers of friends who will be supportive. I leave early the next day. Evan, not a big word man, has brought food and videos to distract me, but I careen around the apartment, trying to rush the morning into existence.

"Let's just go to bed," Evan says. I let him undress me, and put me down on the futon, and cover me with a quilt. He sleeps in his underpants, a fresh pair he changes into just before sleep, which I usually find amusing, but not today.

Evan lies next to me, but his cock doesn't seem to know that I am in grief.

"I don't want you inside me," I say, though I can feel him poking behind me, nuzzling my neck. Evan is not usually like this, but death charges the air with electricity; his cock is trying to balance the energy. Evan's father is dead, too, but not quite like my father. He left Evan's mother for Evan's mother's best friend when Evan was twelve, and then promptly dropped dead of a heart attack. Fathers are not reliable people in our world. Either they leave you and they die, or they die and they leave you. Evan's father was his first big teacher in detachment.

"I'm pissed you don't want to come to the funeral."

"I met you six weeks ago," he says.

"I miss him, and I want to drink," I say.

"Well, don't," says Evan. "It won't make him any less dead."

"You sure know how to comfort a grieving . . . what? Fuck buddy?"

Silence. Evan is snoring. The first man I have ever known who can doze off in the middle of a fight. That's how fast his energy shifts. Normally I'd be pissed, but this is my chance. When I am sure Evan is deeply asleep, I reach over his body and grab the mermaid bottle, where the gin has begun to sing to me. The glass is blue, but the gin, I am sure, is clear and lovely, just the way it used to be. No one would judge me if I drank this night. No one.

"What are you doing?" Evan hisses. And snatches the bottle from my hand. We wrestle. I bite him. He slaps me. He holds me down with one arm across my throat, a leg to either side of my body. And suddenly, I feel how hard he is.

"Give it to me, fucker," I say. "It's none of your goddamned business."

"I say it is," says Evan.

The mermaid glitters in his hand as the moonlight leaks from the edges of the curtains. Evan moves in and out of the light. I realize I'll have to give him something to get the bottle.

"Oh, fuck me," I sigh.

"Really?" I can't see Evan's face, but his voice is full of electricity.

"It'll help me sleep."

"I don't have a condom."

"Well, make something up."

Evan shifts. I can see him staring at the blue mermaid. He runs the bottle, cap side first, across my breasts, and they leap to attention, even though all my brain can hold is the smell of my father's skin in the creepy hospital room, the sound of him getting my name wrong.

Evan sets the mermaid down, picks his own bottle up. He pours the oil into his hands and rubs them together as if he were trying to make fire. He lets me up. I don't try for the bottle right now. I'll let him fuck me first, and then I'll drink.

He smears oil across my belly and my cunt, and suddenly I am hot. Evan takes the mermaid bottle and puts it in me.

"Oh," I say.

The bottle's too big to really fit entirely into my cunt, and Evan doesn't even try, he just wedges the beginning of it in. Then he urges, with his hands, his mouth, his skin, for me to relax. He knows all my pressure points, my chakras, my energy centers. He makes short work of me. He's a professional.

The metal cap is cool, the glass cooler. I shudder at the chill. Metal and glass: dangerous, but not as deadly, I think, as cells gone wild inside a man's brain.

And though the bottle is sliding in and out of my cunt, utterly intact, though the citrusy oil is all over my body, I smell gin.

I smell the gin my father used to drink in the living room of our big lonely house, I smell the gin my mother is probably drinking right now as she stares at the suit the undertakers will put my father in, I smell the gin I used to drink to finish poems, to start poems, to have sex, to have a life, to end my goddamned thinking, thinking, thinking.

Evan puts one hand on my mound and stops fucking me. He leans into my ear.

"I'm sorry he's gone," he whispers. "I really wanted to meet him." Then silence, and the mermaid swims deeper up into me, and away, and in. And I come, but I don't cry. And Evan rolls away from me.

My body glows from the orgasm, but the part of me that wants to drink still wants to drink. The bottle, where is the bottle? I lean over Evan, and touch his cock, groping, really, for the mermaid. He pushes my hand away.

"Later," he says. I hear him put the bottle back on the night table, and then he falls asleep.

Now is my chance. I slither off the bed. I pick the bottle up from the table. It smells like me.

I go to the living room, where all my bags are packed, and I stare at them. Evan did this. I go to the kitchen, where the dishes dry on the rack, so neat I know I had nothing to do with it. I hear Evan snoring. It's the first time we've had any kind of sex without him firing up the Internet after.

I look at the mermaid and for a moment I think she's looking back at me. In the fairy-tale version of the story of my life, she would speak and ask me to release her into the sea. Or at least into the East River. But she says nothing.

I take a glass from the dish rack and bring it and the bottle to the living room. Already I'm rehearsing my AA relapse story, deciding whether I will include the bottlefucking part of it. I imagine the meeting I will go to, to repent.

But I see my father at that meeting, and suddenly, I don't want to tell any part of that story. I put the glass down. But I still hold on to the mermaid.

It's begun to snow. I open the window and feel the air, cold and wet. I lean out, careful to make sure no one's below. I let the bottle go. It shatters on the wet sidewalk, and the glass sings like Charlie Parker's tenor sax. I wish my dad could hear this music.

And then I turn, and Evan is there. I fall into his arms and weep.

Experimental Writer Gets Sucked Off in a Field

Homage to *Straight to Hell*, for Kevin Killian

Robert Glück

I was just about to graduate from Berkeley. It was 1969.

I'd had plenty of experience rioting, but I had no news about Stonewall, let alone an inkling of what Stonewall would come to mean. I had not come out yet. I sort of planted myself in the way of known fags, hoping and fearing to be seduced.

One day I hitchhiked a few hours north just to get away from my hippie commune and out of Berkeley. I took my shirt off and became flesh on the freeway. I was quickly offered a ride in a green Buick by a pudgy check-and-plaid middle-aged (perhaps he was thirty) optometrist's receptionist. Even with the windows open my underarms smelled up the car. My B.O. felt like a hot blush on my cheeks. He put his hand on my knee and it was just that easy—in an instant we were parked in a dry field under a hot sun.

So here is a homosexual, I informed myself. Bad body, dreary life, no friends, isolation, aging alone, poor, no cultural interests. What the hell, I was just a straight young guy letting some old fag blow me. How well I remember that bleached weedy field and stupid sky—twenty years later I would have thought, "Shallow grave." He went down on me and produced orgasms again and again like it was his work to do, that is, single-minded, intent as a mole. "Can you do that?" he asked. "Just trigger yourself as often as you want?"

I had no attraction to him *whatsoever,* and I felt no cultural allegiance at all. I was a hippie and twenty-one years old. I wondered why people over thirty bothered to buy new clothes. Every time I came, he opened the car door and spit my cum into the weeds. That unlovely gesture and my picture of his stifled, small-town life seemed so hopeless that I thought rather grandly, "I am getting blown by the misery of the world." I was an English major and that's the way we thought. It was just before the time when the meaning of life would migrate to secondary sources. But then he wanted *me* to blow *him* and I balked. Blowing the misery of the world was something else.

He grabbed my balls to threaten me, but seemed to cave in on his own, as though I'd put up a fight. He tried a second approach: He took a pair of sunglasses out of his glove compartment—thick black frames and extra-dark lenses—that were exactly the same as the ones I was wearing. He was showing me that we were united, we had accessorized as sisters. He said, "Do you come here often?" Here? I looked out at the discouraging universe. He asked if he could see me again. "Pervert glasses!" I thought in self-horror, I could recognize them for what they were, and the next day I threw my pair away. I wish I hadn't—they'd be right in style now.

Sour Berry Juice

Shu-Huei Henrickson

Mother told us to watch Little Black and make sure she didn't have it with that ugly mutt down the alley. What if she did have it? No, we couldn't keep the puppies; we'd have to give them away. When Little Black left stinking, reddish-brown spots all over the house, we tried our best to keep her off the streets. But it was hard to keep Little Black happy inside. That mangy white dog with black spots frequently lifted his leg in front of the house during Little Black's natural cycles, making her whimper with longing.

Occasionally, Little Black managed to sneak outside. Once my sister and I caught them in the act. We heard Little Black's painful yelping and thought she had gotten run over by a motorcycle. When we hurried out to see what had happened, it was too late: Little Black and the mangy mutt had their rear ends glued together. I ran inside to describe to Mother what I had seen—in incoherent gasps. Mother rushed out with a broomstick to separate Little Black and the mutt.

"I told you kids to keep an eye on her," Mother growled.

Afterwards, Mother took Little Black to a vet to have an emergency contraceptive injection. Despite the expensive injection, Little Black had her first litter.

The second time came as a surprise; we didn't even know when Little Black misbehaved until Mother noticed the swelling of her nipples. Little Black produced only two puppies each time. Both times, the first puppy to come out was bigger, stronger, and better-looking than the other. The little one of the first litter had a protruding lower jaw. We blamed the unfortunate jaw on the injection and ended up naming him Stupid. The little one of the second litter had an unusually wrinkly face; we called him Wrinkle. Even before they opened their eyes, the big one would bully the little one, climbing on top of the little one, pushing his little brother away from Little Black's nipples. We found homes for the firstborns, but Stupid and Wrinkle were so ugly that nobody would take them.

Stupid and Wrinkle probably didn't live with their big brothers long enough to hate them. But I lived with my sister, Jade, long enough to hate her. All my life I wanted to get the best of her. Jade was the firstborn and the better-looking one. She wasn't particularly good-looking. One can't expect to look like a fairy queen when one has ugly parents. But Jade was still better-looking than me. Jade and I were both built like peasants—dark, thick-boned, and healthy. But while she looked like a normal woman, with normal facial features, I looked like a pug, like someone had taken a boxing glove and smashed my face flat. Above all, Jade was confident. Her confidence won her many admirers in her late teens. She knew how to flirt with men, and when she got pregnant, she knew how to get the villain to marry her. I had a hard time getting men to stay interested in me. When I got pregnant, the scoundrel wouldn't marry me. I had to turn to Jade, who withdrew from her savings for me to get rid of the bastard flesh.

Jade wasn't just better-looking and better at handling men; she was equipped with a better brain. I still remember a high school chemistry teacher who asked me why I couldn't be as good as my sister. "You two eat the same five grains and the same variety of foods, but"—she shook her head as she patted mine—"your brain is filled with tofu." While Jade received awards for her accomplishments at school, I developed firm leg muscles from the cruel punishment of jumping frog when I did badly on tests.

Jade was only eleven months older than me. Eleven months! It occurred to me lately how impatient Father must have been.

Maybe that's why I was defective in every respect—all the nutrients had gone to Jade. If Father had waited for a few years for Mother's body to recover fully, I might have turned out differently.

Mother believed Jade also had a good heart which would win her eternity. Mother loved telling the story about Jade defending me from the alley bullies. Jade, hands on her hips, pushed her chest right up to the bullies and said, "How dare you make my sister cry? Who do you think you are?" Mother told this story many times after I revealed to her that I wished Jade dead. "If Jade died, you would have no sister to play with. And what a good sister Jade is," Mother said. I covered my upper lip with the lower lip and thought it would not bother me a bit to have no sister to play with.

Besides, I didn't believe Mother's story. Jade was often mean to me. I remember Jade teasing me, making me scream until I became hoarse. Once she ran her tongue over a guava I had picked out, so I wouldn't want to eat it anymore. When we fought, she went straight for my pigtails and pulled them so long and so hard that I learned about headaches when I was very young. When Mother gave Jade some chocolate candy to share with me, Jade would hide somewhere and devour the candy. Finally, my humiliation and powerlessness were complete when Jade succeeded in marrying my first date, the man who got her pregnant.

I wish I could forget what happened on my first date, but how could one forget something like that? I was nineteen and had not had a date, not even an arranged date. When matchmaker Wu came, she seemed to be interested only in marrying Jade off. I knew I had to do something for myself. The temple boy, plain and hormone crazed, seemed my ideal candidate. I had noticed that he had a tendency to cast longing glances at my breasts. His father was the shaman in our temple. The boy was an assistant during his father's weekly séance. I only had to show up at three séances in a tight bodice to encourage him to act. At the end of my third seduction week, instead of handing me the usual cursive magic word, the boy handed me a note: "Would you go see a movie with me tonight?" I was so excited, my earlobes became feverish and my hands shook. I ran home, immediately burnt the note in a clay pot, mixed the ashes with water, and drank the mixture for good luck.

That night I walked back to the temple and hid myself behind an old willow tree. My date must have been waiting for me, for he came out right away and was speechless as he watched the rise and fall of my full breasts squeezed tight in my red bodice.

At the theater we watched Tarzan rescue Jane. I waited for him to hold my hand and stole glances at his big nose. He too was stealing glances at me, only not at my face, but my breasts. I laid my right elbow on the arm of my seat, hoping he would pick up the hint. He did. But he did more than I had hoped for. He slid his left hand across my back, wiggled it out through my left armpit, and tightened his thin hand on my breast. I was paralyzed by this powerful squeeze. The thick air in the theater became suffocating and I heaved at every squeeze of his hand. "Ah, so big," he sighed from time to time. He squeezed my left breast for a long time. My eyes were closed; I no longer knew what Tarzan was doing. Then he reached for my right hand and guided it to his groin. The touch of something alive under his pants gave me a jolt. I withdrew my hand while giving him a puzzled look that annoyed him. "Playing innocent," he said. He unzipped and proceeded to pump himself. I couldn't take my eyes off what he was doing to himself. He squeezed my breast and pumped until the end of the movie. When the lights came on, I felt like my left breast had been pulled away from me.

On the way home I walked close to him, touching his arm every now and then, but he carefully moved a step or two away from me. I grew increasingly lonely smelling the frogs and the moist dirt road. In front of our coffee berry tree, I put my face up close to his; I looked at his thick lips and half closed my eyes. But without even saying goodnight, he escaped into the night.

My breast hurt for a couple of days. The touch and the squeeze, which had felt so good at the time, seemed so impersonal, so mechanical in retrospect. And yet, I wanted him to touch me again. I went to the séance three more times after the date. I would have liked to let him touch me again; I would have liked to touch him;

I would have liked to see if the second time or the third time would be better. But he pretended nothing had passed between us. I stopped going to the temple altogether. I don't understand why I can't forget that night, even today. Was it because nothing developed between us? Nothing at all. It wasn't until much later that I learned what real lovemaking was like. I continued to long for him, for his touches. I dreamed that he would send me a letter, show up at our door uninvited and unexpected.

When Mother announced that Jade was to marry the temple boy, I climbed up the coffee berry tree. I plucked out the soft black berries and squashed them between my gums. When the little tree ran out of ripe black berries, I swallowed the raw red ones. With every swallow of the berries, I deposited my hatred of Jade in my stomach, until my stomach became so full that there was no more room for hatred. I ran my tongue over both sides of my teeth and tasted the fuzzy film of sour juice. Later, after Jade moved out to establish her new family, I was to associate her with sour berry juice and a disagreeable film over my teeth.

Mother finally managed to marry me off to a garbage-truck driver who had very poor hearing and was much older. He was fifty. I was thirty-five, not a prize by anybody's standards. I had to shout at him when I had important things to tell him. Less important things, I kept to myself. I got used to him shouting back at me as though I too had a hearing problem. We got along very well. We were able to satisfy each other's physical needs and we both longed for children. For a long time we tried every day to make children. There was one thing I wouldn't let him do: He was not allowed to squeeze my left breast. That breast belonged to my brother-in-law.

I often thought about that movie night with my brother-in-law. The more experienced I became as a married woman, the more I fantasized about what could have been. But almost always, when I fantasized about my brother-in-law, sour stomach juice would creep up my throat and give me a burning sensation. Then immediately I would remember Jade, remember the berry tree. I was afraid of Jade. Even in my dreams and fantasies she stood between my brother-in-law and me.

I was forty when I became pregnant. My old husband was so overcome with joy that he got drunk and was killed in a collision. I was even more bitter toward Jade when she came to help at the funeral. What had I done to deserve losing my husband? Why did misfortune only plague ugly people? Jade was still beautiful, composed, and elegantly plump. My brother-in-law too became better-looking with the accumulation of age. His eyes wandered lustfully when he was around some of our younger cousins. Looking at Jade, I was made conscious of how I walked: thighs so fat that my legs parted, making me resemble a duck the way I swayed my behind. I didn't have the courage to look at myself in the mirror. My face had gotten so fat and round that it reminded me of a grease-brushed moon cake. I mumbled gibberish at people. But in my mind, I heard it clearly. My gibberish meant it wasn't fair, Jade had to be made to suffer too. The baby still had five more months to sleep in my womb, but I had made up my mind to lose weight.

I set a goal: my goal was for my brother-in-law to look at me again, the way he did twenty years ago. When the skinny baby came out of my body, the thought of trimming my belly pleased me greatly. When I nursed the baby, all I could think about was that night at the cinema when my brother-in-law squeezed my breast. When I watched the baby's soft hungry mouth, I imagined my brother-in-law covering the nipple that had always belonged to him with his large mouth and taking long, satisfying sucks. When I thought hungrily about him, my underclothing became wet with a sweet fragrance. I wanted him more than ever.

Before I brought my brother-in-law the basket of dyed eggs, I had already worked out my wicked plan. It was my son's one-month birthday and the end of my one-month house arrest when Mother tried to nurse me back to health from the trauma of childbirth. What Mother didn't know was that I ate very little of her herb-reinforced food because I was determined to lose the soft flesh on my body. Most of the food went to our neighbor's dog. I managed it; I managed to lose enough weight that when I sucked in my belly, my breasts gave my middle-aged shape some definition.

Mother bought ten kilos of fresh farm eggs and we boiled

them with red paper. We would give the dyed eggs to friends and relatives to celebrate the one-month birthday of my son. I plotted to deliver the eggs to my brother-in-law when Jade wasn't home. I looked forward to my long-anticipated meeting with him.

I took great care to make myself presentable. Mother hadn't allowed me to wash my hair during the first month to prevent me from getting migraines. Now I boiled up a big pot of water and shampooed my hair three times to rinse out the grease and dust collected during the month. Then I applied a generous amount of jasmine balm on my scalp. I pulled my shoulder-length hair back into a tight ponytail while the hair was still wet and twisted the tail into a bun secured by a net and a dozen pins. I painted my eyebrows with a charcoal pencil and applied orange wax on my lips. For my top, I chose a red bodice that resembled the one I wore twenty years ago.

When I arrived at their little grocery store, I sucked in my belly, straightened my back, and marched straight to my brother-in-law, who was reading a newspaper at his desk toward the back of the shop, toothpick hanging off a corner of his mouth. When he saw me, he squinted and slowly put his paper down.

"You look different today," he mumbled with the toothpick still in his mouth.

"Where is Jade?" I asked in a false sweet voice that screeched in my ear.

"She went out for lunch with some friends from high school."

"Where should I put these eggs?" Now I sounded more normal to myself, having been reassured of Jade's absence.

He got up and started toward the kitchen. I followed, my palms sweating. I left the eggs on the counter and followed him back down the hall. I decided I had to act; I had to act before Jade came home. Before we came back out to the shop, I tightened my jaw, pulled him back against the wall dividing the shop and the little TV room, wrapped my arms tightly around his neck, and kissed him hard on the mouth. To my surprise and disappointment, he put up a fight and eventually pushed me back.

"Be careful of my sore, you animal," he said.

It took me a few seconds to get used to the dark room and to recover from the dizziness that penetrated my head when I kissed him. I looked at his lips carefully and saw a reddish sore the size of a dime. I had broken the soft scab. The sight of the open sore so repulsed me that I didn't want to kiss him anymore. But I didn't want to tear myself from him either. After all that anticipation, I couldn't end before I had even started. I continued to press against him without feeling amorous and surveyed the boxes stacked up high against the wall next to us. "Strengthen the Liver and Nourish the Kidneys," one label read. Several boxes contained "Revive the Sperm, Foster the Chi." Suddenly his hands traveled under my bodice, ran along my spine, and gave me little shivers. I was aroused again. I guided his hands to my breasts.

"Let's finish what we started twenty years ago," I whispered.

He continued to stare at me, not adding any pressure on my breasts. Worrying about when Jade was due home, I proceeded to touch his sensitive parts. But to my disappointment, I found him not at all aroused. He could see the disappointment on my face and pushed me away.

"Why are you doing this to me? You *know* I am incapable," he growled.

I stared at him in disbelief.

"You are just as animal-like as your sister."

"But twenty years ago . . ."

"Why did you think I didn't go further twenty years ago?"

"But you got Jade pregnant?"

"I did *not* get her pregnant. Some other bastard did. Your sister couldn't get him to marry her, so she came to me. She knew about my problem and knew I would appreciate the marital arrangement. You two are both animals."

"She knew? Jade knew?"

I straightened up my clothes and smoothed out my hair. I backed away from him slowly. I couldn't hold back my grin. Poor Jade was married to this useless human.

"ANIMAL!" my brother-in-law shouted after me as I left his little shop.

It's Never Too Late in New York

Nelson George

There's a part of me that's always envied my good buddy Walter Gibbs, so whenever we played ball, I always came hard. An elbow in the lower back, a kick toward his groin on a jumper, a move to inflict a bit of pain and give me an edge. After all, Walter was a better athlete than I was. I was taller and had longer arms but Walter had strong legs that gave him more hops than a rabbit. I knew that if I let up on Walter for even a moment, he'd win.

So whenever we were matched against each other, I found that if I beat on him enough, Walter would fold. I'd use my legs to cut off his drives. My elbows to push him off the perimeter. My whole body to keep him from spots near the basket when he posted me up. If I brought it like that, Walter would give in. Not quit exactly, but just not care as much as I did. So on this Super Bowl Sunday afternoon, I beat Walter in three games of one-on-one, not by outshooting or even outplaying him, but by making one or two hustle plays—getting my own rebound on a missed shot, knocking a ball off his leg, anything that gave me an edge. I never won by much—one point, two points tops. But it meant something to me every time.

Later, as we sat in the steam room, Walter, in his humble way, remarked, "Niggah, you ain't shit."

"Then why did I win the trifecta today?"

"You won three games because my mind was on ass. I was holding back for tonight."

"Since when do you have to marshal your strength to get busy, Walter?"

"I have a special treat coming my way, that's why."

"I take it you're not talking about going to Andy's for the game?"

"Nah. But you know what, Dwayne? I'm gonna put you down."

"You mean 'in-there-like-swimwear'?"

"You know you're really showing your age right now, niggah. You sound like a Heavy D record. This is the twenty-first century. It's time for some new slang. Word?" I laughed at that. Walter was getting as old school as I was. So for effect he capped his riff with, "Yes, home slice, word."

In a cab downtown Walter gave me the details of his post-game strategy.

"Her name is Medina."

"As in 'Funky Cold'?"

"Yes, yes, and you don't stop. Met her at the Paradise Strip Club. Right as she rubbed her pussy against my dick she realized she'd seen my picture in *Vibe*."

"Wait a minute, I met this girl. Her real name's Beatrice. Remember, we all went to the movies together?"

"Oh yeah. Beatrice. I like Medina better myself. When'd she tell you her real name?"

"I think when you went to get popcorn."

"Okay, good," he said, not really sounding pleased. "She must have liked you."

"I guess so."

It was about two months back. He'd just wrapped production on a movie and was chillin' in town. He'd met me at the Sony on Sixty-eighth Street with Medina, aka Beatrice. She was petite with skin the color of a ripe tangerine. She wore outrageously high black platform boots—the kind Japanese tourists usually sport—and a flimsy beige dress under a snazzy leather coat. In her hair were two decorative beige barrettes. Her eyes were slanted and framed with dark eyeliner. Her lips, moistened by red lipstick, seemed to go on forever. Though probably twenty-six, she radiated a baby-doll sexiness I liked. That night she eyed me carefully, pulling me in with her gaze. *Desire me,* her eyes ordered, and I obeyed.

Somehow Beatrice ended up sitting between Walter and me. The protocol for your man and his date is that he sits in the middle. At first that didn't seem important. Not until Walter got a page on his two-way and left to make a call in the lobby. Nothing should have happened. I was attracted to her but I wasn't gonna kick it to my man's date. All I did was lean over and say something innocuous to her about "too many commercials and not enough trailers." She responded by brushing my knee with her hand and then letting it rest there. I covered it with mine and then, impulsively, brought them to my lips and kissed her fingers. She took her hand out of mine and, using both hands, held my face.

Wordlessly, we tongued each other as images of coming blockbusters flicked across our faces. I hadn't known this girl more than ten minutes and we'd made this quick, curious connection. Maybe it was because we both knew that Walter had a high-profile girlfriend. Maybe we just felt like being naughty. I wondered what the people behind us were thinking.

By the time Walter came back with his arms full of bottled water and a huge bag of buttered popcorn, our lips had parted. But, despite Walter's presence in the darkened theater, I still let a hand rest on her thigh, and she'd brush it even as Walter chuckled at Eddie Murphy's latest. When he went to the restroom, about halfway through the movie, Beatrice whispered her real name to me along with her number, but alas, all I could recall later was her warm breath on my ear.

After the movie Walter, not an unperceptive man, gave me a hug and then whisked her away in a taxi while I went home with a very hard dick.

"So, you're meeting her, huh?" I said, feeling jealous. "Sounds like fun to me."

"Oh, Dwayne, that's not all. She's bringing her lover to meet me."

"Who, based on your grin, is a female."

"Yes, niggah. And because of your fine performance on the hardwood I'm gonna give you an opportunity to express your hard wood. You feel me?"

"Oh shit."

"Yes, niggah. Oh shit."

Walter and I had been friends some fifteen years. With admiration and envy, I'd watched (and sometimes helped) his rise from movie novice to edgy low-budget film producer to Hollywood hack capable of making $20 million jammies. Along the way Walter developed an amazing skill for orchestrating nontraditional, multipartner sex. Just as Walter had a knack for finding the right young director to give voice to black rage and humor, the man had a gift for plucking the inner freak out of otherwise seemingly conventional women. I'd seen him fuck models in Porto Sans in Bryant Park and entice the collegiate daughters of potential investors back to his crib. I'd also received a few three A.M. phone calls from my stoned friend in some posh hotel with the voices of many women groaning in the background.

As a pop music journalist now turned screenwriter, I'd bedded my share of singers, models, actresses and wanna-be stars. Yet, in all my years in the entertainment game, I'd never followed Walter's lead and indulged in orgies. There seemed something, well, unsanitary about more than one person penetrating a woman at the same time. Two dicks in the bed, in my opinion, meant two testicles too many.

A couple of girlfriends had suggested we add another woman to the mix, but I'd declined. I think of myself as a one-on-one kind of guy. Yes, I'd cheated on women—sainthood was not my destination—but to me sex demanded full concentration and abandonment into the depths of a woman's body and soul. I simply didn't believe I could split my focus and be a good lover. But, yes, of course I was curious. And I already knew I desired Beatrice and that she desired me.

"Come correct," Walter said a half hour later as the cab stopped in the East Village in front of Bowery Bar. "I know you're new to this orgy game but it's never too late to learn. That's why I love this city. It's never too late in New York, niggah."

Inside, a huge TV screen set up in the back of the restaurant was projecting the interminable pre-game hype that hard-core football fans savored. A few of the mostly male downtown-hipster crowd were making wagers on the Titans versus the Rams. Thankfully, instead of sports chatter, light r&b was playing as the commentator's words ran across the bottom of the screen. However, if you looked to the right of the screen, there was a much better show under way.

Swinging her hips in a slow, seductive motion was Beatrice. She was dancing alone to the music in front of a small table where an attractive thirtyish woman sat sipping wine. She had an oval face with hooded eyes, slim lips and skin the color of a harvest moon. Her breasts were full and, from what I could see under the table, she had thick, shapely legs. To the envy of many at Bowery Bar, Walter strolled over and kissed Beatrice as I stood anxiously behind him.

"You remember my man, right?"

Beatrice received me with a light kiss and a long hug. Then she said, "This is Sonja—the friend I told you about."

"She talks a lot about you, Walter," Sonja said, locking eyes with him.

"Likewise," he replied, and then sat down next to her. After I was introduced I squeezed in on the other side of Sonja as Beatrice went back to her dancing. Sonja and Walter traded endearments and then gazed at Beatrice, the lovely link between them. I watched Sonja laugh, then softly touch Walter's lips. "Yeah, sweetness," he murmured. "Yeah."

Walter's two-way buzzed. He checked the message and grinned. "I'll be right back," he said. "Why don't you two lovely people make friends." And so we did. I went first: Ex-full-time music critic; author of the critically acclaimed black-music history *The Relentless Beat;* single; childless; writing a screenplay for Walter's Idea Factory Productions called *One Special Moment.* I told my story neatly with an emphasis on my professional résumé.

Sonja, in contrast, took time with all the details, especially the personal ones: Trini immigrant family; raised in Hempstead; Cornell undergrad; New York Law; a day job at Universal Records in business affairs; an IBM executive boyfriend with a crib in Jersey; and a nightlife that had nothing to do with contracts and depositions.

"My boyfriend," she said at one point, "would love this big-screen TV and this conversation. He's always watching documentaries on jazz and blues and all that. He probably knows your work."

"Really," I replied, not knowing how to respond. "It's a shame he's not here."

She smiled and turned her gaze from me to Beatrice. "Now that's not what you really think, is it?"

"No, counselor, it isn't."

"The truth is always a good thing. How long have you and Walter been friends?"

"Known him fifteen years or so. Way back before his first music videos."

"So you must have a lot in common."

This was an encouraging line of questioning.

"As much as good friends do. As much as you and your good friend have in common," I answered.

"Well, it's only been two months but we already share so much." She had more to say but Walter walked up to the table.

"Let's go, team," he said, gesturing for us to stand. "I have a new recruit."

Walter led Beatrice by the hand while I guided Sonja behind them, my hand resting in the soft curve of her waist. We moved around the chairs of envious men to the bar where a barely post-college chocolate-brown cutie awaited us. Her name was Robinette and she was dressed in seventies retro style—plain hip-hugger slacks, a beige turtleneck, a brown leather jacket, black platform shoes and yellow-tinted shades. A woolly natural silhouetted her baby face.

"Walter," she whined, "I'm supposed to be meeting some friends."

He took her by the hand like a father would his child. "No, Robinette, that's dead. You're coming with us." She didn't resist, but wore a petulant scowl as we headed for the door. A bouncer looked at me and joked, "Y'all planning your own personal Super Bowl party, huh?" I nodded like it was my game plan and headed out the door.

Outside we commandeered two taxis. Walter got into the first one with Robinette. "Let me get her head straight," he whispered, and then instructed me to jump in the second cab with the other two women. As we drove west across the Village to Moomba, Beatrice nestled in between Sonja and me, turned and began kissing her friend. As their tongues tied I at first watched like an intruder until, timidly, I started rubbing the insides of Beatrice's legs. I then progressed to kissing her neck. She opened her gams wider in encouragement. By the time we reached Moomba my fingers had traced some delightful geometric patterns inside her panties.

Up on Moomba's second floor we dined on seafood, artfully arranged vegetables and a medley of alcoholic beverages. The seating was strategic: Sonja and Beatrice sat next to each other, nuzzling like deer. Walter sat at the head of the table, beaming and pouring Moët like water; Robinette and I sat to his right. Robinette stared, mesmerized by Beatrice and Sonja, while Walter and I soothed, cajoled and whispered to her about the joys of being sexually open. Robinette's eyes looked a bit glazed and it hit me that "getting her head right" probably involved drugs. Walter was an old hand at this game, so I just noted it and said nothing.

Initially I'd just followed Walter's lead in seducing Robinette. But, as the evening's possibilities became apparent, I grew more animated. I softly rubbed her legs, gazed deep into her brown eyes and listened empathetically to her frustrations with the fashion game. "Yes, I worked at Condé Nast two years before I got to go on a shoot," she complained. As I nodded that I understood her frustration, mentally I was licking my lips.

Unlike Sonja, a seemingly practical girl with an extravagant inner life, Robinette was obsessed with the surface. It was clear why she fancied Walter—he represented power, opportunity and mobility. Still, I wasn't sure we would pull Robinette in until she bragged about her close relationship with a Eurasian model and her white photographer hubby. At this couple's mention Walter's eyes widened.

"Have you been out to their house in East Hampton, Robinette?" He leaned in close to her.

"Yes," she said haughtily. "They were kind enough to ask me out."

"And did you stay the weekend?"

"Of course, Walter. I wouldn't go out for just one day."

"No doubt. Now," he said matter-of-factly, "who ate your pussy first—him or her?"

Her reply was a guilty giggle. So now it was on. All our predatory eyes gazed hungrily at young Robinette. Walter pressed on.

"Did you enjoy more eating or being eaten? C'mon, darling. Everybody at this table likes the taste of pussy."

Walter's frankness must have melted Robinette as a dreamy look replaced her earlier self-absorption; it was now clear she had officially joined our party.

"Let's go," Walter announced, the check disappearing under the weight of his black AmEx card.

Robinette asked, "Where are we going?"

"My place," Walter answered. "After all, it's Super Bowl Sunday."

Outside Moomba we snared a cab. Now the rules of the New York taxi industry preclude carrying more than four passengers at a time. Sonja, the attorney, sweet-talked Pierre, the Haitian cabbie, into taking us. Walter, Beatrice, Sonja and Robinette squeezed snugly into the backseat and I, the fifth wheel, sat up next to the driver. The taxi's two sides were separated by a bullet-proof partition. There was a wide hole in the center for exchanging money. Soon after we pulled off I glanced into the back and saw the most remarkable things.

From left to right sat Sonja, Walter, Robinette and Beatrice, as tightly packed as the dot on an i.

Walter kissed Beatrice by leaning across the body of a very uncomfortable Robinette. With his left hand he reached back toward Sonja, who began sucking his fingers. Beatrice reached down and across Robinette to unzip Walter's pants. Then she bent down and placed her mouth around his dick. Sonja and Walter locked lips as Robinette sat motionless and the taxi's windows began to fog.

And then, as if someone gave a signal, Sonja, Beatrice and Walter descended on young Robinette. Walter unbuttoned her blouse. Beatrice unzipped her slacks. Sonja reached over and pulled down Robinette's leopard bra, revealing her tiny, hard black nipples. Her matching leopard panties showcased a flat, smooth stomach and a thin wisp of carefully shaved pubic hair. Her moans filled the now-steamy car as I stuck my hand through the opening in the bulletproof glass, stretching my fingers to touch Robinette's soft, slender legs. But that was all I could really do, aside from peer at the proceedings like a poor child outside a bakery. Pierre, our very focused driver, didn't flinch, slow down, complain or even seem to care. He just rolled up unconcerned to Walter's apartment in a smooth, efficient manner. As we drove I could hear the Super Bowl starting lineups being announced on the radio.

Outside of very well-cast porn videos I'd never seen anything like this. I was involved, but then not really. What could be worse than being three feet away from an orgy? I was just a horny-ass voyeur, separated from the action by steel and plastic and leather.

When we stopped at Walter's building on West Thirty-fourth Street, I paid Pierre as the lord of the manor and his three concubines sauntered inside. I have no idea how much money I gave Pierre, 'cause I was not getting left behind again. I had never been in an orgy before—hadn't even had a threesome. Now I was ready to lose my "virginity."

Walter was reserved in the lobby, speaking politely to the doorman, before checking his mail even though it was Sunday. Even in the elevator, when a glassy-eyed Robinette tried to smother him with kisses, he seemed more interested in the security camera than her.

Ah, but once he closed the door to his apartment, he dropped the mask and returned to his true lecherous nature, doling out orders as if he were a drill sergeant.

"Ladies, there are two guest bathrooms. Why don't you make any necessary stops while Dwayne and I get refreshments."

The women dutifully retreated to the bathrooms, which were located along the apartment's long central corridor adjacent to two guest bedrooms. Walter's main bedroom was at one end of the corridor next to his gym. Beyond that was the kitchen. At the opposite end of the hall was the entry to the living room and dining area. Walter locked the door to the master bedroom and opened the door to one of the guest rooms.

He then turned to me and spoke with great seriousness. "If anyone asks, you spent the night here. Unknown to me you took advantage of my generosity and brought some ass up here. You with that?"

"Of course."

Walter then dropped down to the carpeted floor and began furiously doing push-ups. I laughed. "Laugh now, niggah. In twenty minutes you'll be singing my praise," he huffed between sets.

I went back into the hall. One of the bathroom doors was open. In Walter's gym, Robinette stood staring at herself in the floor-to-ceiling mirrors. I came up behind her, placing my hands on her hips and my lips on her long brown neck. She moaned as I nibbled softly, but never took her eyes off her image. She ran her hands up her body, finally stopping at her chest. Then she cupped her breasts through her blouse. My hands followed her trail and then blazed new territory by sliding inside her blouse and under her bra. Together we slipped out one breast and then the other. My groin pressed between her small buns and my hands pinched her nipples. Slowly, like we were dancing to an old-school jam, I turned her around until we were in profile in the mirror. Watching the spectacle of my hands on Robinette's girlish body and shining ebony skin, I felt like a vampire preparing for the first bite.

But I knew that for Robinette I was just a tool being employed to achieve pleasure—a pleasure that her hazy eyes suggested wasn't necessarily dependent on me. This moment was more about her mind, her fantasy, than me. I went down to my knees, pushing aside her leopard panties, savoring her taste with my mouth. As I slipped my tongue under the crotch of her panties she opened her mouth and a moan escaped from the back of her throat, a beautiful sound I remembered from the taxi. But now I was the reason she made it.

As Robinette rocked in my mouth an animal sound came from down the hall. It was primordial. It came from deep inside someone, from down where the larynx meets the lungs.

For the first time since Moomba, Robinette's eyes seemed focused. "What was that?" she asked, her voice hushed.

"Sounded like either Sonja or Beatrice?"

"Who?"

Now I was pulled out of the moment. This woman—a girl, really—didn't know anyone here except Walter. Not even the guy who was currently eating her pussy.

This was really crazy.

"Let's find Walter," I said, pulling her clothes up around her as I stood up. We walked down the hall, drawn by the heaving of bedsprings. We entered the guest bedroom and stood there staring at the bed. Walter was on the bottom. Sonja was above him, her pussy enveloping his dick. Beatrice was behind Sonja humping her ass with a black strap-on dildo. As Sonja was penetrated from below and behind, shock waves of pleasure moved through her fleshy body. Walter smiled as he saw our faces and motioned Robinette over. When she reached the bed he pointed at Sonja.

An obedient Robinette then leaned forward and began fondling Sonja's breasts and kissing her neck.

At that moment I vowed, "This is not gonna be the mother-fucking cab all over again!" After ripping open a packet of my favorite green-and-white Trojans and doffing my coat, I placed myself behind Beatrice's active little ass and found her sweet spot.

The other four bodies had to adjust to my presence and, for an awkward moment, I felt like an intruder, like a DJ playing Bach at a down-home blues joint.

But then we found our collective rhythm. Beatrice adjusted her stroke to mine, Sonja arched her back higher, Walter thrust his pelvis differently; and Robinette, well, she didn't do anything but close her eyes even tighter. For a time we were all in harmony.

After a while it felt like I was standing outside the pile, just marveling at the beauty of these five undulating brown bodies. It was gorgeous in the way of some erotic African wood carving—the kind they keep under wraps at the Metropolitan Museum of Art. My mind took mental snapshots of this moment, moving around the bed like the camera in *The Matrix*. It was sex, but not sex as I'd experienced it in my previous thirty-plus years. It wasn't just fucking—it was a full-fledged never-to-be-forgotten freaky-deekey-funkadelic jam. I was already nostalgic for it and the night wasn't even over.

It was like a sequence of edits in a film as we shifted from person to person, position to position. It seemed like I spent most of my time with Sonja, doing a duet that was deep and funky, while Walter somehow handled Beatrice and Robinette in a balancing act involving fingers, mouth and penis.

Things took an even stranger turn when I became aware I was kissing a leg that was a touch hairier than it should have been. I looked up to see it belonged to Walter. "Go ahead," urged Beatrice as she returned my lips to his leg. "Lick it," she ordered. "Now kiss it and use your tongue."

And so I did, as the three ladies murmured their approval. Walter sniggered and said, "Don't be a trick, Dwayne."

"Shut up," Sonja said.

"And," Walter responded, "what does he get for licking me, ladies?"

"Yeah, what do I get?" I chimed in.

"Sonja, go help him," Beatrice commanded.

And, like magic, a soft hand took control of my dick and a mouth engulfed its head. I tongued Walter's leg right up his knee, and then asked, "Is that all I get?"

No, it wasn't. Robinette took one nipple and Beatrice began licking the other, and I was caught up in a series of new, joyously weird sensations. My mouth opened and my body wiggled and I could feel blood twirling inside me as I licked Walter and was licked by the ladies. The feeling was of total abandon. I don't know that I'd ever felt so free, yet so passive. I was a vessel, a cup that pleasure was being poured into. And, happily, I was overflowing.

I didn't sleep for long. Maybe a half hour. But there had never been a sleep like that in my life because I'd never had a night like this before. So satisfied, so calm. I opened my eyes slowly. It was quiet. To my right was Robinette. I saw her swallow a little black pill and follow it with wine.

"Are you all right?"

"Ah-huh," she replied.

"Where'd they go?"

"The girls said they were hungry."

"No doubt."

"But they told me to stay here."

"Really?"

"Yeah. That Beatrice girl is so bossy, but it's all right. I'll have my time with Walter, too."

I rolled onto my back and took inventory. Had I already had my Super Bowl? Was I out of the game? After that experience, what did I have left? Not much, it seemed. Yet Walter was somewhere in the house still getting busy with two women. Again I was envious of Walter, but I guess that's why he was a mogul and I wasn't. There was a certain hunger for conquest in Walter I just didn't possess.

I rose gingerly off the mattress and felt dizzy when I stood up. I'd come so hard my head was still spinning.

Down the hallway, past the two bathrooms and into the gym I stumbled toward the strange, sexual sound coming from the kitchen. It was different from the moaning and grunting from before. It was a man's voice. Not a moan or groan, but a weirdly contented whimper. Didn't even know that such a sound existed.

I stepped into the kitchen doorway and, for the third time tonight, witnessed sex as I'd never seen it before. My eyes widened. I almost stopped breathing. Sonja was sitting on a chair with her legs around Walter's neck. So far, so good. Walter was on his hands and knees, jerking himself off with one hand. No surprise there. The tricky, heart-stopping, world-wrecking part was Beatrice, who was bent over Walter's back, slowly humping his ass with that black strap-on dildo. In and out she stroked, moving as expertly as she had with Sonja, but with a more leisurely, almost luxurious stroke. Not only hadn't I ever seen anything like this, I'd never even imagined it was possible. I guess I was more innocent than I wanted to admit.

Beatrice saw me standing there, smiled and then bent her finger in a "come here" gesture. Before I had been stunned. Now I was horrified. I stepped backward, turned and almost ran back down the hallway.

The guest bedroom was a mess of rumpled sheets, wet spots and condom packages. In the air hung the aroma of sweat, perfume and sex. Robinette had disappeared into a bathroom. I slipped on my pants and T-shirt and sat on the bed feeling numb. I decided to do something normal. I went into the living room, sat down and messed around with the remote, hoping to find the Super Bowl and try to blank out what I'd just seen. It was the fourth quarter and the Titans were mounting a comeback led by quarterback Steve McNair. It was shaping up to be a memorable effort; commentators predicted this could be one of the greatest endings of all time. But obviously, the game, no matter who won, wouldn't be what I'd remember about tonight.

To my surprise Beatrice, in panties and an open robe, walked in and sat down on the sofa beside me. She wanted to know the score.

"The Rams are winning but the Titans are making a game of it," I said. "You like football?"

"A little. I watch it at the club with customers. It gives men something to talk about. But I find it too violent."

"Sometimes," I suggested, "a little violence is good?"

"A little pain, yes," she replied. "But not violence."

"Okay," I said, and then took a moment to really study her. Her face was moist and her eyes tired. Still, if I didn't know what she'd just done, nothing about her manner would have revealed it. She looked like someone's flirtatious girlfriend. We pass people every day on the street, people who have done the most unusual things. We think they are just ordinary people but we don't know who they really are or what they're truly capable of. I thought I knew who Beatrice was. A freak. A stripper. She's still both. But on this Sunday it was clear the lady was also one hell of a head coach.

She said, "You know, I think you're cute."

"Are you being sarcastic?"

"No, Dwayne. Don't be so insecure."

"Did Walter ask you to do that to him?"

"Do what?" She wanted me to say it.

"You know. What you did in the kitchen."

"No," she said slyly. "I asked him and he agreed. I've done a lot for him. Things you don't know about. It was something he owed me. A little returned favor, you know?"

"A little favor. Wow. You sure move through the world differently."

"I don't know. Everything's about exchange. If we get closer, Dwayne, I may ask a favor of you, too."

"You already had me kissing Walter's hairy-ass leg. Isn't that favor enough?"

"And that wasn't so bad, was it?"

"I was, you know, distracted."

"That's how it starts, baby. One distraction leads to another."

*   *   *

On the TV McNair was driving the Titans. The clock was ticking. A field goal wouldn't do. A touchdown was the Titans' only shot. Walter ambled in and sat next to me, requesting an update on the game. Sonja appeared next, seating herself partly on Beatrice's lap and partly on mine. We sat there and, for a funny moment, we were just any close American family watching the big game.

Sonja asked for the phone—something about calling her boyfriend. I suppressed a chuckle and watched her ass bounce as she exited. A moment later Beatrice left, too. When they were gone Walter leaned over and said, "Soon as the game's over, you say you're going home and take all the freaks with you. I gotta call Daria."

Daria Dinkins, black ingenue, decent actress, all-around cutie, was shooting a sci-fi/martial arts flick in Thailand. She was "the black girl" in a multi-culti cast.

Whatever "favor" Walter felt obliged to do for his bisexual gal pal was in the past. The bass was back in his voice and he'd reverted to mack mode. But now, of course, I would never, ever, see Walter Gibbs the same way again.

Still, he sounded, looked and acted like the Walter I'd always known; like the guy I'd played ball with that afternoon; like the man who'd seen more ass than a toilet. Besides, wasn't I the one who'd been licking his leg not too long ago? Yes, I had been "distracted." But then again, licking a man's leg and being ass-fucked by a stripper are not exactly the same thing.

"Mum's the word on this, right?" I said.

"Niggah, we shouldn't even have to have that convo. But you got a big mouth, which is one reason I never put you down before."

"Like I can't be trusted."

"Like you're CNN. I only tell you shit I want known. In this situation I expect you to tell lots of niggahs everything. Shit, I expect you to be a big man in every gym or bar in the Apple. Just leave my motherfucking name out of it. Aiight."

"No doubt. By the way, that girl Robinette is talking like she expects to stay."

"Yo Dwayne, you got to take her. She wants to be my girl. Now, she's talented for her age—"

"Which is?"

Walter ignored my question and just said, "I just don't wanna be alone with her right now. That girl's trying to get ahead in life. You never know what ideas she might get about how to do that. Tonight was cool. Two weeks later I'm in the motherfucking *Post*. As long as you guys are all in it with me, I'm safe. You feel me?"

"I got you, dog. You have the most to lose."

"And you have the most to gain, so keep my name out of it and we'll be stacking paper for a long time to come." He held out his fist and I met it with mine.

We looked up and saw that a Titans wide receiver was being tackled by the Rams linebacker one yard short of the goal line. The gun sounded. The Super Bowl was over and bettors all around the nation were scrambling for their phones. Back in the bedroom I began searching for my shoes and socks, all the while keeping an eye on Robinette, who had emerged from the bathroom and was sprawled lethargically across the bed.

"Robinette," I said, shaking her. "Robinette."

"Yes," she said in a sleepy voice.

"We're all getting ready to leave."

"Oh."

No movement, not even an effort. Sonja and Beatrice, now dressed, walked in. Beatrice placed her slender hands on her hips and surveyed the situation. "Why don't you take a quick shower?" she suggested. "I got this."

The water rolled over places of my pain—a bite on my left forearm, scratches on my back, a sore right shoulder, a rawness of the left side of my dick from someone's teeth. I put my clothes on gingerly, like a running back after a hundred-yard game. In the mirror my eyes were red and my face flushed. I craved my empty bed.

By the time I was dressed the ladies were gathered in the living room. Robinette, now fully dressed, sipped apple juice. Walter was nowhere to be found. Beatrice stood by Robinette and clearly had our young friend under control. Perhaps the god-momma of decadence had found a fine young disciple. Meanwhile, Sonja's demeanor had changed. I could see the well-bred, highly motivated, ambitious Buppie in her had now reemerged. She'd freaked enough for the week. I guess it was time to put her mask back on.

"I just spoke to my boyfriend and he does know who you are," Sonja said excitedly. "He saw you on something on A&E about Prince."

"That's what I used to do," I said. "I was a talking head for years."

"Well, I need to get an autographed book for him."

"Not a problem," I replied, as if we'd just met at a book signing.

In a perfect world I would have met Sonja at a conference on African-American something or other. Maybe at a dinner party via a mutual friend. There we would have talked about our families, our careers, our past lovers and what we liked for dessert. We would have gone to the movies. Some theater perhaps. Had sex on the third or fourth date and vacationed in Cancún or Negril. But this wasn't a book signing.

As we stood on Thirty-fourth Street hailing cabs, I mused that Sonja was outwardly the type of sister any man would aspire to marry. Her shape, her gig, her complexion were a black man's ideal. But then Sonja was no stereotype of upwardly mobile accomplishment. There were other shades to the lady. And then there was that boyfriend.

As if reading my mind, Sonja asked if I had a card. I didn't, but I wrote my digits on the back of hers and put another one into my pocket. Beatrice watched without comment, though there was a twinkle in her baby browns. The ladies hopped into the backseat but I didn't get in.

"You're not going with us?" Beatrice wondered.

"No, ladies, I'm gonna stop and grab some food and then take the subway home."

"See you soon," Beatrice said warmly.

"Call me," Sonja commanded. "I want an autographed book for my boyfriend."

Robinette offered a listless "Bye" and then sank into the back-seat as the cab pulled off.

I stood on the curb watching the departing cab and then slid out my celli. By the time I was in Mickey D's I'd raised Walter.

"Yo niggah, I'm still on the phone with my girl."

"Just wanted to say that was unbelievable, my man."

"No doubt."

"No doubt, indeed."

At this point in the conversation I tossed a fry into my mouth and wondered if I should mention what I'd seen in the kitchen. Should I bring up the fact that my longtime friend and current employer had just an hour ago been looking like a *Man Date* magazine cover boy? Eventually I would ask him. I would. Just not on Super Bowl Sunday.

Instead I mumbled, "Okay, Walter, I'll let you go."

"Aiight. My niggah."

"Yeah. Peace."

I sat there, munching on my fries, remembering the pleasure and trying to forget that damn dildo. A brother came in wearing a Tennessee Titans snorkel. "Tough, my man," I said to him.

"Naw, dog. Nothing like being in the Super Bowl. Don't know when you'll be back. Getting in the game is all you can ask, you know?"

He held out his knuckles. I met them with mine. Then I stood up luxuriating in how sore my whole body was and smiling at how it got that way.

Brontitis

Maria Dahvana Headley

I'm romantic, all right, though I've spent my whole life vociferously denying any romantic tendencies. My mother is a romance novelist aspiring to great literature: everything she writes has winds whistling through moors and consumptive heroines bursting from bodices. She heard me say this once, and sighed for Branwell and his possibly incestuous relationship with Charlotte. In the course of my childhood, we had three hamsters named Mr. Rochester (one female), whether for their brooding manners or their tendency to eat their young, I don't know.

There's nothing that can ruin a girl's tender nature more thoroughly than a mother who wore lace-up corsets all through the shoulder-padded 1980s, and who once subsisted for several months on thin gruel and saltines as a show of solidarity with beleaguered literary heroines.

No way in hell I was going to turn out to be a withered poetess, my maidenhead intact at the age of thirty-five, tumbling into a grave packed full of gray woolen underwear. At thirteen, I Lolita-ed my first Humbert. At fourteen, I'd drilled my way through three construction workers. By fifteen, five college professors had professed their love, and by sixteen I was sick of men altogether and onto women. By seventeen, I'd dyed my hair purple, gotten a few tattoos, and was dating the first of two Chloes.

From nineteen to twenty-three I was the sort of celibate girl wet dreams are made of—in short, a terminal tease. It's amazing how easily people can be had, men and women alike. I was shell-shocked by the simplicity of sex appeal. My life had become a reverse Brontë. Where buttoned dresses and whalebone ignited the throttled desires of Jane Eyre and her ilk, my drooping camisoles, incessant cleavage-enhancing devices, and painted-on jeans all served to make my libido terminally bored. I was a eu-thanized sex kitten, a lukewarm tamale, a woman who preferred going to the dentist to going to her lover's bed.

Then, of course, as you've been expecting, Romance came along, shuffling his feet, bearing roses and wine, humming to himself. I saw him coming and my gorge got an erection.

"I want to court you," said Romance in a voice I wanted to wrap around myself. "I don't want to do anything until we're married. We'll be chaste."

"Do you really think that's going to work?" I asked.

"Yep," Romance said, flashing the devil's smile. "It always works."

Let me tell you how Romance looks to a woman so jaded that jade's no longer a shade of green. Romance is six feet four. Romance could throw me over his shoulder like a Continental soldier. Romance is wearing ripped jeans and a T-shirt, and Romance is the sort of man who could be embossed on stationery, the sort who could be used to sell many products, even embar-rassing ones, because he's that male. Romance has dark hair and blue eyes and big hands and never wears shoes.

Romance, against my better judgment, makes me drip. I hate Romance. And I love him. I want to jump his bones. Of course I do. I'm deprived. Depraved. Depilated. There's nothing like a fresh bikini wax to send you off on a mortification-of-the-flesh tangent. My latent Brontitis kicked into gear. Use me, abuse me, and stow me in the attic! Pace the moors in whipping storms, show me your dark and morbid soul! Screw me in a snowstorm, Romance; lick me in a landslide!

Of course, Romance would not. Romance would take me to dinner and the movies, Romance would lean across the table and whisper in my ear, Romance would focus his blue gaze on me for hours at a time. I was a fly rolling in amber, suddenly discovering that its fragile feet are stuck and a couple of legs are missing. Fucking Romance. Fuck Romance. I wanted to fuck Romance. Unromantically, of course. No fade-out fantasy here, I wanted the real deal, ripping of bodices, sweat and claw marks, on my knees on the floor. I wanted him to Wide Sargasso Sea me, not Jane Eyre-ate me.

Romance called me thirteen times a day and referred to me as "Hey, Beautiful . . ."

I pressed Romance against the wall in my apartment one day when he arrived bearing perfume, lingerie, and armfuls of frothing flowers. I told him I could no longer be patient.

"Too bad," said Romance, and grinned the grin.

I was reminded of all the cartoons in which one's bad self and one's good self war on opposite shoulders. The right side has the cherub, the left has the demon with the little red horns and the tail lashing, smirking. I found my demon blathering its mouth off all day, so loudly I couldn't think, telling me stories about how Romance might kneel in front of me to propose and how I could slowly unzip my jeans at that point, and how he would be looking adoringly up at me, enumerating his love, and how I would scoot forward and bury his mouth in my cunt.

The demons. Damn them. I couldn't think about true love when the demons were thinking of true lust instead. And then there are the angels. Most people's angels tell them the right thing to do. Most people's angels would tell them to get married, as Romance wants; most people's angels would tell them that getting fucked whilst bent over the back of the couch prior to marriage is an unethical thing to want, and that I shouldn't even think about it. My angels couldn't speak. They'd start to open their mouths, and melted butter would run out. They'd sit on their hands and end up fingering themselves.

The demons made me do things like yank up my skirt in places like the library, trying to get Romance to notice.

Romance looked at me, smiled, and said, "That's beautiful, I wish I could sketch you." He didn't touch me. He didn't move. Romance's entire goal was to drive me insane.

He did things like develop a thin layer of sweat on his upper lip, making me want to suck him until I reached the rind. "Fine," I said incoherently, "I don't need you to knead me, I can make my loaves turn to fishes all by myself." I made sure he was watching and then slid a couple of fingers into my pussy. "Ooh," I said, spying on him from the corner of my eye.

"Yeah, right," he said, knowing very well I was faking. My capacity for giving myself pleasure was gone. I only wanted him.

Finally, I cracked.

Romance had arrived at my apartment and was reclining on my couch. Romance, that asshole, was wearing a long black coat. Romance was not naked beneath the coat. Romance would not let me wear him. Romance was reading Proust. Romance had become my madeleine. He was the cookie I would never be allowed to swallow. I eyed him from the kitchen while burning dinner. I heaved. I quivered. I trembled. I fell to my knees.

"Marry me," I bellowed gracelessly, jamming onto his finger the ring that cost me the money I was saving to get the tattoos proclaiming me, in ninety-seven languages, forever single. It was like the end of *Taming of the Shrew*. My hand wanted to go beneath his foot. I unknit my threatening, unkind brow. I prostrated myself at his feet. I wanted to wed, to wantonly wive, to whore, to wend, weave and wallow.

He smiled. He said, "But, do you love me?"

No. No, I didn't fucking love him. He is Romance. You don't love Romance. You love spaghetti. You love Branwell Brontë, if Branwell Brontë is the name of a cereal, not a man. Look at what happens in *Jane Eyre*, for example. The mad wife in the attic. The fire. The weather, for fuck's sake. No one wants that weather. No one wants the wind wailing over the moors. No one wants the boning in the corset that causes your internal organs to go squish and start looking like half-priced meat. No one wants the bedbugs and the terrible little dogs and having to be not seen and not heard ad infinitum. No one wants to be a goddamned maiden schoolteacher. No woman wants the drafts and the gruel and the dark brooding hero who can't do shit for himself.

I correct: every woman wants the dark brooding hero who can't do shit for himself. Just as I wanted Romance. "Marry me," I whimpered. Triumphant music played. The sun came out. The wind started humming something possibly from *West Side Story*. And we got joined in holy macaroni.

Now he lies on the couch all day reading Colette and languishing. If consumption were still fashionable, he'd be coughing up specks of blood into a silk handkerchief. Romance failed to mention that he's never owned a checkbook, never had a job, never even owned a goldfish.

I sit in my steel chair and write smutty novels to pay the bills. It's actually much better money than you'd imagine, and I sign my name Jane. At night Romance makes love to me by candlelight. I drip the hot wax onto his chest and he slides the candle into my cunt, and all in all, it's a fairly good deal.

Still, of course, he won't actually fuck me. He is waiting for me to really love him, waiting for unity of our souls, waiting for me to be reduced to an amoeba of desire. Waiting for me to take some vows of some sort, though I'm not sure what.

I'm thinking that if I become a nun, he might love me. I've gone through seventeen bodices, ripping them and shredding them. As I become more and more enslaved, as his packages arrive from Amazon.com filled with first-edition leather-bound French novels, and as his deliveries of orchids and champagne bubble over, he says, smiling the wicked smile of a man with pussy wrapped around his fingers, "It always works."

What can I say? I'm romantic.

Robots of the World, Unite!

Karl Iagnemma

I t was toward the end of their relationship. "Relationship" was too strong a term—they had been fucking once or twice a week for the past three months, but lately the shimmer of excitement had dulled, and now the sex was perfunctory and rushed, not even desperate, as though desperation was too strong an emotion to conjure. Still, it was sex, and Gerald, a male graduate student in a world of male graduate students, prayed that it would never stop. He was, in some minor, embarrassing way, in love.

Her name was Luba. From the beginning, she'd been fascinated with his robots. Gerald figured her Russian ancestry might somehow explain it; *robot,* after all, was a Czech word, and perhaps all Eastern Europeans liked robots, with their vague whiffs of sadness and communism. Luba was tall and pale, swan-like, with a cloud of fine blond hair. She smelled like lemon and soap, and baby powder. It was what Gerald imagined angels must smell like.

Luba liked to rendezvous in Gerald's lab, the Robotics and Automation lab, a damp basement space cluttered with ratchets and rusted soldering irons, stacks of busted oscilloscopes, intestinal snarls of wire. The room reeked of cutting fluid and bare feet. Luba would tap on the door at midnight or one A.M., after her shift at the Drunken Schoolboy Saloon, then wander bemusedly among the various broken-down robots, touching their battered metal shells, before she kissed Gerald, dropped her coat, and scooted onto the rickety prototype table.

That night, she was late. At one-thirty, Gerald grabbed his backpack and flipped off the lights, allowing himself a moment of silent self-pity in the lab's greenish LED glow. There was a rap at the door. "Sorry," Luba said, touching his elbow as she brushed past, "I had laundry issues."

She yanked off her woolly hat and scratched her scalp, shrugged off her coat and tossed it over an empty acetylene tank. Gerald stepped behind Luba and kissed the bony knob of her spine, then peeled her sweatshirt over her head. He unbuttoned her jeans, knelt, and yanked down her pants and panties—the yellow Raggedy Ann ones—then steered her by the hips to the prototype table and hoisted her aboard. Luba hissed at the steel's chill. Gerald shucked his pants down to his ankles. He had been hard, on and off, since noon.

He licked his index finger, then touched Luba between the legs, like some obscure tribal greeting. He had always loved her scorn for foreplay—she was like a man that way, unencumbered by patience—but now something in her passive willingness made Gerald's stomach twine into a knot. He pressed into her—a warm, tunneling handshake, a rush of homecoming, of relief.

Luba said, "Hang on."

"What?"

She wiggled up the table, let her legs flop shut.

"What? What's up?"

Luba shrugged. She lay on her back, her hair scrawled on the studded table, her panties puddled at her feet. "I dunno. I sorta don't feel like it."

"But you came here—*you're here,*" Gerald said, immediately regretting the note of anguish in his voice. Now she would pull on her jeans and sweatshirt, smiling stiffly, assuring Gerald that everything was fine, no problem—why would he think there was a problem? Next week there would be a telephone message, full of pity and false cheer. *You're an awesome guy, Gerald. I'm still going to call you, okay?*

Now he said, "Let's try something different—what do you want me to do?"

Luba shrugged again, staring past Gerald at the lab's clutter.

"Anything," he said. He dropped to a squat and pried her knees apart.

She said, "Start one of the robots."

Gerald followed her stare to the Schilling Titan II, a titanium manipulator with sluggish servovalves and leaky hydraulics; the Puma 560, a battered blue gantry with a mangled end-effector. The brain-dead microbots. And, of course, Amelio, the animatronic head, the topic of Gerald's dormant Ph.D. thesis.

He said, "What's up with you and robots?"

"I dunno." A playful grin tugged at the corners of her lips. "I just like them. Make one move."

He supposed it could be arousing, the talk of elasticity and friction, balls and sockets, stress and strain. He supposed it could ignite a spark, seeing lifeless bodies move and talk and act vaguely like people, though without the half-truths and indecision, the forgotten promises, the stony threats. He supposed.

He hiked his jeans with one hand and shuffled to the controller PC, flipped the Puma circuit breaker and popped the safety relay. He called up the initialization sequence, and the Puma's motors whirred, its joints slewing to a home position with the arm pointing upward at a sixty-degree angle. Luba lay on her side, hands tucked beneath her chin, staring. She said, "That's it?"

"Well. Pretty much. Yeah."

"That's all it does?"

"What did you expect it to do?"

Luba shrugged. "I dunno."

"It doesn't like, *dance* or anything."

"Dancing would be cool."

Gerald called up the homing command, and the Puma shuddered, its detents locking. He snapped the circuit breaker shut, then leaned back in the chair. He gestured vaguely, then dropped his hands in his lap. "Well. Sorry."

"Turn on that one."

She pointed at Amelio. Once, years ago, Gerald had dreamed of Amelio as the world's first social robot—a talking, interacting creature! Friend of children! Beloved by pets!—but now it was just a shit-heap in the corner, a monument to failure. Amelio had an aluminum head with wide freakshow eyes, and a one-degree-of-freedom jaw that clacked when it spit phrases from its tiny lexicon: "Stop that." "I don't understand." "I like it." Amelio could track gestures and hear voices and obey simple commands, but his brain—Gerald's thesis—was soup. And yet Gerald was fond of Amelio: he felt, at least, that Amelio understood him, in a way that he would never understand a woman like Luba.

"That's Amelio."

"Ah-mee-lee-oh. Good name."

"It's Latin for something."

Gerald shuffled to Amelio's terminal and flipped the breaker. Amelio's head jerked to an upright quiver, panning leftward until his eyes found a feature to track—Luba's lolling feet.

Amelio said, "I like it."

Gerald shuffled back to the prototype table. His balls touched the chilly steel, sending a shiver through his spine, and suddenly—strangely—recalling for him an image of himself as a young graduate student, standing naked in front of a mirror, performing an experiment. He'd been flapping his arms at varying frequencies, watching his stomach and balls jiggle in response. At a certain frequency his balls had begun vibrating *out of phase* with the jelly around his midsection. What joy! His body was a dynamic system, explainable by physics! Now this memory caused in Gerald a twinge of sadness. He was, he realized, a tremendous geek.

Luba clasped her ankles behind Gerald's back, her gaze fixed on Amelio's jittery mouth, and Gerald dropped his jeans with a pang of scruffy guilt. He worked his way inside her. She'd shifted positions, and the hole pattern on the table's surface had quilted her bottom with blotchy scarlet bumps. Gerald adjusted his angle, letting gravity tug him faster.

Amelio said, "I don't understand."

It must be confused by the repetitive motion, Gerald thought, the periodic velocity vectors in its field of view. Luba giggled. He gripped her hipbone, the immaculate skin that looked like it had never seen sun. He thought: I could marry this girl. It was a vintage sexthought, a quarter-millimeter from insanity—but down there, somewhere, was a sober nut of truth.

Amelio said, "I don't understand."

Luba's jaw and fists tightened. She thrashed, her back pressing into an arch, a glaze of sweat on her sternum. She tore at Gerald's wrist. A small thrilling birdsound escaped her throat, and she squeezed Gerald, a warm viscoelastic clench—and then her body seemed to collapse into tiny, precise shudders. Gerald's stomach fell away. She looked like a woman riding out a hurricane. He couldn't look away from her pained face.

Finally Luba blinked, her eyes slowly focusing.

He said, "Pretty cool, huh?"

Luba giggled. "I like Amelio." Her chest was marbled with orgasm rash. "Why doesn't he say more?"

"That's all he knows."

"Sad."

"Yeah. Sad."

He could teach Amelio—couldn't he? He could teach him to say "Come here," and "Go faster," and "Tell me more"—that part was easy. He could teach him how to recognize affection— was *that* possible? Had anything similar been reported in the literature? And she could help him, Luba, this strange girl, this lover of machines. And, yes, it would be possible to grant Amelio memory—of laughter, of good deeds done to him, of people he liked—so that eventually, one day, he might say, "You. Yes. I like you. I love you."

Gerald said, "Luba, please: come back. Tomorrow night. I want to teach him something new."

The Bounty of Summer

Carol Queen

We stop at farmers' markets whenever we're on the road, especially in July when the peaches come ripe, timed with the Perseid meteor showers. We get enough fruit to sate any summer hunger, not just peaches but whatever is juicy and sweet, bearing it away in brown bags as if we are smuggling jewels.

At the bed-and-breakfast we get a room overlooking the Pacific—we can see it from our bed and from the huge Jacuzzi in the bathroom. It's the honeymoon suite, though we are not married, just fucking like it's the only thing we will have to do for the rest of our lives. We've come equipped with candles to make the Jacuzzi room a wet cathedral of fuck. We stay in the water all weekend, except when we're in the bed. We get out to pee and refill the water bottle so we don't pass out and drown.

We float one at a time, holding each other's heads. He can reach my pussy too because his arms are so long. He sits on the tile edge while I suck his cock, then we switch places. I brace myself on the edge while he fucks me, and we fuck as often as possible. It doesn't matter if he's hard—we both have fingers and tongues, and a bag of sex toys too if it comes to that.

He tells me to close my eyes: His voice is my blindfold. His hands roam on me everywhere, warm, wet as the water. He has turned on the jets and positioned me over one. Everything about me is open, so open, except my eyes. I can picture him anyway, his hands covering my breasts, sliding down, sliding back up to grasp the back of my neck, pulling me in for a wet and melting kiss. I float in his touch, in our sex, like a lotus on a pond, anchored.

A cold something interrupts the warm. Cold and completely smooth, not icy, but a shocking cool compared to warm water and hot kisses. He runs the thing up and down my body, rolls it, really; it seems round or ovoid. I still do not open my eyes. Over my nipples, the coolness tugging them into even tighter erection. Down my belly, giving me the ripply butterfly feeling I sometimes get when I'm touched there. Between my legs, of course, everything we play with goes between my legs, smooth and chill on my clit, nuzzling my cunt lips apart.

It feels like it wants to enter me, nudging the way his cock does, and rounded like a cockhead; but so much cooler than his cock, a little bigger too perhaps. Pushing in—he's lubed it, whatever it is, it stretches the lips, slides in and in. He makes sure it happens slowly. It is big, I realize, wider than his cock, big enough that I have to fight with myself a little to take it.

Suddenly it slides all the way in—it's passed the midpoint and the slide is unstoppable—I'm filled.

He tells me to open my eyes.

There on the edge of the tub one of our paper bags of fruit sits open, full of gleaming red plums not quite the size of a small fist.

"Do you want another one?" he asks, and holds one up for me to bite, juice running down my chin, down my tits.

Ah, the bounty of summer. We eat more plums while he fucks me, his cock nudging the fruit and barely fitting, juice running everywhere. Laughing.

Charles Sykes' *Spirit of Ecstasy*

P. S. Haven

I love Charles Sykes' *Spirit of Ecstasy*. Andy knows this. I love every last inch of her, and knowing this, Andy sneaks me out to the garage to look at her after his grandfather has fallen asleep. He indulges me as I gaze upon her sensual silver form, her fluttering robe frozen behind her. She's as beautiful as the first time I ever laid eyes on her. We stare at her, and the 1934 Rolls-Royce Phantom II she adorns, lovingly—both of us, Andy and I, admiring her lithe shape, her bewitching beauty, the light from above glinting off her plating, causing her to sparkle and glow almost magically. I love Charles Sykes' *Spirit of Ecstasy*. She's beautiful, absolutely gorgeous.

Andy finally coaxes me back into the house and into bed. I like it up the ass. Andy knows this, too. I bend forward, my ass parting, opening up to reveal to Andy the tiny pucker of my anus. I groan (softly, so as not to wake up Grandpa) as he enters me, grateful for the familiar ache, the fullness of having a cock in my ass. I let him fuck me as deeply as he wants, even when he pins my hands helplessly to my back, the full weight of his body pushing his cock into me, pressing me into the mattress. Andy comes forever, and when he's empty he can do no more than lower himself onto the bed beside me and fall asleep. I use his sheets to wipe the sticky deposit from my asshole.

I leave Andy asleep in the bed, put on the Brooks Brothers

dress shirt he'd cast off before fucking me, and then steal down the hallway past his grandfather's bedroom and out the back door. I dash across the street-lit backyard; the grass is cool and wet with dew. (Andy has done an amazing job of ignoring his grandfather's hints to mow it.)

I love going out to the garage. Maybe it's that my dad was a mechanic. The garage itself is small, especially compared to the house, just enough room for the Rolls. There are dusty Venetian blinds on the windows and inside the blue light of the boulevard is striped across the wooden shelves lined with vintage repair manuals and old oilcans. I check over my shoulder instinctively, making sure I had locked the door behind me, making sure I was alone. I was, of course. I turn on one row of the fluorescent fixtures above and look at her, poised at the prow of the bonnet, bravely pointing the way into 1934's promising future.

I almost can't believe this is happening. I almost can't comprehend how things have come this far, this fast. I am so nervous I am trembling. How long have I fantasized about just this? How long have I searched for her, built up to her, waited for her? I think of casing antique car shows by day, only to jump fences and infiltrate fairgrounds after dark and mount a 1933 Plymouth or a 1951 Nash to fill myself with one of Avard Fairbanks' flying mermaids or George Petty's winged goddesses. But never Charles Sykes' *Spirit of Ecstasy*. I think of the time I almost bought her, disembodied, from a member of the Rolls-Royce Enthusiasts' Club. And how the thought of her like that, severed from the rest of her Rolls, her enchantment taken out of context, suddenly repulsed me, and I practically fled.

Then I think of Eleanor Thornton, a young woman with beauty, spirit and intelligence, but not the social status to marry the man she loved, John Walter Edward-Scott-Montagu, heir to Lord Montagu, English automobile pioneer. I think of Lord Montagu, commissioning the creation of a mascot to adorn the radiator of every Rolls-Royce he produced, a commission filled by one Charles Robinson Sykes, sculptor and close friend and confidant of John. Charles knew of John's love affair with his secretary, Eleanor, and like the lovers themselves, he used utmost discretion. Lord Montagu was none the wiser when, in February 1911, he was presented with a sculpted figurine of his son's forbidden love. Christened *Spirit of Ecstasy,* young Eleanor Thornton's likeness has graced every Rolls-Royce henceforth.

I let Andy's Brooks Brothers shirt slip from my arms and onto the dusty concrete below like some burlesque ecdysiast, somebody Eleanor might have known. The undercarriage creaks and sinks as I climb carefully onto the front bumper and between those two huge headlamps. I can see myself in the windshield, my nude body pale and ghost-like, my reflection translucent, the steering wheel and driver's seat visible through me. I gaze at my reflection, my eyes locking with themselves, childlike with anticipation, flashing in the intermittent bands of light sweeping across them as cars drive by outside the garage.

I turn my back to her and lift myself onto the bonnet, pushing my ass out behind me, spreading my legs until I feel Eleanor's outstretched arms brush against the insides of my thighs. I use her arms as my guide, positioning myself over her, lowering myself until her fluttering robes press into my skin. I hover over her for a moment, tensing and then relaxing the long muscles in my thighs, in my back, my ass; the throbbing muscles in my cunt. My sweat drips onto the bonnet, the radiator digging into my palms. I try to toss the hair out of my face. My breathing is almost desperate now and I deny myself no longer.

I descend until I feel Eleanor's head gently nudge against the soft folds of my cunt and press into me there, and patiently I push against her until I feel my body begin to yield. Slowly, certainly, she opens me, my cunt yielding, first to Eleanor's head and then to her slender shoulders, sliding onto her until her entire upper body is within me. I hold her there for a moment, letting myself adjust to her, absorb her, struggling against the desperate urge to plunge straight onto her. I moan at the feel of her, moan louder as I raise my body and then gently lower myself onto her again. Eleanor enters further, her long arms, cast behind her like wings, spread me open. I press my hands flat against the bonnet beneath me and arch my back, pushing my cunt onto her as far as my body will let me.

I begin to fuck Eleanor, bracing myself against the bonnet, my arms trembling with my weight as I work her into me with stuttered, abrupt strokes. I spread my legs further still; Eleanor's head and shoulders sliding in and out of me easily, running into me like a blade, and fucking me thoroughly. I groan as she enters me again and again, slipping into me, through my opening and deep inside, her backswept arms dictating cruelly how far she can go. Tears escape my clenched eyelids, streaming down my cheeks as Eleanor's entire torso slides into my cunt, puncturing yet connecting at the same time.

I fuck her relentlessly, desperate to come. I listen to myself grunting, almost barking, echoing in the empty garage as I plunge myself down onto her again and again. Suddenly I think of Andy, and for a moment I feel sorry for him. I had never behaved this way with him, had never performed like this. He would understand, I told myself. He would.

The feel of Charles Sykes' *Spirit of Ecstasy* in my cunt, so much harder than Andy's cock could ever be, fills my senses. With my moans I try to show her how much I love her, how much I love what she is doing to me. I need her and I know if I stop fucking her, I'll die. I enclose her, envelop her in my body, and try my best to literally consume her, wanting only to reward her with my orgasm.

I work Eleanor into my cunt, fitting every last inch of her into me now. I'm loose now and Eleanor moves in and out easily. I drop the full weight of my body onto the bonnet of the Rolls and weep uncontrollably, the pain exhilarating as it fades into an almost unbearable pleasure. I can feel Eleanor's entire body inside of me, filling me completely. My breath flees me in a continuous moan, my body twisting and contorting as if I've been speared. The tightness is agonizing, and I begin to buck frantically against the bonnet, Eleanor sliding in and out so fast I can't catch my breath. I impale myself on her, giving myself to her fully, spreading my legs wide to accommodate as much of her as I can, as deeply as I can.

I look down between my legs at the *Spirit of Ecstasy,* the distorted shape of my cunt around it as it gets fucked. I slide two fingers into my empty ass and push at Eleanor through the thin membrane that separates ass from cunt. I can feel her on the other side, her shoulders pushing back, and for a moment I fear that I might tear; that Eleanor might actually, physically rip me open, but I keep fucking her.

I am slowly becoming aware of the orgasm building deep within me and I fuck Eleanor harder still. It hurts, but I'm going to come, nonetheless. All I can think about is coming; how good it's going to feel when I come, how it doesn't matter that it hurts, how nothing matters but coming. Suddenly my entire body buckles underneath me, my climax washing over me like a tidal wave, and it feels like the hardest come ever. I sound like I'm drowning. Eleanor doesn't stop. She keeps on fucking me. Hard. Harder than anything can fuck. A burst of grunts escapes me and, with my thighs trembling helplessly, I come all over Eleanor. My fluids drool out of me and onto Eleanor, leaving her coated in a thick, white froth.

I think again of Eleanor Thornton and how her life had been lost off the coast of Crete, on passage to India aboard the SS *Persia,* torpedoed by a German submarine. She didn't live long enough to see the success of the statue she had inspired.

I dismount Eleanor and lie on the bonnet and kiss her until I can no longer taste myself on her. Maybe it's a coincidence, maybe it isn't, that Andy is awake when I come back to bed. It takes me a long time to fall asleep. But it's mostly because I don't want it to be the day after I fucked Charles Sykes' *Spirit of Ecstasy* yet. I want it to still be the day itself. When sleep finally comes, I dream I'm silver-plated.

Surviving Darwin

Alicia Gifford

I met Curtis Greene in AA. He told me he'd gotten too fond of his Pouilly-Fuissé despite his dry Southern Baptist upbringing. He said he'd started to drink socially after moving to California, and then he'd started to look forward to getting home at night for a glass or two every day. He never wanted to go to restaurants that didn't have a good wine list. He figured he had a problem, he said, and started to come to meetings.

We got friendly and I could tell he liked me by the way he'd look for me and save me a seat. He'd get red and tongue-tied talking to me. He told me he was a pharmacist and owned three drugstores in the Los Angeles area, Greene's Pharmacies. He drove a new BMW the color of midnight and he smelled good, like money. He was married, he said, and had a little boy named Alex.

I got caught stealing large amounts of Vicodin from the hospital floor I worked on as a nurse. I'd pop a few and get to work, tending to my patients' needs while loaded on their pain meds. I loved my job when I was high. I felt connected. Actualized.

Things were great as long as a couple of pills would get me loaded, but then I needed six, and then ten at a time, to get the kind of buzz I needed. I started to wake up feeling like shit until I could get a few Vicodin in me.

Nurses are in such short supply that they can't get rid of all of us druggies or the patients would be wiping their own asses; or worse yet, the supervisors and administrators would have to do it, so they send us for our shot at redemption to a program called Diversion, a rehab for licensed health professionals operated by the state of California. They assign you a color and make you call a phone number every day, and if it's your color you have to go piss in a jar for random drug testing. You have to go to Diversion meetings once a week and AA or NA meetings the other six nights, and every six months a committee of tight-asses evaluates you to see how you're progressing with your little problem.

NA was full of street drug addicts—meth freaks with open sores and junkies with the jitters. I found the AA crowd more to my liking but I was desperate for a way out of this mess. I hated Diversion and, without Vicodin, I hated nursing.

One night I walked to the meeting about a mile from my apartment and then I asked Curtis for a ride home. I leaned my head back against the leather headrest and laid my hand on his thigh. Fifteen minutes later his cock was in my mouth and he was telling me that he thought about me night and day. I saw possibilities.

We started an affair. He told me about his wife, how he and she were high school sweethearts back in Benton, Arkansas, where they grew up. His wife, the only woman he'd been with before me, was prudish and frigid, he said. I was forbidden fruit, a wild California girl, free-spirited and comfortable with my body. After sex the first time, he asked me if I'd felt "warm."

"Do you mean: did I come?" I asked.

He winced. "Yes," he whispered. I taught him the marvel of the clitoris and buried his face in it. He'd bawl after sex with me, blubbering how much he loved me, how lucky he was to have found me. He said he loved his wife too, and his son, and that he was just so torn up inside.

"If you love your wife so much, why are you here?" I asked him. He blinked bewildered blue eyes. "Have you ever thought about divorce?"

He startled. "I couldn't divorce Susan," he said. "I could never leave my boy."

I laughed at him. "You don't divorce your *kids,* silly."

I lied and told him that a doctor at work had asked me out. I said he was cute and single and crazy about me, and that I hoped everything would work out between us. Curtis didn't hide his emotions well.

I said, "Honey, you're married. I can't put my life on hold for a married man."

He sat there with his head in his hands. "I can't stand the thought of you with someone else," he said, looking like a dazed, sick cow.

"I'm not going to *sleep* with him," I said. "Not on our first date."

"I can't get a divorce, I just can't." I had to keep boxes of Kleenex everywhere because Curtis was always bursting into tears.

Later I got together with my ex-boyfriend Artie. We were still good friends and still had an intense sexual relationship even though he was living with an older, wealthy woman who supported him.

He lit up a joint.

"Get that stuff away from me," I told him. "You'll contaminate my urine." It smelled so good. I love drugs, to tell you the truth. I miss Vicodin, the stony bliss of it. If I could get away with it, I'd be using—not out of control like last time. Now and then. A sensible habit. But I had five years of Big Brother in the form of Diversion in my future.

"So what do you get out of torturing this guy?" Artie asked.

"I like him," I said. "Plus, you never know."

"Right," Artie said. "A hayseed from Podunk is right up your alley."

I waved my hand like a game-show hostess toward my new wide-screen TV and Bang & Olufsen sound system. "He also paid for my transmission."

"Any good in bed?" Artie asked, stoned now, yanking at my sweatshirt.

"He's sweet. And a good learner," I said, mimicking Curtis's Arkansas lilt. "And extremely grateful." I had to stop talking then, Artie had his fat tongue in my mouth and was digging into my pants with his fingers. Artie kissed a lot of puckered, old-lady ass to live like he liked, and when we got together, he took control and I submitted. I found humiliation cleansing somehow, absolution for something blistered in me.

I got the box out from under the bed and he trussed me up with leather straps. He put alligator clamps on my nipples and gagged and blindfolded me. Artie was fun that way.

Curtis didn't look too good. He'd lost fifteen pounds in the three months since our affair started, and bags hung under his eyes. He said he couldn't stop thinking about me, and that his wife kept asking him what was wrong. She wanted to go to couples' counseling. He told me that if it wasn't for his son he might consider getting a divorce. They were so young when they got married, he said, and he'd become a different man. His wife was still the same Arkansas piano teacher who went to church every Sunday and Wednesday nights. Her throat had never experienced a warming swallow of alcohol or the blunt thrust of a penis.

Alex was six. Curtis showed me pictures of him, a towhead with Curtis's water-blue eyes and pouty red mouth. He showed me pictures of his wife Susan, too, your basic Midwest Baptist, dressed in crisp, buttoned-up pastel shirts and tailored slacks and loafers. I scanned through the photos, a tic jerking my upper eyelid like a pulse.

He wanted me to meet Alex, so one Saturday he took him to the mall and we staged a coincidental meeting. Alex was bored and fidgety while Curtis and I drank coffee. At one point he looked at me with his crusty little eyes and said, "My mom is prettier than you."

Curtis said, "Mommy's very pretty but that's not a nice thing to say. Ms. Nolan is very pretty too."

I smiled at the little prick. "All good little boys think their mommy is the prettiest in the whole world." Curtis beamed at me, and when Alex wasn't looking, he blew me a kiss. My eye was twitching again. I craved a Vicodin.

Afterwards, he phoned me. "See why I couldn't break up my family, even though I love you so much I can't function?"

"He's precious," I said, trying not to vomit. "Maybe it's best if we stop seeing each other." I hung up. I ignored his calls and didn't answer the door when he came pounding on it. He left me notes in my mailbox, desperate missives that Artie and I giggled over.

"So it's over with the hayseed?" Artie asked, flopping on my sofa.

"Hardly," I said.

"You're not going to break up his family, are you?"

"*I'm* not. He might though. He's not as happy as he thought he was."

"What about the brat? You're not exactly the mommy type."

"He's a bit of a problem."

"It'd be awful if something happened to him," Artie said, undoing his belt and wrapping it around my neck.

"Awful," I said. Artie cinched the belt and I saw stars.

Now, Curtis is at my house. He's weepy and tiresome with his professions of love and angst over what to do about it.

"Life is short," I tell him. "I'm turning thirty-five next month. I can't be wasting my time on dead ends."

"If it wasn't for Alex—"

"Look, we've each got to do what's right. I love you but you're taken." I let my voice break a little. I'm fond of Curtis, or maybe it's his desperate adoration that appeals to me. I offered to let him tie me up but he was shocked, wouldn't do it. He said he couldn't enjoy degrading me that way. Artie would pistol-whip me unconscious if I let him.

"I can't live without you," Curtis says. "I'm going to ask Susan for a divorce. We can share custody of Alex. You'd be such a good influence on him, I just know it."

"Baby—are you sure?"

"I love you, Nina. I want to marry you, take care of you. You could quit your job and we could have babies together, little brothers and sisters for Alex." I feel a dark, thrilling victory. I hide my face in his shoulder and cry real tears, not from happiness but for something I can't name. My skin burns and itches like I've rolled in dried grass.

He tells Susan he's in love with another woman and that he wants a divorce. She goes berserk in a quiet, Midwestern way, developing a taste for vodka and taking to her bed. He says that Alex has started to wet his pants.

Susan begs Curtis to reconsider. She calls his mother in Arkansas, who calls him and implores him to come to his senses.

"I'm in love, Mother. Life is short. I'm divorcing Susan, not Alex. I'll always be his daddy and he'll spend half his time with me." He's talking to her on his cell phone in my apartment and I listen to the conversation with my head lying on his bare genitals. I lick the head of his penis while he consoles his mother. "Susan will be fine. Everyone in California gets divorced. She'll be financially secure, and Alex will still have both of his parents plus a wonderful new stepmother. Wait until you meet her," he says, closing his eyes, his cock rigid against his belly.

After Curtis's lawyer serves Susan divorce papers, she takes Alex to a neighbor's house. She fills her car with gasoline and then drives into their snug, weather-stripped garage. She closes the door and drinks a pint of vodka with the motor running; a photo of Curtis, Alex and her laughing in front of a Christmas tree is on the dash. When Curtis phones to tell me of her suicide, I'm shocked, but then it occurs to me that he won't have to pay her alimony or divide their assets—we'll have it all. And then it hits me that Alex will be with Curtis twenty-four/seven now. Artie is right—I'm *not* the maternal type. I can't help wishing she'd taken Alex with her.

Curtis flies to Little Rock with Alex and Susan's body to bury her there. He phones to tell me how awful and sad the scene is there, how much he misses me, and how he wants to get married as soon as decently possible, to create a stable family environment for Alex.

"I can't take care of someone else's brat," I tell Artie.

"You are some piece of work, girl," he says. "Do you have any guilt at all?"

There's something in me that cringes to think of Susan alone in her car, breathing in carbon monoxide and gulping down vodka. And there's another part of me that revels in it, finds a black satisfying thrill in her despair.

"The way I see it," I tell Artie, "it's dog-eat-dog, survival of the fittest. Susan wasn't a survivor."

"Brrr," Artie shivers. "I never want to get on your bad side," he says, getting undressed.

"Too late," I say, reaching for the box under my bed.

Curtis wants Alex and me to get to know each other slowly. We go to the zoo. We go to the beach. We rent Disney videos and watch them at Curtis's five-thousand-square-foot home in La Cañada-Flintridge, an affluent suburb of Los Angeles. It's done in a kitschy country decor that makes me want to gag. I see black granite and silk-covered walls. Chrome and nickel and sumptuous wool carpeting to hide the cliché of peg-and-groove oak.

"Why don't you take him out by yourself this Saturday?" Curtis says. "I have to attend a seminar."

"Sure, honey," I say. "Good idea."

I've been having bad dreams and sleeping poorly. I have a blotchy rash on my chin and my joints ache. I'm getting migraines. I don't feel like hanging out with Alex, who snivels all the time, but Curtis doesn't want me to move in or get married until he feels Alex is comfortable with me. I ask Alex what he'd like to do and he shrugs. I get him into the car, the Range Rover that Susan killed herself in, and buckle him into his seat belt.

We head to a coffee shop to get some breakfast. As we're driving I look at Alex and see tears streaking his face.

"What now?" I ask.

"I miss my mother," he says. All Alex knows is that his mother is dead.

A dazzling scotoma appears in my field of vision, harbinger to a migraine. And me without a pain pill.

"I'm sorry about your mommy, honey," I say to him. The first throbs descend on my brain. "But she's in heaven. With God. She must be happy there." My mouth has a metallic taste, like I've been sucking a lead pipe.

"She's not happy, not without me and Daddy," he says. "I hate you. I wish *you* were dead." His small body convulses with sobs. My head hurts so bad I have to pull the car over. I'm nauseated and break into a sweat. I've just enough time to open the car door and vomit the coffee I had earlier, then bile. I'm drenched, my shirt sticks to my body and sweat streams from my armpits. I feel a tapping. I wipe my mouth on my sleeve and turn to see Alex, who's undone his seat belt and is kneeling on the seat, rubbing my back and shoulder with his hand, his face anxious and tear-stained.

"I'm sorry," he says. "I didn't mean it." He covers his face with his hands. I put my arms around his sturdy little body and my nose fills with his boy smell. He hugs me, trembling. Each beat of my heart is a wrenching explosion in my brain. I left some Excedrin Migraine back at Curtis's house.

"I have to go back to the house and get my headache medicine," I tell him. I can't see; the scotoma is like a sizzling white starburst that takes more than half my field of vision from each eye, leaving me with blind spots. I hang a U-turn, careening the car crazily. Despite the headache it occurs to me that Alex has left his seat belt unfastened. I imagine hurtling into one of the thick, old elms that line the street—a horrible accident while crazed with a migraine, and poor little Alex, his seat belt undone, becomes a Scud missile. I envision him shooting through the windshield, impacting the tree. A lightning storm of pain blazes in my brain.

I pull the car over.

"Put your seat belt on, Alex," I say, panting, leaning my head on the steering wheel. Snot streams from my nose to my lap. "Safety first," I say. He nods and fastens it, and I manage to get us back to Curtis's house.

"I'm going to take my medicine and rest," I tell Alex. I lie down on the living room sofa and he goes to watch television in the den. I fall asleep and wake to find him standing over me, pale and worried-looking.

"I'm okay," I say.

"Do you want a drink of water?"

"That'd be nice." He brings me water in a plastic Pokémon cup, arranges his blanket on my legs and puts his hand on my forehead. I tell him again that I'm fine and he goes back to watch TV. I think of how his body felt in my arms, how it pulled at something in me. I wonder if I could ever love him, if I could ever love anything. I vomit the water I've just swallowed and Alex brings paper towels and mops it up. I tell him again I'm fine.

By the time Curtis gets home in the afternoon my headache is gone and Alex and I have eaten pizza and watched cartoons. I tell Curtis about the morning, how sick I was and how Alex took such good care of me. Alex listens, pink with pleasure, his eyes downcast and shy. Curtis, of course, is crying.

Later I'll go home and write Curtis a letter to tell him that it's over. He won't recognize it as the only decent thing I've done for as long as I can remember. I'll call Artie and tell him I've gotten off the gravy train and he'll come over. "So," he'll say, "I guess we're back in business."

I'll get the metal box from the bottom of my closet, the one I keep locked up. I'll find the key in my jewelry box and open it.

"Make it hurt," I'll tell him.

Sit

Bernice L. McFadden

He was hearing talk. Whispers that sounded like palm tree leaves brushing against each other. He'd grown up hearing this type of talk. When he was a boy the women talked over and around him. Now those same women spoke directly to him and eyed him with interest, wondering if he was the same type of lover his father had been.

His mother's friends, some cousins, not so distant, his brother's wife, his sister's classmates and the women who walked the beach offering to braid the white people's hair for two dollars a plait.

There were others. Many, many others.

He'd been back only a day and a half. His skin was still pale from the cold German winter he'd spent making love to a rich white widow.

He hadn't wanted to go; he hated the European winters and the bright sunshine that lent no warmth at all.

But he went anyway because she'd promised him her dead husband's brand new BMW if he'd come and stay through the New Year.

Now he was back, a little heavier from the rich foods he'd eaten during the two months he was gone, but still solid—still, according to what he was hearing, desirable.

"He back on the island."

"Nah, man! That ain't true!"

"How you meaning? I saw him myself, in town near the stop post!"

"He look just the same, you know! A little bigger, but—"

"But?"

"But still sweet as hell!"

Butler laughed to himself. They all wanted an invitation to sit, but he was particular, and so there were only two or three from the island who had experienced it.

He jumped into his car and started down Highway 1, beeping his horn and waving his hand in greeting when people stared wide-eyed at the slick black car and then, recognizing the license plate number, yelled out to him.

The news would spread quickly about his return and the new car. There would be plenty of jealousy and malice. But Butler was used to that and mentally prepared himself to deal with it.

He took the right turn sharply and screeched onto Spring Garden Highway; Square One's "Faluma" pounded out from the car speakers.

Turquoise water to his left, brightly colored wall houses, palm trees and uniform-clad schoolchildren to his right, he smiled at the beauty of his surroundings. Barbados was more than an island to him; it was a beautiful woman, full of lush, deep valleys and salty curves.

Barbados is the only place for me, he thought as he came to a stop in front of Bombas Beach Bar & Restaurant.

The lunchtime crowd filled every table and stool in the place. Butler stood at the end of the bar closest to the doorway, perusing the crowd. There were so many different ethnic groups there that the chattering voices sounded like a conference at the UN.

A group of German men, their skin seared red by the sun, sat ogling three English girls who Butler was sure were all under the age of eighteen. A family of Italians sat nearby, their waitress sucking her teeth as she explained to them for the third time that she could not take lire as payment. Across from them two Frenchmen sat quietly smoking cigarette after cigarette while sipping wine, openly amused by everything going on around them.

The rest of the people were locals, except for a golden brown Yankee girl seated at a table closest to the railing. She had her feet propped up in a chair, her head moving between the blue ocean before her and the open magazine that lay in her lap.

The sea breeze was teasing the colorful material of her wrap, flipping it back and forth, allowing Butler to see that her thighs were thick.

Butler tilted his head to try to see what the rest of her looked like.

"Lemme have a Banks," Butler called out to the bartender for the national beer.

"Well, look who's back."

The voice was soft and he recognized it immediately. Still, he was annoyed at the interruption and took his time moving his attention between women.

She looked good, even better than before he'd left. Her dark skin was smooth; her eyes were large, round, and clear, with long eyelashes that feathered out. She was short, thick and tight with a behind so broad you could amost sit a plate on it.

"What you saying, Sandra?" Butler reached out for her, but she stepped away.

"Can't shout. And you?" She gave him a wicked smile.

"I all right, you know."

There were no more words between them for a long time. Butler could see the remnants of her disappointment still clinging beneath her eyes. Could tell by the sharp cut of her jaw that she had cussed him plenty of times over the few months he had been gone. He had decided that he would invite her to sit, but she had spoiled it, and all the desire he felt for her had slipped away.

She needed a lift from the supermarket and Butler had obliged. It was safe; he knew his cousin, her husband, was away.

She told him he should stay awhile, that she was going to make coo-coo and steamed fish and he was more than welcome to some.

"Some of what?" he asked, allowing his eyes to move from her face to her breasts and then down to her center.

Sandra smiled, shook her head and walked into the kitchen.

They'd known each other since first form, and he'd always yearned for her; but back then he was small, shy and unsure of himself. By the time they were grown, his cousin Ian had her, and Butler had put his desire for her away. But things had begun to change between Sandra and Ian, and whenever Butler found himself in her company, their eyes often wandered over each other and old familiar feelings began bubbling to the surface again.

Butler strolled through the small living room, looking at the framed photographs on the wall and end tables. Wedding pictures, Ian looking scared, Sandra glowing and jubilant. A family portrait, a pregnant Sandra, a sober Ian and their grinning one-year-old daughter, Fay, between them.

"You need help?" he called from the living room as he straightened the lace doily on the arm of the chair.

"No, I'm fine."

The sky was darkening and thunder sounded in the distance. The rain, even the thought of rain, made him horny. He moved to the doorway of the kitchen and watched as Sandra bent over to retrieve the frying pan from the cabinet. Butler smiled and took a seat at the table.

Sandra dumped the okra into a pot of boiling water and began to stir.

"Work all right?" she asked, her voice wavering a bit. She could feel Butler's eyes on her.

"Yeah, man." Butler's response was slow, his words thick. Sandra felt a stirring in her belly.

Five minutes passed and no words moved between them. Sandra wiped at the perspiration on her forehead and then dumped the cornmeal into the pot.

Butler enjoyed watching Sandra turn the coo-coo, her strong arms working the cornmeal and okra together, her hips moving in rhythm with her limbs. She was nervous and excited; he could tell by the way she kept shifting her weight from foot to foot and the small hisses of air she released after every fourth breath. Butler stood and made his way toward her. The tiny wall house vibrated beneath his footfalls.

She kept stirring.

His hands were on her hips, pulling her backward against him.

She kept stirring.

He kissed her neck and moved his hands over her thick belly.

She kept stirring.

He took the heavy wooden spoon from her hand and turned her around to face him. The coo-coo bubbled behind her, and she felt the heat of the flame on her backside.

He pulled her to him and Sandra's breath quickened; she could feel him hard against her. Butler softly kissed her eyelids, her cheeks and the tip of her nose. Sandra felt dizzy and reached over to grab hold of the counter.

Butler ran his tongue slowly across her lips and then down her chin, before bending his head to kiss the space above her breasts.

Sandra could no longer contain herself and flung her arms around his neck; she showered his head and face with kisses before finally finding his mouth and swallowing his tongue.

She felt hungry and primitive in a way Ian had never made her feel.

Butler moved away from her; it was Sandra's turn to reach out for him, but he gently pushed her hands away.

His eyes never left hers as he slowly unzipped his pants. Sandra's breath caught in her throat when he reached in and pulled out his penis.

It was large and long and Sandra thought she'd never seen a more beautiful piece of flesh in her life. "Mercy," she whispered when her breath returned.

Butler stepped forward and took her hand; it was shaking. "Touch me," he whispered.

Sandra placed her trembling fingers on him.

His eyes still held hers, urging her on, and she obeyed, wrapping her hand around it and closing her eyes as the flesh pulsed against her palm.

Butler smiled; he had decided he would extend her the invitation to sit.

"Come," Butler started, but Sandra had dropped to her knees; she wanted him in her mouth, she wanted to taste him.

Butler looked down on her as she gently kissed the tip of his penis; it jerked and Butler let out a groan. "I love you," Sandra whispered.

The invitation came to a halt on the tip of his tongue.

He pushed her away.

Sandra, confused, looked up into eyes that had grown as dark as the sky.

Butler zipped up his pants and looked over at the stove. "The coo-coo is sticking," he said as if she hadn't just had him in her mouth.

"When Ian coming back?" he said as he walked over to the table and sat back down.

Sandra was still on her knees, her eyes searching the tile floor for answers.

"Next two days." Her response was quiet and filled with shame.

"Where he gone again . . . Canada?"

"No. Miami."

She stood, dragged her hands across her face and turned off the stove.

"All right, then." That was Butler's way of saying good-bye. He slapped the table and jumped up from the chair.

"Yeah, man," Sandra said, still unable to look at him.

She heard the door slam shut, the car engine turn over and the rattle of gravel as Butler sped away.

Sandra had not forgotten that embarrassment, and now, standing there before him again, her face flushed with the memory of it.

"Ian all right?" Butler asked before tilting the beer to his mouth.

Sandra looked at Butler for a long time before responding. "Yeah," she said, her voice dripping with disgust.

"Kids good?"

Sandra didn't answer. She just turned and walked away.

* * *

Butler shook his head and drained the contents of the bottle. Women always put their hearts in situations where they didn't belong. Sandra was still hurt and confused, but Butler knew she wouldn't always feel that way. *She'll get over it,* he thought. Just then the basket weavers, fish women and silver peddlers who used Bombas as a shortcut to the road came up the steps that led from the beach.

Butler looked at the women and smiled. They were gray-haired, but their skin was still as smooth as silk, their legs and arms muscular.

"He look like his daddy spit 'im out, ya know!"

"Pretty, smooth and dark like chocolate."

"Lips like pillows!"

"Dem eyes! You could lose yourself in dem, ya know!"

"Jes like 'im father!"

"Hmmmm . . . Wonder if he hung the same, too?"

"Ya too old for that nonsense, Judy!"

A flurry of giggles surrounded him and he turned to face five brown, smiling women who no longer looked at him as a child. Their eyes moved over his body slowly, seductively drinking in every inch of him. The women breathed him in and then moved away. Butler looked at their retreating wide hips and round bottoms before calling for another beer.

Butler's father, Errol, was a seaman. He was shorter than Butler, stocky, with rugged good looks and a passion for rum and women. Errol bragged about having had more than three hundred women in his lifetime, and Butler, who idolized his father, set out at a very young age to accomplish the same.

"It sweet, eh?" the fish woman shouted over her shoulder at him before stepping out onto the road.

Butler felt sure she wasn't referring to the basket of fish she balanced on top of her head.

The lunch crowd began to thin as people returned to their hotel rooms for a midday nap, or back to their beach chairs and books. But the stranger remained and so did Butler.

"What the lady drinking?" Butler asked Peter the bartender while nodding toward her table.

Peter was tall, dark and lanky with a pleasant smile. The customers loved him, and after a few of his special rum punches, almost always ended up revealing their deepest, darkest secrets to him.

"She?" Peter pulled at his chin while his eyes moved slowly from Butler to the woman. "Well, she don't talk much. 'Hello, afternoon, night.' That's all I hear from her and this the third day she been in here."

"Uh," Butler said, pulling at his own chin.

"She look good, though. Thick, nice eyes. Gray, I think. Maybe contacts, I don't know."

Butler tilted his head once again in order to try to get a better look at the woman. Something about the way she held her head and the rigid line of her back told him that she had not been touched for a very long time.

Butler was entranced; it was rare to stumble upon a woman like that. It would be, he thought, almost like having a virgin.

"Well, what she drinking?" Butler asked again, reaching for his wallet.

"She drinking some of everything. She call for something different each time and only take a sip or two from it. She waste it, the ice melt down and the waitress take it away," Peter said, and then dropped his voice and leaned closer to Butler. "I don't think she really a drinker."

They grinned together. They both knew that a woman alone on an island was either running from something or looking to run into something.

"Well, send over a bottle of champagne, then," Butler said, and placed a hundred-dollar bill on the counter.

Peter's eyes widened. This type of behavior from Butler was usually reserved for the white women he was trying to pick up. This would be the only money he would spend. After the champagne, the talk and the sex, they all but handed him their credit cards.

The beach boys didn't usually try to hustle black women,

especially American black women; those women had a thing about spending money on a man.

"Ya sure?" Peter asked, looking down at the money and then at the woman.

There was no indication that she had money; she wore no jewelry, she paid her bills with a credit card that wasn't platinum or even gold.

"Yeah, man." Butler said. "Very sure."

Haydree watched the surf roll and a sense of calm washed over her. This trip was everything she never knew she needed. Barbados and its gentle breezes, crystal-clear waters and star-filled nights seemed to be the perfect tonic for all that ailed her.

She could live here, she thought, as a smiling Rastafarian waved at her from the beach. Haydree nodded her head and then looked down at her magazine.

She did not want to encourage conversation, even though every night since her arrival she'd been stricken with a heavy sense of loneliness. It was a temporary dilemma; her fiancé, Griffin, was back at home in Brooklyn, waiting for her.

"You want to go away?" Griffin asked her for the fifth time. "A month before we get married, you want to take a trip to an island without me?" He was confused for the first few days, and then angry, the closer it came to her departure date.

"I just need to do something totally for me, Griffin. I can't make you understand. Just accept it," Haydree had said as she stroked his hand.

Griffin did just that—he accepted it, just as he accepted their sexless relationship.

Griffin hadn't pressed her about it. They were, after all, both in the Church. He understood, he said, even when their kissing moved to heavy petting and Griffin would push her back into the couch, climb on top of her and begin a slow grind that made his already stiff member larger and harder, so hard she thought it would cut through his jeans and the soft silk skirts she'd taken to wearing whenever she knew they would be together.

She'd allowed that, as well as his hands beneath her blouse, but not beneath her bra. He could cup her Victoria's Secret–clad breasts, kiss the lace material, even the soft mounds of flesh the bra did not cover, but nothing else.

Anything else would definitely lead to sex, and they were, after all, both in the Church.

Griffin always said he understood, even after Haydree finally pushed him off.

She would clear her throat, nod at the clock and then the door. He'd grimace, reach out for her again; she'd laugh and slap his hands away before moving from the couch to the wing chair on the other side of the room.

They'd meet up again at the front door to exchange good-byes and small kisses while Griffin checked to make sure his shirt was buttoned right and his tie was straight, and worked to adjust his still-stiff penis to a comfortable and unnoticeable position in his pants.

Haydree had decided when she met Griffin at the church social eight months earlier that she would not give herself over to him, not before he said he loved her, not before the engagement ring and not before she walked down the aisle and said I do.

If she'd learned nothing else from her relationship with Curtis Anderson—the incident, as she referred to him—she'd learned restraint.

Curtis was a hard two years ago. She was only twenty-four, working part-time at Macy's and going to school full-time to finish her degree in fashion merchandising. Curtis was thirty-two and worlds ahead of her on every level. She was taken with him immediately; he was so different from the men her age she'd dated. He was suave and debonair, like the men she'd read about in the Arabesque romance novels that were piled high alongside her bed. She told him she loved him after their second date, and two months later he invited her to move in with him.

She'd expected that living together would be sweet and sticky-good like the chocolate ice cream they'd shared after the first time they'd made love. She'd expected the long sweaty nights with him between her thighs, the headboard thumping rhythmically against the wall while he called her name over and over again until he climaxed and moaned, "B-b-baby."

After lovemaking they took long hot showers, him bathing her breasts and the small pointed flesh between her legs with the sponge and soon after, with his tongue. Her fingers would grip his shoulders for a moment, her nails boring into his tight brown skin. Then when the orgasms began to rip through her and she could feel her body slipping against the tile, her hands would find his head, her fingers becoming entwined in the dreadlocks she had encouraged him to grow as she screamed, "Yes, yes, yes!"

It had been that way all through the summer, lusty and wild, Haydree showing up at work without panties and calling him from the stockroom to tell him so, hiding behind boxes and touching herself as she cooed to him over the phone.

When she'd told him the color green made her horny, he took her to Central Park, where there were hundreds of shades of green. They spread a blanket out on the grass near the lake but far enough away from the sun-worshiping, thin white women with their large breasts in tiny bikini tops.

When the sun dipped and the droves of people thinned, Curtis guided her to an out-of-the-way bench and had her straddle him there.

Curtis kissed her chin, her eyelids, and then deeply on the mouth. His hands held her behind, guiding her in a slow grind against his hips. Haydree shuddered and her panties went damp.

He slipped his hands beneath her short sundress and pulled her thong to the left, while his right hand cupped her vagina. "Ooh," Haydree squealed. "No, Curtis, no," she exclaimed, becoming more excited. She was panting by the time he slipped himself free of his sweatpants and moved inside of her.

He did nothing for a long time, he just held on tight to Haydree's waist as she rolled her hips against him. Her eyes were closed and her head thrown back as she sucked hard on her bottom lip to keep from screaming. A dog howled off in the distance and for a brief moment Haydree felt ashamed of herself. Her hips slowed to a stop.

"No, baby, please," Curtis panted before arching himself upward and easing himself deeper inside of her.

Haydree felt a rush of pleasure rip through her, everything around her began to spin and meld, she felt pain and joy all at once, and for a split second her mind danced on death and then heaven. When she cried out his name, the birds fluttered from the treetops and Haydree's body went limp against him. She sobbed into his neck and wailed like she'd lost her best friend, instead of having finally found the orgasm she'd spent years reading about.

Yes, she thought living with Curtis would always be like that; and it had been, for a while. But then September came along and the nights grew cool, and so did Curtis.

He didn't look at her the same; most times he didn't look at her at all. Their lovemaking, when he did decide to touch her, was mundane. He would climb on top of her, peck her once on the lips, shove himself inside of her and ride her for three minutes before rolling off and going to sleep.

Curtis said it was work. He said she needed to understand that his job was demanding and that it drained him mentally, emotionally and physically.

Haydree bit her tongue and tried to understand.

Fall moved to winter, allowing night to creep in at five; Curtis followed at ten, sometimes eleven. An indecent hour for a married man, Haydree's mother, Doris B., had said. "But not for a man who is getting the milk without having purchased the cow."

Haydree knew that her mother really wanted to say, "He got another woman, fool." But all Doris B. did was roll her eyes and suck her teeth in that signature Bajan way.

Haydree just folded her lips and looked down at her thighs, which had grown thick with satisfaction. Happy weight is what she called it, those extra pounds a woman always seemed to pile on when she was enthralled in a relationship that had her grinning like a fool all day long. Now she supposed the misery that was growing inside of her would soon melt it all away.

There were business dinners, client socials, and even a ski trip that wives and significant others were not allowed to attend. "Sorry, baby," Curtis said, and pecked her on the cheek as he packed the new Shetland sweater she'd bought him for Christmas.

When she shared these things with Doris B., her mother huffed, gave Haydree a narrow look, then finally said, "Wake up, child, he got another woman.

"I said ya should have never moved in with him. A good man, a decent man would have asked you to marry him, not shack up with him," Doris B. said as she sliced a thick wedge from the mango she held.

Haydree just looked down at her thighs, which were growing thinner by the week.

Reality came tumbling in when she found the hair. She had touched it to make sure she was seeing right. She slid her pinkie across the length of it to make sure it wasn't a streak of soap or a piece of thread clinging to the tile. After touching it and being sure, she felt dirty and turned the hot water on high, shoving her hand beneath the steady rush of it and scrubbing her hand until it was raw.

"You're imagining things," Curtis said as he moved about the bedroom trying his best to avoid Haydree.

"Do you see them?" Haydree screamed as she held up eight strands of blond hair between her thumb and forefinger. She'd gone searching, finding two more in the bathroom, three on the couch, one on the floor in the kitchen and two on her pillow.

"Yeah, I see it, Haydree, but I don't know where they came from."

Curtis's composure was breaking down, his voice was beginning to waver and there were small beads of sweat forming around his hairline.

"The bitch is white and going bald!" Haydree screamed and rushed at Curtis, smashing all eight hairs into his face.

"Bastard." She spat and walked out of the house.

That was two years ago, but she still carried around that hurt; and even though Griffin was a good man, she knew he would never have her the way Curtis did. Her bruised heart wouldn't allow it.

"This is good," Doris B. exclaimed after Haydree showed her the two-carat diamond ring. "Yes, yes, this is good, this is the right way to do things!"

Haydree didn't know about all of that, but she did know that Griffin loved her more than she loved him and that was a good thing, a safety thing.

So what was she doing, just a month from becoming Mrs. Griffin James, on a romantic island all alone?

She was here to give herself her own little private bachelorette party, a final stupendous send-off from single life. She was here to get her groove back, take it home, and share it with Griffin on their wedding night.

But she was already three days in and no one had tickled her fancy. She had received a lot of attention. Island men could do wonders for a woman with low self-esteem. They showered you with compliments and looked at you like you were the most beautiful woman they had ever seen.

Haydree was waiting for a sign, something inside of her that would let her know *he* was the one.

"From the gentleman at the bar." Peter set the silver bucket down on the table, smiled and walked away.

Haydree stared at the foiled neck of the champagne bottle. She'd had beer and cocktails sent over to her, someone even had Peter bring over a branch of hibiscus blooms—but champagne, this was a first.

Haydree turned to meet the dark, smoky eyes of the stranger who smiled casually and saluted her with his beer bottle.

He was good-looking, not pretty, but striking in a way that made you want to look at him longer than would be considered appropriate. His dark skin glowed and his teeth stood out bright and clean against his complexion. His chest was wide, and Haydree could see the sharp curves of his well-developed chest through the thin material of his tank top.

He was more than striking; he was beautiful.

Haydree smiled and mouthed, "Thank you."

Though the sun had started to slip from the sky, the stranger still had not approached.

Haydree thought she would have to take the champagne back to her hotel room, maybe enjoy it after dinner in her private Jacuzzi. No, champagne was meant to be shared. She would invite him to do just that.

But when she turned around, the stranger was gone. Peter was alone at the bar, arms folded and grinning.

Haydree's mouth dropped open.

"His name is Butler. I think he wants to invite you to sit, but you never heard that from me," Peter sang out to her, and then began to wipe at the wet spots on the bar.

Haydree just stared at him. What the hell did that mean?

Two days passed and Butler had not made an appearance. Haydree found herself staring into every dark male face that walked into Bombas. She squinted her eyes against the bright sun in order to make out the dark figures moving up and down the beach. She even strolled over to investigate a group of men congregating beneath a coconut tree, allowing her eyes to move slowly over the faces that looked back at her.

"Nice lady."

"Beautiful!"

"You alone, can I come?"

Haydree felt like a fiend in need of a fix; but her preferred dealer had disappeared, and soon she might have to settle for something less.

She had even dreamed about him and had touched herself while sleeping.

What did he sound like, how did he feel, what would he smell like? Haydree had one more day and night left; she had to know.

"So where is your friend?"

Peter's eyes went wide with surprise as he looked quickly over his shoulder to make sure she was speaking to him.

Haydree dropped her beach bag down to the ground and settled herself on a stool.

Peter smiled knowingly. "Uhm, who would that be? I have lots of friends, pretty lady."

Oh, it was a game, Haydree thought. She would play along.

"The man who sent over the champagne the other night."

Peter scratched at his chin and looked up into the sky. "Champagne?"

"C'mon." Haydree laughed.

"Ah yes, Butler! Well, I don't know where he's at. Why, are you looking for him?" Peter grinned.

"Well, yes, I guess I am. I mean, a bottle of champagne . . . well, that was very nice of him. I'd really like to thank him."

"Yes, it was, he's a very nice man." Peter's tone was playful, teasing. "If I see him, who shall I say is looking for him?"

"Haydree Sanders," Haydree said, thinking she sounded a little too eager.

"Uh-huh, the pretty Haydree Sanders. The American, Haydree Sanders?"

Haydree didn't know where this was going, but she would continue to play along. "My parents were born here."

"Oh, a Yankee Bajan."

"I guess," Haydree said, shrugging her shoulders.

"And where would the pretty lady be staying?"

"Why?" Haydree's New York instincts kicked in.

"Just curious."

Haydree looked at him for a while; he seemed harmless. "Sandy Lane."

Peter grabbed his chest and stumbled dramatically backward. "Well, the only people that be at Sandy Lane looking like me and you get a paycheck at the end of the week."

Haydree laughed. It was true; there was one other brown guest at the hotel and Haydree suspected he was Iranian.

Peter rubbed his thumb and forefinger together. "Expensive," he said.

"Yes it is, but I'm worth it." Haydree was surprised at the boldness of her response.

"Well, it looks as if you are," Peter said, nodding his head in agreement.

Haydree had to make a decision. Butler had not returned to Bombas, and she was leaving the island in the morning. There were the doorman, the pool guy and the front desk manager. All of them appealed to her and they had made it known that she was quite appealing to them, but she still couldn't get Butler out of her mind.

Maybe it just wasn't meant to be, she thought, as she swung open the French doors and stepped out onto the marble balcony.

She had just showered; her body was wrapped in a thick white towel that barely contained her wide hips and broad behind. The foliage around the balcony was thick, so Haydree was not concerned with a strolling guest or hotel employee seeing her from the winding stone path below.

The air was warm and languid, wrapping her in the sweet scent of hibiscus. Haydree's body swayed to the gentle sounds of the steel band as she sipped champagne from a crystal flute.

She was debating whether to order dinner up to her room or join the forty or so couples in the main dining room. The captain was always very gracious to her, and he was good-looking, too. She had noticed a few lustful looks sent her way.

"Maybe him," she said aloud just as she heard soft tapping at the door.

It was seven-thirty. That would be Claudia the maid, there to turn the bed down, fluff her pillows and don them with chocolate mints.

Haydree didn't ask who, just flung the door open.

"Good night."

Haydree took two steps backward and then her hands flew up to her mouth. She didn't know if she was going to scream for help or shout for joy.

Butler stepped in and closed the door.

"We say good night here; I know in America you say good evening."

Haydree could neither speak nor take her eyes off him: the smooth black skin, thick arched eyebrows and those lips, she could live for days off those lips.

"How did you get up here?" Haydree said when she was finally able to speak.

"I took the stairs, of course." Butler grinned.

Haydree cleared her throat and took another step backward. She was more than happy to see him, but at eight hundred dollars a night she thought security should be a little more scrupulous.

Butler read her mind. "Everyone knows Butler." He purred and Haydree felt her knees begin to knock.

"I hear you were looking for me," Butler said as he walked past Haydree and out onto the balcony.

Haydree was stunned at his boldness, but found herself following him like a cat in heat.

"Well, I, uhm, yes, I wanted to thank you for the champagne. That was very nice of you."

Butler leaned over the balcony. "You could make love right here and no one could see." He turned to face Haydree; his eyes danced over her body, reminding Haydree of her attire. "They would hear, though," he added, and ran his tongue slowly across his top lip.

Haydree felt her skin begin to heat.

"Are you a screamer?"

Haydree's face flushed. "I think you should leave." She supposed that was the right thing to say, something a decent woman would demand.

You didn't come here to be decent, did you, Haydree? the little voice in her head reminded her as she tugged the towel tightly around herself.

"Okay." Butler began to move toward her. She could smell the sweet, subtle scent of his cologne.

"I mean, you come here unannounced, you say these things . . . what am I supposed to do?"

The words fell from her mouth like rainwater. She didn't want him to go; she wanted him to stay. She wanted those lips on her body.

Butler stopped in front of her and placed his hands on her bare shoulders; they were hot and Haydree thought that she would melt beneath them. He looked deeply into her eyes. "I have something you need. I know this because I see it missing from your eyes."

He bent and kissed her. He kissed her passionately, as though they were longtime lovers, and just like that Haydree began to melt.

The towel fell to the floor and Butler stepped back to admire her. "Lovely," he said as he slid his hands down her hips and then her thighs. Haydree was shaking. Butler walked around her like she was a statue in a museum, commenting on the beauty of her backside, the arch of her back and the small mole on her shoulder blade.

When he came face-to-face with her again, his shirt was off. Haydree had never seen a more perfect chest; his nipples were ebony against his mahogany skin.

Butler cupped her breasts, tilting his head so he could lick each nipple with the tip of his tongue before sucking it into his soft, warm mouth.

He guided her through the French doors and toward the bed. There he eased her downward, kissing her as she went. He stood over her, slowly removing his watch, sandals and pants.

"Don't be afraid," he said when Haydree's eyes widened. She had never seen a penis so large in all her life—well, not up close and personal. She wanted to tell him that it wouldn't fit, no way, no how!

Butler slowly parted her knees and then pushed her legs apart. Haydree turned her head away with shame. The lights were on and bright. "Hmmmm," he crooned as he ran his index finger between her legs. "You are so wet."

Haydree moaned. He hadn't even penetrated her and already there was a wet spot spreading beneath her.

Haydree reached out and took his penis in her hand. It pulsed like the beat of a heart, and like dozens of other women Butler had had, she too thought it was beautiful.

"I don't need sex," he said as he positioned himself beside her.

Haydree turned to look at him. "What?"

"I don't need sex," he said again.

Haydree felt a tinge of fear rip through her. If not sex, what did he want?

Butler stroked her hair and then moved his hands over her breast and down between her legs. His eyes held hers even as he slipped his index finger inside of her and began moving his thumb rhythmically back and forth across her clit.

Haydree's mind began to bend.

"I want to invite you to sit," Butler breathed into her ear before pulling her earlobe into his mouth.

"Yes, yes," Haydree groaned. She didn't know what she was saying yes to, but the good feeling he was creating between her legs didn't let her care.

She was almost there, almost there, her back began to arch just as Butler pulled his hand away.

Haydree shot straight up.

Butler just laughed and rolled over onto his back.

Haydree jumped up from the bed, looked down on him for a moment and then went out onto the balcony for her towel and a bit of sobering air.

"What the hell am I doing?" she whispered to herself as her senses slowly returned to her.

"Haydree, come, sit." Butler's voice floated out to her.

Haydree spun around. The lights were off, but she could make out Butler, his body bathed in the cool blue moonlight. He was sprawled out on the bed, his cock stiff and reaching for the night sky. Haydree's mouth went dry.

"Shit," she said as she dropped the towel and headed back to him.

"Come." He urged her over.

"Condom?" Haydree asked, wondering if he had any, or was she going to have to go for the pack she had hidden in her tampon box.

"No need. I told you I don't want sex."

"What?" Haydree was really confused now.

"Come, woman. Come and sit."

Haydree eased closer and closer, like a small child unsure if she should accept the candy that was being offered by a stranger.

Their knees touched.

"C'mon." Butler indicated his stomach.

Haydree straddled his legs and slid forward, hoisting herself high enough to clear Butler's towering penis, before coming to rest on his stomach.

He grabbed her behind and began pushing her forward, forward until his chin rested in the short hairs that covered her vagina.

Haydree understood now.

She had been loved that way before, but never in this position of power, of total control.

Butler inhaled her and then eased his hands beneath her and suspended her.

He raised his head and kissed her in the place that no man had seen or touched in two years. He took her clit between his lips and rolled his tongue across its pointed tip. Haydree's body shook. "Oh God yes," she moaned as a searing jolt of pleasure moved through her.

Just when she didn't think she could take any more and her throat was almost raw from screaming, Butler eased his head away from her and the invitation rolled from his mouth.

"Sit."

Haydree took a deep breath, eased herself down and felt her body explode into a million pieces as Butler slid his tongue deep inside and swallowed her.

Haydree gazed out onto the blue Caribbean waters as the jetliner climbed away from the island. Her body jerked every so often at the memory of it all. She would try hard to put those thoughts away before she landed, but she had four hours to replay the whole scene over and over in her head and that's exactly what she'd planned on doing.

"S'cuse me?"

Haydree turned to see an attractive white woman looking down at her. "I was wondering if this seat is being used, I hate sitting so close to the flight deck. Would you mind?"

Haydree shook her head no and moved her pocketbook from the seat. "Come, sit," Haydree said, and didn't know why she'd phrased it that way or even used that tone, his tone.

Haydree's eyes locked with the woman's and she knew from the expression on her face that she had been extended the invitation, too.

The woman nodded her head knowingly. Haydree just grinned.

Loved It and Set It Free

Lisa Montanarelli

In 1985, my first dildo drifted out into Baltimore Harbor on a broken bookshelf. I'd owned this dong for less than a day, but we'd been through a lot together. The night before, I'd eased it inside me, while my high school best friend lay next to me faking sleep. Most people keep their first dildos until they rot. But I was different. I loved mine and set it free.

"The Boss" was a single piece of beige rubber shaped like a billy club or toy sword—with a handle, a cross-guard, and a ten-inch dong in place of a blade. The label on the package said "anatomically correct," but even then I knew ten inches was a little on the long side.

I first laid eyes on The Boss when my friend Kim took me to a porn shop on East Baltimore Street. Kim was a born comic with gawky limbs and a wide, pouty mouth. The summer before our senior year, she carried bottles of Sun-In and hydrogen peroxide wherever she went. When we weren't swimming, she poured them over her head and lay in the sun.

By the time we went back to our all-girls school that fall, Kim's hair hung in clumps like bleached snakes. People said she dyed her hair orange to match the school colors—orange and green. So she dyed it green for one of the field hockey games. This was in the mid 1980s, before grunge rock.

Around that time, Kim and I were playing "I Never"—one of

the few games you can win through sheer inexperience and naïveté. In "I Never," players take turns confessing things they've never done. If the other player has done something you haven't, she owes you a penny. I won two cents easily, because I'd never bleached my hair or dyed it green.

It took me a bit longer to come up with my third confession. Finally I said, "I've never really gotten a good look at another person's genitals."

This was true. Although I'd made out with both boys and girls, we rarely took off our clothes. Instead, we groped each other in dark, semipublic places—fumbling with buttons, bras, belt buckles, and zippers, and glancing over our shoulders every few seconds, expecting our parents to catch us in the act. I'd even lost my virginity in the classic sense on the floor of a toolshed. In short, I'd had plenty of action, but little chance to look at naked bodies or genitalia. I had rarely ever seen boys naked, except when our neighbor little Billy ran across our backyard with his babysitter chasing him. I saw girls' bodies in locker rooms, but felt much too self-conscious to stare.

I expected Kim to question my confession, but she just nodded and tossed me another penny.

"You should come over and watch porn movies the next time my parents go away. That'll give you plenty of chances to check out other people's genitals."

Unlike my parents—the last in town to buy a microwave or any new appliance—Kim's family owned a VCR. When her mom and dad went out of town, Kim rented porn. We planned our porn adventure months in advance and waited for her folks' next vacation.

Kim rented porn videos from a seedy shop on "the Block." The 400 block of East Baltimore Street is Baltimore's red-light district, where the locals go to see naked girls dancing and buy porn. Growing up in the sub-suburban sprawl of Baltimore County, I'd never been to the Block, so we drove me past it one night, when Kim borrowed her mom's Honda Civic.

"That's the Block." Kim pointed out the window. "Look now, or you'll miss it."

I pressed my face against the passenger window. Neon lights danced against the starless sky; then darkness swallowed the neon as we dove back into the night.

"Was that it?"

"Yeah. It's only one block. I'll go around again."

The second time, she drove more slowly, so I could read the neon signs: Golden Nugget Lounge, the Crystal Pussycat, Gresser's Gayety Liquors, Savetta's Psychic Readings, Crazy John's, and the Plaza Saloon. Glamorous names—at least for kids growing up in Baltimore.

We didn't rent videos that night. We just drove by, and Kim pointed out Sylvester's Videos, the store where she rented porn.

"They have booths in the back where you can watch videos, but you don't want to go in there. The walls are sticky and gross. Let's just wait until my parents go away, and we'll rent videos to take home."

Finally Kim's parents scheduled an overnight camping trip. They left on a Friday; my heart and stomach fluttered all day at school. After our last class, Kim and I met in the locker room and changed out of our school uniforms and into jeans.

"Hurry up," said Kim. "I want to get down to the Block while it's still light out, so no one will break into my mom's car." Kim had her mom's car for the weekend. We slung our backpacks over our shoulders and walked out.

As we drove downtown, I pressed my face against the window and marveled at the dirt on the streets. City dirt is different from country dirt. Where I come from, dirt is brown like mud or red like sandstone. In the city, black grit cakes under your fingernails and sticks to the concrete. The wind writes messages on the sidewalk with black dust and dead leaves. I soon realized we were driving in circles, passing the same buildings.

"Are we lost?"

"No, I'm looking for parking."

"Where are we?"

"The Block, silly."

I winced. "It looks different by day."

While night had hidden everything but the neon signs, the sun exposed gray concrete buildings and trash in the street. Turned off, the neon signs were only pale plastic tubing and dusty electrical cords. We passed the same ones I'd seen at night—the Crystal Pussycat, Savetta's Psychic Readings, the Plaza Saloon. At night, they had seemed intimidating, but seeing them by day was like watching a flashy porn star sleep in her underwear and snore.

"Why didn't you take that parking space we just passed?" I asked.

"I want to park in front of the porn shop so I can keep an eye on the car."

After we'd made several more loops, a car pulled out right in front of us, across the street from Sylvester's Videos. Kim pulled up alongside the space.

"That's tiny. You can't fit in there."

"I'm going to try." She cranked her steering wheel all the way to the right and backed into the space much too fast. As her back tires rammed the curb, her elbow struck the horn with a loud honk. A siren squealed in the distance. Across the street, the door to Sylvester's Videos creaked open, and a guy with beady eyes and slicked-back gray hair stepped out of the store and glared at us.

"Shit, Kim. Let's get out of here."

"Get out and direct me," she said calmly.

Trembling, I climbed out of the passenger seat and motioned her into the space. When I glanced over my shoulder, the beady-eyed man had vanished. Kim got out of the car.

"That's the first time I've parallel parked since my driver's ed test," she said.

I followed her across the street. The door to Sylvester's Videos was covered with ripped, faded posters and random thumbtacks. The paint was chipped. It hadn't been painted in years.

I looked at Kim.

"Come on, let's go in." She hoisted the door open—revealing a heavy black plastic curtain. Glancing at me, she pulled aside the curtain and slipped inside. I followed her into a dimly lit square room. Videos lined the walls floor to ceiling.

The beady-eyed man—the same one who had glared at us outside—sat behind the cash register.

"Howdy, girls." He smiled with crooked yellow teeth.

At the sound of his voice, two customers in the front room turned and peered at us. Both were bent over videos, with their collars turned up and hats pulled down over their eyes. Kim and I were the only two women in the store—perhaps the only women who had been there in a long time.

Kim took me on a tour of the narrow, low-ceilinged rooms, pointing to X-rated videos with titles like: *The Penile Colony, Hannah Does Her Sisters, Astropussy Strikes Back, Public Enema Number One, Two,* and *Three*.

"The booths are in the back." Kim pointed to a man slipping behind a black plastic curtain. "You can rent your video, close the curtain, pop your video in the slot and jerk off—Lisa . . . Lisa!" She poked me.

I had frozen facing a wall of rubber penises and sundry other body parts, including hands and arms. I had never looked at a penis this way before. For the first time in my life, I could look at it without worrying about what the person attached to it thought of me. At the time I was too inexperienced to know that one never quite looks at penises the way one looks at dildos, propped up on shelves, strapped onto harnesses, or packaged in plastic, hanging from hooks on walls—like in Toys "R" Us, or meat in a butcher shop. Through my entire childhood, I had been looking at Ken dolls without penises. Suddenly I was looking at the opposite of Ken dolls: penises without bodies attached.

Given my deprivation, this wall of "anatomically correct" models—in black, brown, and beige, complete with rippling rubber veins—was an embarrassment of riches. Some of them, labeled "stints," were hollow and attached to elastic straps. One even had leather straps. What were they for? Then I saw the flying-saucer-shaped "butt plug." Why would anyone need that? Plugs were those things you put in sinks to stop the water from draining. Was a butt plug the opposite of an enema? I was used to things having practical purposes. This was the first time I'd encountered something intended strictly for sexual pleasure, and I just didn't get it.

"Haven't you ever seen a dildo before?" asked Kim.

"N-no," I stammered.

"Check this out." She pointed to a plastic package containing a foot-long rubber forearm with the hand clenched in a fist. I'd never seen anything like it, except those dismembered arms you find in Walgreens at Halloween.

"What do you think you're supposed to do with this?" Kim asked. "Bonk somebody over the head?" I was pretty sure that wasn't what you were supposed to do, but before I could say anything, she yanked the plastic package off the hook and bonked me over the head with the rubber forearm.

"Kim! Stop!"

She clasped her hands over her mouth and burst into giggles, shoulders shaking uncontrollably. Customers in the store turned and stared.

"You're going to get us kicked out of here!" I hissed.

"Shhh! Lower your voice!"

"Look. Here's the description." We huddled over the package and read the label in excited whispers:

12.5 inches long, 3 inches wide, 9 inches around
Size: Huge
Product Category: Anal stimulation
Color: Black
Made of: Rubber
For use in this part of the body: Anus

"It's for the . . . the . . . anus?" I asked in disbelief.

"That's the butt," she whispered smugly.

"I know what an anus is, but I don't see how it could fit."

She shrugged. "Don't ask me."

"Do all these things go up your butt?" I gestured to the wall of dildos and butt plugs.

"They don't go up my butt," she giggled. "But you can put dildos up your vagina. Haven't you ever put vegetables up there?"

"No. Have you?"

"Of course."

"You're kidding. What kind?"

"Cucumbers, carrots, and zucchini. When I was about twelve, I used to sneak them out of the vegetable drawer in the refrigerator and put them back when I was done."

"Ew! Yuck!"

Kim hung the rubber arm back on its hook. "We're not getting this," she whispered. "Let's get some dildos. Here's a thin one. It's eight ninety-nine."

Kim handed me a package. I stared at the label: THE BOSS: ANATOMICALLY CORRECT DONG.

"Are you suggesting I buy this?"

"Why not? I'll buy one too."

"How do you know it'll fit?"

"You just have to try your luck. You can't try it on in a dressing room like a pair of jeans."

I laughed nervously.

"Come on," she said. "Let's move on to the videos. That's what we came here for."

I followed her back into the front room, where we rifled through hundreds of video boxes and decided on two orgy movies: *Farm Family Free for All* and *Group Grope 9*.

Growing up in the seventies and eighties, I had become familiar with the made-for-TV Roman orgy—where toga-clad patricians get it on with priestesses of Isis in the Roman baths (made to look like contemporary Jacuzzis). My parents allowed me to watch these programs due to their so-called historical significance. Hence much of my early sex education came from *I, Claudius,* and the head of a penis still reminds me of a Roman centurion's helmet. When you watch orgy scenes in historical dramas, perhaps you are supposed to think, *My god, how decadent,* and believe rampant orgies caused the fall of Rome. Modern libertines should learn from history and beware! But I watched the orgies and wondered, *Why don't people do that anymore?* I thought Roman orgies, like Egyptian mummies, were ancient history. *Farm Family Free for All* and *Group Grope 9* were my first signs that the orgy lived on, at least in contemporary porn.

After nearly an hour of X-rated shopping, Kim and I finally carried our lurid wares to the cashier and spread them out on the counter. The beady-eyed man winked at us.

"You want some K-Y Jelly for those dongs?"

"That's not a bad idea," said Kim. "We'll take some."

Outside, dusk had fallen, and the neon signs flickered on in orange, pink, and green. We crossed the street. Kim's mother's car was still intact. As we drove back to her house, I shivered when a cop car whizzed by. What if they pulled us over and found the porn videos and dildos? I pictured our mug shots on the front page with photos of The Boss underneath.

When we finally made it back to Kim's, we emptied our bags onto the living room rug and tore open our dildo packages.

"Hey, this isn't very realistic. It doesn't have balls!"

The Boss, as I mentioned earlier, had no balls. Instead, the penis-shaped shaft ended in a handle and cross-guard, like a toy sword. I looked down at the dildo in my hands.

"Darn. I really wanted to see what balls look like."

"You'll see them in the movies," said Kim. *"En garde!"* She held the dildo by the handle and brandished it like the sword Excalibur, but the rubber weenie just flopped around.

I giggled. "That's one lame weapon."

"Oh well. Let's watch the videos." Kim switched on the TV and took the videos out of their plastic boxes.

"What do you want to watch first, *Farm Family Free for All* or *Group Grope 9*?"

"How about *Farm Family Free for All*?" We unzipped our sleeping bags and curled up side by side, propping our heads up on pillows so we could see the TV. Punching buttons on the remote control, Kim fast-forwarded to the opening scene, where a well-endowed hottie, looking much like Heidi with a blond mullet and cleavage, skipped through a cornfield in an astonishingly low-cut blue gingham dress. The scene changed to the inside of a barn, where two men in plaid flannel shirts and overalls were milking cows. The younger man stood up and stretched.

"Gee, Paw," he drawled. "Ah wish Sissy would git here with those vittles. Ah need a break."

Outside, the blonde in blue gingham peeked through a crack in the barn door. Seeing the men, she slipped one hand up her gingham skirt and opened the door.

"Did Ah hear y'all say yuh need some refreshments?"

The men turned and gaped as she stepped into the barn, toting a straw basket in the crook of her arm and fondling her breasts.

I shook my head. "God, Kim! Can you believe these accents? Nobody talks like that."

"Watch this." Kim pointed the remote control at the TV. The video flew into fast-forward. Three more people in plaid flannel, calico, and gingham speed-walked into the barn, where they all tore off each other's clothes, sprawled on the hay, and plugged themselves into each other's orifices, fucking and sucking as fast as an assembly line.

"Dammit, Kim! I'm never going to see genitals this way!" I grabbed the remote control and pushed "play." My jaw dropped. Two tanned, tight-bodied girls, locked in a 69, were licking each other. With identical big boobs and blond mullets, they looked like twins. In fact, they were twins. This was *Farm Family Free for All*. My heart beat faster. I'd never seen two girls having sex, even on screen. Out of the corner of my eye, I peered at Kim. Did she know this was going to be in the video? I knew orgies meant sex scenes with more than one man, more than one woman, or several of both. Somehow it hadn't dawned on me that girls would be getting it on with each other. I gaped at the screen transfixed, crotch tingling under the covers. I crossed my legs and squeezed my thighs together. Finally, I couldn't stand it anymore. I slipped my hands between my thighs. Kim's elbow brushed against mine, so the tiny hairs on our arms stood on end. She was doing the same thing I was, but I didn't dare look at her.

I wondered if the people at school would be able to tell we'd watched lesbian porn. Would they see it in our eyes?

In English class earlier that year we had been talking about Virginia Woolf. The class was sitting in a semicircle around the edge of the room, facing our teacher, Mrs. Byrd. My mind was wandering, when someone mentioned the word *lesbians*. Patty raised her hand.

"Have there ever been any lesbians in our school?"

"Yes," said Mrs. Byrd. "We've had some."

"How can you tell?"

"Sometimes two girls are . . . closer than normal."

"Does the school do anything about it?" asked Patty.

"We try to split them up," said Mrs. Byrd. "Sometimes we tell their parents."

A hush fell over the room, as we all exchanged nervous glances. I looked at Kim, who sat across the room from me doodling. She didn't look up.

If they found out, would they separate us? Tell our parents?

Meanwhile, on *Farm Family Free for All,* the rest of the family joined the girls with mullets. The scene turned into a more traditional orgy with writhing bodies—a monster with multiple arms and legs. I circled my clit with my fingertip, less interested in the family scene, but barely admitting—even to myself—the girl-on-girl porn had turned me on.

Kim grunted next to me. She was snoring.

"Come on—I know you're not really asleep."

No answer.

"Kim?" I put my hand on her shoulder.

She was really asleep. I thought about waking her up, then changed my mind and circled my clit faster, feeling lucky and slightly out of control. My back tensed and my heart quickened, as I tried not to make any noise or move anything except my hand. I had played this game before—many times. The goal was to come without waking the other person. Sometimes, no doubt, the other person woke up and just pretended she was still sleeping. I had faked sleep myself when someone was masturbating beside me.

On screen the camera zoomed in on the girls. A man fucked one of them from behind, while she licked her sister's pussy. Next to me, Kim was breathing slack-jawed—either sound asleep or damn good at pretending. Her legs twitched under the covers. Reaching my arm outside the blankets, I groped around on the icy hardwood floor. My hand landed on the dildo—cold, hard, and ribbed with veins. I dragged it into the sleeping bag and pushed its cold head against the wet lips of my cunt. With a deep breath, I tried to ease the rubber cock inside me. It didn't fit. I pushed, took another breath, and pushed again. Still no go. Suddenly I remembered the K-Y Jelly. I ran my hand over the floor and found the K-Y. It looked like a tube of toothpaste. I squeezed a glob of clear lube into my palm. I couldn't believe how cold it was. I thought of Kim's refrigerated cucumbers. I didn't want anything that cold near my pussy, but if I wanted The Boss inside me, I knew I had to get the lube in there first.

I soaked the head of The Boss in K-Y, then—wincing—squeezed the cold lube directly into my cunt. It spilled onto the sleeping bag, spreading out in a puddle under my butt. Shivering, I glanced at Kim. Her eyelids fluttered. She was dreaming. With several deep breaths, I shoved The Boss inside me. My whole body shook—my cunt was so full, it almost burned. I looked at Kim again. What would it be like to kiss her? I brushed my lips against her cheek. Mustering all my courage, I stretched out the tip of my tongue and licked her hair.

Kim stirred and turned over on her side. I froze. Was she awake? I listened for her breath. I was sure she was awake, but I couldn't stop now. I eased the dildo in and out of my cunt. The woman on the screen came like a swimmer gasping for air. The man squeezed his cock and squirted white jizz on her tits. I came with them, melting into the scene. The cock inside me was his cock. My sounds shot out of her mouth. My wave of pleasure rocked her body on the screen. My cunt contracted and spit out the dildo—wet between my thighs. Warmth spread through my belly, heart, and limbs. I sank into the floor—and yet I was floating.

Someone nudged me.

"Stop it."

"Wake up."

"What? What time is it?"

"Five-thirty."

"What the fuck?" I glanced around the dark, unfamiliar room.

"Wake up." Kim's shadowy form bent over me.

I suddenly remembered where I was—sprawled out on Kim's living room floor. I must have dozed off after I came.

"Lisa, listen to me. We have to get rid of these now."

"Get rid of what?"

"These." She bumped me on the cheek with something rubber. I winced as the overhead lights blinked on. What was she talking about? Then it dawned on me. *Jesus, what did I do last night?* I remembered the wall of dildos, The Boss, and licking Kim's hair—shit! Was she awake when I did that? What did she think of me?

"Lisa!" Kim repeated, bonking me on the head. "We've got to get rid of these things before my parents get home. They'll be back early this morning."

"We can't just throw them away. They weren't cheap."

"Do you want to take them home with you?"

"Shit." I peered at the dildos as my eyes adjusted to the light. "I don't think I can."

"What should we do with them then? We can't just throw them in the trash, or bury them in the backyard. The dogs'll get at them."

"Can we burn them?"

"God, no! They'd stink."

"Well then, let's just walk a few blocks down the street and throw them in someone else's trash."

"Good idea. We can take the car and drive a little ways away. We'll take the videos back to the store too." She put the VCR on rewind.

It was still dark outside. The crickets were chirping as we stepped out into the cold, wet air. Kim drove. I dozed in the passenger seat with the dildos in my lap wrapped in newspaper. The car screeched to a stop.

"Where are we?" The sky had turned dark blue. I rolled down my window, tasting the salt air.

"We're at Fells Point. I was thinking we could throw them in the water," said Kim. We climbed out of the car. I followed her to the edge of the pier. Water was lapping at the dock, and the seabirds called out, flapping their wings. One swooped within inches of the water, a white ghost.

Holding the dildos wrapped in newspaper, I peered down into the black water.

"It's a shame to let these sink to the bottom of the harbor."

"I know! Let's float them out to sea on one of those boards over there." Kim darted away and came back seconds later, dragging a dismantled bookcase. She pulled off the top shelf and dislodged several long rusty nails.

"We'll put the dildos on a raft. That way, someone might find them."

We lowered the board into the water. Kim tore off a sheet of newspaper and wrote: "S.O.S. Free to a Good Home."

I leaned over and placed the dildos side by side. Wrapped in newsprint, they looked like twins in swaddling clothes. I thought of Romulus and Remus—the twins abandoned to the elements, who washed up on shore and founded Rome. Who knew what great fortune or conquest lay in store for our dildos? Would they be suckled by she-wolves? I watched them float away, convinced that some lonely soul, who desperately needed dildos, would find them.

After the Beep

Simon Sheppard

The voice on the answering machine is deeply masculine and commanding: "I know who you are and I know what you're going to do for me. You're to follow these and all further instructions exactly. You'll strip down now, right now; stop the tape until you're completely naked."

He's just gotten home, is still in his suit, has a bag of groceries in one hand and the day's mail in the other. It's crazy. A joke. Even so, the hand with the mail reaches over and pushes the Stop button. What harm could it possibly do? No one can see him. He's had a hard day at work. He's come back to an empty apartment. He was thinking of beating off when he got home, anyway. What harm could it do? Might as well play it through.

Being a methodical sort of fellow, he carefully leaves his clothes in a neat, folded pile on the chair in the hallway. He's down to his Calvins before he realizes that his dick has gotten as hard as it gets. He steps out of his briefs. Hard-on wobbling ahead of him, he walks back to the telephone and pushes the Play button on the answering machine.

"Good. Now that you're naked you're going to start playing with your cock. Very gently at first. Just take your forefinger and softly rub the little flap of skin under your dickhead. Feels good, doesn't it? Okay, now run your forefinger down the underside of your cock." His dick does a little spasmodic dance as he teases the tender manflesh. "Thumb and forefinger now, in a circle around your dick. Still gently. Just tease it. Now rub a little faster." A sticky pearl of precum forms at the piss-slit. "Good, now I want you to spit in your hand and slowly rub the spit around your cockhead. Squeeze down. Harder. Now run that wet hand up and down the shaft." He's leaning against the wall next to the front door, eyes closed, following every command of the unknown man's voice. "Okay, now I want you to really get to work on that boner. Wank it hard. Rub that cock of yours from the piss hole all the way to your blond bush." So the man does know who he is, knows he's a blond! The man is able to picture him there, jacking off on command. The man is . . .

He groans loudly, tenses his stomach. His thigh muscles tremble. He shuts his eyes tighter and shoots a big load of cum all over the kilim on the hallway floor. The message machine is still running. " . . . know you enjoyed that. To acknowledge your pleasure, you'll change the outgoing message, incorporating the phrase, 'If this is Jack calling, please be sure to leave a detailed message.' Now go wipe up. I'll be in touch." There's a beep, then the whir of the rewinding tape.

This is crazy, he thinks, going to get a handful of paper towels to mop up his congealing cum. He pops a Lean Cuisine into the microwave, half watches an animal show on PBS, and gets ready to put himself to bed. But before he turns in, he goes to the answering machine, pushes a couple of buttons, and speaks into the handset. "Sorry, I can't take your call right now. Please leave a message after the beep and I'll be in touch as soon as I can. And if this is Jack calling, please be sure to leave a detailed message."

The next day, he has to restrain himself from picking up his phone messages while he's at work. But when he gets home, he's rewarded by the blink of the messages-waiting light on his answering machine. There are three messages, actually. The first is from his mother; he fast-forwards through that. The second is from his friend Anthony. Fast-forward button again. And then the voice, insistent, maybe gently mocking, sexy as hell.

"I see that you enjoyed last night as much as I did. If I know you, you're already getting undressed without waiting for my instructions. Well, I'll let it go this time. And I'll bet your cock is already hard." Right on the money. "Once you're naked, I want you to turn off whatever lights are on in the apartment. Then you're going to go into the living room, pull up the center Levolor, and turn on that little lamp on the writing desk." My God, the guy's been in the apartment! "Do it now. Leave the machine running and keep it at top volume so you can hear my instructions." He's reluctant to do what he's been told. He's shown off a few times in the steam room at the Y, been to a few sex clubs, but standing buck naked in the window of his own apartment . . . "Do it. Do it now. What are you afraid of? Do it or you'll never hear from me again." What *is* he afraid of? His apartment is several floors up. With only that little lamp on, no one who's not looking for him is liable to see him from the street. He's switching on the lamp when the voice speaks again. The high volume has made the voice sound harsher. "Good, now stand there facing out to the street. You don't have to press yourself up against the glass, but you must be within sight of someone standing across the way. That's right. Now, play with your tits, gently at first. Just lick your fingertips and rub them over your nipples. Now press down harder. Grab 'em, pinch with your thumbs and forefingers. Go on, pinch harder." He shudders with pleasure. He wonders if anyone can see him. No one on the sidewalk is looking his way, but the unlit windows in the buildings across the street stare back at him like rows of dark eyes. "Now keep your left hand on your chest and move your right hand slowly down over your belly." His moist palm starts stroking his tautly muscled abdomen, ruffling the trail of very blond hair that gradually widens as it expands into a curly bush. The edge of his hand presses up against the base of his hot, achingly stiff erection. "Now your balls. Use your right hand to hold your dick up against your belly while you squeeze your balls with your left. Yeah, stretch 'em out. And squeeze harder." He watches his reflection in the window, watches his naked body as it obeys the voice. Outside that window, beyond his ghostly reflection, the city is going on about its business. In a weird way, he thinks, he's having sex not just with himself, not even with just the unknown caller, but with everyone out there. He squeezes his nuts harder and with his other hand begins to stroke his shaft. His dickhead becomes slick with precum. He brings his left hand up, sticks his fingers in his mouth, and licks them clean. "You're doin' good, real good. Now take your hand away from your balls and get the forefinger real wet with spit. Then reach on back and just slide that wet finger all the way up that slick asshole of yours. All the way up. Now turn around so your butt is facing the street. And take that finger and slide it in and out and in and out. And play with your dick while you're finger-fucking yourself. Now turn back around. Keep your finger up your ass. No, why don't you take it out for a second, get some spit on your middle finger as well, and stick them both up your butt?" He stares out at the city as his fingers penetrate his own wet heat. A light goes on in a window across the street. A middle-aged woman in a nightgown shuffles into view. She looks in his direction as she reaches up for her window shade and slowly pulls it closed. Has she seen him? "Now get some spit on your right hand and start working that dick real good. Work that piece of meat till you come. Do it. Do it because I'm telling you to." And his hand works the wet shaft, faster and faster, till his asshole clamps down around his fingers. He gives a wordless shout, and arcs of cum shoot through the air, hitting the windowpane and running down the glass. He feels woozy, puts his wet hand against the window frame so he won't lose his balance. In a minute the voice speaks again: "Now that was fun, wasn't it? You can go clean up now. And after you do, change your outgoing message again. Make it, 'Jack, my meat is yours.' Just that. Talk to you soon." And a beep.

The next day, he spends much of the afternoon thinking about getting home from work and checking his answering machine. The hours crawl by. He's so horny he has to go into the men's room and beat off. Within a half hour, he's horny again.

When he finally gets home, the light on the machine is blinking. Two messages. His dick is getting hard. He pushes the Play button and reaches for his fly.

"Honey, this is your mother. I almost thought I had the wrong number, till I realized it was your voice. Who is this Jack? Oh well, give me a call, please. You never returned my last call, and I'm starting to worry. Is anything wrong? You know I worry." *Beep.*

Second message: "So I guess our little arrangement is working out. But maybe it's time you had a rest. You've been working so—hard—to please me. Go out, treat yourself to a nice dinner. I'll be back in touch soon. Keep your hands off your dick till then. Don't shoot a load, or you'll never hear from me again. Oh, and I really liked it when you licked your precum off your fingers. Very nice." *Beep.*

So he was being watched last night! The voice was there, could see him. The thought makes his dick swell even harder. If he could, if he were allowed, he'd reach down and . . .

The phone rings. He doesn't pick up. Outgoing message: "Jack, my meat is yours." *Beep.*

"Honey, it's your mother. When you get home . . ."

He picks up. "Yeah, hi, Mom . . ."

The rest of the work week drags by. No message. By Friday he's so horny that he's bouncing off the walls. Once, he catches himself humping his crotch against the underside of the desk. Luckily, his co-workers seem not to have noticed. He leaves work early and rushes home.

Yes! The light is blinking! He pushes the Play button. The tape rewinds itself and plays. He hears the familiar, commanding voice. "I'm sure you've obeyed me since our last encounter. Now I have some very specific instructions for you. You're to follow them to the letter. Got that?" He finds himself nodding agreement. "After dinner you're to change into a T-shirt and 501s. Wait until midnight. I don't care what you do till then, just as long as you keep your hands off your cock. Then you're to go to"—he gives the name of a well-known sex shop in the warehouse district—"and buy yourself a cock ring and a buttplug. Go into the video arcade in back, enter one of the booths, drop your pants, put the cock ring on and the buttplug in. Button up, leave the shop, turn right, and go down the street a few blocks till you reach the playground. There's a pay phone at the northwest corner of the park. Wait there for further instructions. Got that?" He finds himself nodding again, which is silly, since the caller can't see him. Or maybe he can. *Beep.*

The place reeks of Lysol. The bored, pierced guy at the register rings up his purchases: a black leather cock ring with chromed studs, a shiny black buttplug, and a small bottle of lube. He buys a handful of tokens and heads back to the video booths, shopping bag in hand. A few guys are roaming the corridor between the booths. A cute, fat guy in a business suit. A man in a T-shirt with a well-developed body and an attitude to match. A tall, skinny student type wearing glasses.

He ducks into a booth and latches the door. Dropping a token in the slot, he pulls out his prick and plays with it while two L.A. surfer types go through the motions on the blurry screen. When he's half hard, he puts the leather band around the base of his dick and balls, cinches it tight, and snaps it shut. He's opening the lube when he hears the door rattle. Someone's trying to get in. He squirts a big gob of lube in his hand and reaches back to his butt. The door latch gives way. It's the skinny student. In the bluish light of the video screen he looks a little scared and awfully young.

The intrusion nearly makes him stop, but then he looks in the kid's eyes and the kid sort of smiles and rubs the crotch of his jeans. So he turns around and, back to the young guy, he slowly and deliberately works the lube into his ass. With his dry hand, he grasps the buttplug and starts working the tip of the plug into his slippery hole. Feet spread, back arched, he grabs his ass with his free hand, pulls his asscheeks apart, and pushes the plug deeper and deeper till, with a little pop, it goes in all the way to its base. His dick is rock-hard as he turns back to the tall, skinny kid. The boy's prick is just fucking huge, and he's jacking it for all it's worth. Reflected in the kid's glasses, tiny little surfer boys are having sex.

"Sorry," he says to the boy, reaching for his pants, "I gotta save my load."

The boy's hand is moving at the speed of sound. "Just . . . one . . . minute . . . please." Pound pound pound. "Just . . . let . . . me . . . looook . . ." And the kid shoots, a little ocean of cum forming on the dirty floor between them. "Thanks, mister," the kid says, tucking his big, half-limp meat back into his jeans and walking toward the exit. The video screen's gone dark. The horny surfers have gone back to wherever good little surfers go.

At this hour, the streets around the playground are deserted—too late for basketball, too early for cruising. He's only there for fifteen minutes or so when the pay phone on the corner rings.

He picks up the receiver.

"Very good. You follow directions well."

It's the first time he's actually had him on the line, the first time he can talk back. "Who are you?" he asks, but the voice on the other end just keeps talking, and he realizes he's listening to a tape.

". . . reach down and play with your dick through your jeans. Stroke it until it gets hard." It's already hard. "Now unbuckle your belt and undo the top two buttons, and reach on down into your pants." His hand slides over his hairy belly, down to the moist hardness of his dick. "Start jacking off. Slowly. Go real slow." He concentrates on playing with his swollen cockhead, stroking the sensitive flesh. A gooey drop of precum oozes from his piss-slit. "Now then, keep one hand on your dick and use your other hand to unbutton your pants all the way down." Awkwardly cradling the phone on his shoulder, he does as the voice commands. His pants sag to his thighs. "Now peel down your briefs." The streets are empty, but still . . . He looks around. There, across the street, just beyond a streetlight's glow, stands a man. A handsome, bearded black man, muscles bulging beneath a white T-shirt. Looking his way.

He pushes his briefs down to midthigh.

"And now you'll jack off for me. Take your time. Do a real good job. I'll be watching." He grabs his stiff dick. The cock ring has made it extra hard. Staring straight at the man across the street, he starts massaging his manflesh. "Right. You have permission to come. Eventually. In fact, you *will* come. That's an order. Hang up now. And stay there till after you're done. I'll be back in touch." He hangs up, brings his hand to his mouth, spits in the palm. Lubes up his dick with the spit. He looks down; the pale white flesh of his wet cock is gleaming in the streetlamp's yellowish light. He looks across the street. The black guy is playing with his fly, slowly pulling it down. He reaches inside and pulls out a big, dark piece of meat.

Every stroke makes his hole clamp down on the buttplug, sending rushes of sensation deep into his body. The other man is beating off now, too. He thinks he can see foreskin sliding over the man's swollen cockhead. The man takes a few steps back, into the light, and leans up against a building, thrusting his hips forward, never letting go of his big cock.

A car cruises by, a red Miata coming between them, but doesn't even slow down. The black man is pumping faster now, a half-smile on his broad, handsome face. Seeing the smile somehow gets him even hotter. He shifts his weight and his pants fall to his ankles. More spit. He rubs one hand all the way up and down the slick, veiny shaft and plays with his tightening balls with the other. Faster. The black man matches his pace. Beating off harder, faster. The black guy grunts, thrusts his hips forward, and shoots big gobs of cum onto the sidewalk.

He can't hold back any longer. He shoots, too, buttplug deep in his hot ass, hard dick spasming again and again.

When he's caught his breath, he realizes his hand is dripping with cum. Looking straight into the black man's eyes, he brings his hand to his mouth and licks it clean. The bearded man smiles and brings his own hand to his mouth, licking his fingers one by one. Then the guy puts his still-hard cock back into his pants, nods once, and walks off.

The phone rings. He's standing there naked from the waist down, and the nighttime breeze is cool on his butt. He lets the phone ring while he reaches down and pulls up his jeans. Some of his load has landed in his briefs and his crotch feels wet and sticky.

"Nice job. Wouldn't you say so?"

"Yeah, I tried my best."

"I'll bet you did." It's not a recording this time. The voice is actually talking to him!

"So was that . . ."

"The man across the street? No, it wasn't me. He was just a pleasant surprise. For both of us."

"I want to meet you."

"What?"

"Meet you. I want to meet you."

"Are you sure?"

"Yeah. Nobody's ever made me feel the way you make me feel. I want to meet you and repay you. Make you feel good. I'll do whatever you say. Anything."

"Say 'please.'"

"Please." He can't believe it; his dick is starting to get hard again. "Please, sir."

"Tomorrow night. Midnight. Your place."

"You know where it is?"

"I know where it is."

"Of course you do."

He spends all Saturday naked in his apartment, the buttplug firmly in his ass. Every time the phone rings, his dick jumps. Pavlov's dick. At midday he finds himself stark naked, talking to his mother on the phone while absentmindedly stroking his stiff cock.

"Is anything the matter, dear? You sound a little strange."

The afternoon drags by. By dinnertime he's played with himself so much his dick is getting sore. He wasn't given permission to jack off, but then he wasn't forbidden to, either. So he pours a big glob of lube on his cock and goes at it again. But he's saving his cum. For midnight.

As he strokes his slick meat, he tries to imagine who the voice can belong to. He flips through the men he knows. Men from the office. Guys at the gym. Old tricks who might have saved his number. Young guys. Old guys. Fat. Buff. Doesn't matter. The voice is pure, abstract. Whoever it belongs to will turn him on. Every man passing through his mind turns him on. He's vibrating with pure lust. His dick is a tuning fork.

He orders a pizza. Mushroom and sausage. When the delivery boy arrives, he opens the door naked, with a hard-on. The pizza man, a hunky young Latino, doesn't blink; he's seen weirder than that in this city. He gets a big tip.

After dinner, he's too distracted to watch TV. He flips through some old porn magazines. Pictures of Scott O'Hara sucking his own dick.

The phone rings. He rushes to answer it.

"Is Yolanda there?"

Wrong number.

Ten o'clock. He thinks about the messages. The faceless man who tells him what to do.

Eleven o'clock. The anticipation he's felt. The freedom of having sex with no one in particular, and so with everyone.

Eleven-thirty. The mystery. The pure distillation of desire and surrender.

Twelve o'clock, exactly. The doorbell rings. He snaps the cock ring on. His dick has never been so hard. This is it. He goes to the intercom.

"Who is it?"

"Who the fuck do you think it is?" The voice. Even through the tinny intercom, instantly indentifiable.

Long silence.

"Well, buzz me in."

"Y'know, I've been thinking."

"Yeah?"

"Thinking that maybe it's not . . ."

". . . not such a good idea to meet face-to-face, right?"

"It's just that it's been so good, so hot."

"So why ruin it, right?"

"You're angry. Are you angry?"

"I asked if you were sure you wanted to meet. Remember?"

"And I thought I did want to. Then. But your messages . . . your messages are so . . . powerful for me. I wouldn't want to take a chance on ruining that."

"You're jacking off, aren't you?"

"Yeah."

"You're gonna come. For me. And I want to hear you when you shoot your load. I want to hear you over the intercom."

It only takes a minute. He tries to hold back, make it last longer, but he's lost control. Moaning and cursing into the intercom, he has one of the most amazing orgasms of his life. When he recovers, he says, "Are you still there?"

Silence.

Cum drips down the wall.

He spends Sunday in a funk. Has he made a mistake, chased the voice away forever? He rerecords the outgoing message, begging Jack to keep calling. He goes to the gym, the first time in weeks, doing an extra-hard workout to try and relieve his stress. It leaves him so exhausted he doesn't even pay attention to the hot middle-aged man jerking off in the sauna.

When he gets home, the phone is ringing. He fumbles with the key, lets himself in just as the machine is picking up the call. It's his friend Anthony. He never did return Anthony's call. He wants to talk about what's been happening, but he can't tell Anthony. Anthony wouldn't understand. No one would.

At the office the next day he throws himself into his work, tries not to think about the voice. He's still sore from his workout. He owes himself a hot bath when he gets home.

*   *   *

The light on the answering machine is blinking. He presses Play.

"I'm gratified that you want to continue our relationship. Not that I expected anything else from you. I know how much you need to obey me." His dick is hard. "Okay, go run a hot bath, strip down, and then I'll have further instructions."

Half an hour later, as his soapy hands work his dick, he hears it, and thick ropes of cum spurt into the lukewarm bathwater. The comforting sound, the sound that seals his devotion, his surrender.

Beep.

Salt

Bill Noble

The week Shoshanna left her, snow dusted the *pali* for the first time in memory. It was so cold she could hear the year's crop of mangoes plopping green off the trees. Then, with the white still clinging to the cliffs, rangers came and burned her shack down. And nearly busted her, too, if she hadn't run. That was a big deal—and it was a big deal, too, when some hippie in a home-made pigskin vest walked up and found her cold and crying by the ashes.

Mandy wiped her face on the back of a sooty hand and glared, but the hippie wrapped his jacket around her shoulders till she stopped shivering. He didn't seem to need to talk much, and sure as shit she had no need to talk to him, so they just stood, sur-rounded by guava and tangled lantana, listening to the embers pop.

"Nothin' to salvage," he said after a while. And then, looking her nakedness up and down, "Warm enough?"

Part of her wanted to say *Fuck you,* what with the man smell and the pigskin stink, but she managed to keep her mouth shut.

"Got some food in my boat." Her belly cramped at the word *food,* so she turned and looked at him for the first time.

He had a gray ponytail, a lean belly, and a pair of raggedy shorts that must have been white once. No underwear: Mandy could glimpse the crookedy dangle of a testicle.

Salt. That's the other smell. He's a paddler. She pulled the jacket tighter and grunted, "I guess I could eat." She fought some brief internal battle and then looked at him again. "Thanks."

"Hike back to the beach?" And then he seemed afraid he'd overstepped. "Or I could bring stuff up."

"Nah," she said, and turned toward the narrow canebrake trail that led down Kalalau Valley toward the ocean. "You saw the fire?" she asked, half surprised she was talking to him. She shook her tangled hair out and tied it back, shimmying her bare butt as she went down the trail. *Why the hell am I doing that?* And then her grief over Shoshanna slammed back.

"Saw the smoke, and I'd heard about the rangers roustin' people, all up and down the Na Pali Coast. Tryin' t' make the world safe for tourists," he said. "How long were you livin' here?"

She stopped and handed him back his jacket. "What's your name?" she asked.

"Pranha," he said. "Wanna little bud?" He grubbed a small brass cylinder and wrinkled rolling papers out of his shorts.

"I'm Mandy. No, I don't smoke. Don't wear clothes much, either," she said, gesturing at the jacket. "But . . . I appreciate the help." The words tumbled out. She hadn't had much occasion to talk this last week.

They sat cross-legged when they reached the beach and ate Ry-Krisp and pineapple under the steady roar of the surf. The guy never sneaked a look at her snatch, not once. It was making her wet, wanting him to. *Gay?* She shrugged. *Ah, who gives a shit?*

The sun was already flattening on the horizon. "So, how long you been livin' in Kalalau?"

"Six years in Kaua'i, four years out here."

He tore open another packet of crackers and sized her up. Mandy was about as brown as a haole could get, long, tight-curled hair, jujube nipples, bodacious hips. Hippies like her lived all over the islands, in the remotest places. "From L.A.?"

She bristled. *What the fuck is it to you?* But she gave it up and said, "San Bernardino. Sonofabitch husband, fucked-up job, too much dope and loud music. You?"

"Anaheim," he said, and they both snorted.

"My partner left," she said, pissed she'd said it as soon as the words were out.

"Where'd he go?"

"She," she said, testing. The guy didn't flinch. And even letting him know she was a lesbian didn't get him to look at her snatch.

He squinted. "What you plannin' on doing?"

Tears came. She jumped up and stalked away down the beach. When she came back at dusk, he had a tarp spread in the lee of some pandanus. He looked up. "I just roll up in it at night," he said. "Even tonight, that'll be warm enough. Join me if you want, no hassles."

She stomped off again but returned before full dark. A shama thrush was weaving its fluted music with the slow beat of the surf.

"No sex," she said, looking as ferocious as she could with a blurry, tear-stained face.

"No sex," he agreed. It was funny—the guy had hardly any male vibes. He raised the edge of the tarp to invite her in; his nakedness startled her for a moment, then she lay down, naked herself, and he folded the tarp over them. She flung an arm over his chest, challenging him with her eyes. It was good to hold a body, even if it wasn't Shoshanna's. Even if it was a man's.

Mandy woke curled tight around Pranha. He was deep in sleep, mouth open, breath rattling in his throat. He had an erection. She fingered its length, amused at the heat of it, moved by the slow pulse along its underside. Men. Horny even when they're asleep, for Chrissakes. And then she remembered Shoshanna again, the way she'd taken her by the shoulders that very first night—her first woman—and kissed her till they almost fell over. She remembered the sureness and force as her hand went between Shoshanna's legs, and the sounds she brought out of her . . . and Mandy, lying with a strange man, felt the familiar knife of her wanting.

Salt tears spilled over Pranha's sleeping shoulder. She gripped his cock until his arousal faded, and, after, kept him cupped tiny in her hand until sleep reclaimed her.

In the morning Pranha said he was splitting. "You can come," he said. He gestured at his weathered kayak with its homemade outrigger and tattered sail wound around a jerry-rigged mast.

"Where're you headed?"

"Around to Hanapepe."

"I hate that side of the island, Hanapepe and Lihue and all the fucking tourists. I've got friends in Hanalei. I might go there, I guess, if you were going."

"Well . . ." Pranha looked doubtful. "The trades are pretty fresh. Be rough headin' that way. Big seas."

Mandy looked at the kayak, its red deck bleached mottled pink from the sun. Bags of gear were stuffed around the seats in the two narrow cockpits. A scratched marijuana-leaf decal fanned over the bow; a tattered rainbow flag hung on the mast. In that moment, she was overwhelmed by the need to leave Kalalau, to get away from the smell of guava, the memories of Shoshanna, the ashes of her home. The ocean had a sharp tang, urgent, like freedom, and the wind teased her breasts. "If you'll go to Hanalei, I'll go with you. I don't care about the waves."

He reached for his salt-stiffened shorts and pulled them on self-consciously while she eyed the ungainly flapping of his cock. "We could try," he said.

She stood up, showing him her muscled belly, her smooth, solid biceps. "I'm strong," she said. "I can paddle. I'll help you drag the boat down." For the first time, she caught him looking at her breasts.

Pranha looked up to the *pali,* where the snow was only a faint filigree now. He looked out to sea. Big rollers far out, their white backs churning in and out of view. He sat facing the breakers, chin on his knees. He rolled a joint, lit it, and sucked it deeply. After a while he turned and looked at the broad-hipped, naked woman, tear tracks and ash still dark on her cheeks. He took another long toke, studying the sea. "Okay," he said, letting the smoke out. He stashed the joint and stood.

As they dragged the boat to the surf line, Mandy challenged him. "How come you don't want sex with me?"

"You asked me not to."

"Bullshit."

He tested the lashings on the mast. "Anyway, it's not about you."

"Broken heart?" she said, a twist of recognition in her gut.

Pranha's callused, cracked fingers stroked the kayak's flank; he was not looking at her. He unclipped the spare paddle and offered it to her. "Too much of a hassle. All that shit. You can really paddle?"

Sometimes missing Shoshanna was like a knife. "Suppose I asked you to lick me. Would you?"

He was watching the ocean. "Look," he said, "we've got an easy set comin' in," and shoved the kayak bow-first into the surge.

They smashed through three big breakers and found themselves at sea. Mandy was breathless with the effort. The water was a fierce dark blue, and the wind, a scant hundred yards offshore, was fiercer. She craned back to look at him, licking the salt from her lips. "I didn't know it'd be blowing so hard. Is this okay?"

"Paddle. We gotta stay in close, under the *pali*. Farther out it's really blowing. Up at Ke'e there'll be fifteen-foot swells. Mandy?"

Over her shoulder, she raised an eyebrow at him.

"If you wanted, I'd lick you." He looked her calmly in the eye when he said it, then looked away, over the water.

A knot of desire tied itself behind her pelvic arch, and then twisted tighter in refusal. Her old contempt for her husband bubbled up. "What're you, an angel of mercy?" He was leaning hard into each stroke. He didn't look up.

"Or you've got herpes." Acid in her saliva bunched her jaw muscles. *I'll make this son of a bitch respond!*

His pale blue eyes came up to catch hers. "You lived alone much before this?"

It was hard to paddle and keep looking back at him. As the water dried on her bare flesh, the sun began to warm her. She softened her voice. "You had a hard-on last night. I touched a man for the first time in . . . I don't know. Ten years. I kind of hate men. I held you for a couple of hours, I guess, and it made me horny." Sometimes thinking about Shoshanna, about stumbling on her in the little bakery in Kilauea, about kissing her woman's softness, made her feel the knife actually ripping her gut. She raised her gray eyes to Pranha.

"Shit," he said, his eyes wide.

It took her a long minute to realize he wasn't talking to her. She turned, and a dark wall of water was rushing at her. It tore the paddle from her hands and buried her. Deep. The sea forced its way into her stomach, bitter and flat. In the roar of the water, something in the boat groaned, a long, wrenching groan, and the sea spun her over and over, trapped in the cockpit.

Somehow she squirmed free and, after kicking toward the light for far too long a time, broke the surface. She spat salt, cursing and coughing. The kayak wallowed belly-up. One outrigger had snapped; the other had wrenched loose from the pontoon, which was now attached to the boat by only two fragile lines. The mast with its furled sail tipped over a downwind swell and vanished. "Hey!" she yelled, and then she remembered his name. "Pran-HA! Heyyyy!"

"I'm here," he said, and she discovered him clinging to the stern a few feet behind her.

"What the hell! What do we do?" She was still coughing up water.

"Boost the stern and drain her. Then the bow. If we're lucky, we get enough water out to right her." His calmness pissed her off.

"Are we okay?"

"Dunno."

"What the fuck does that mean?"

"Well, we've got one paddle and we can rerig the pontoon. Maybe by the time we get paddlin' again we won't be too far offshore to get back."

"Get back to fucking where?!"

"That's Kaua'i," he said, gesturing into the driving wind. He waved downwind. "And that's the Marianas. Thousand miles. We probably don't wanna go that way."

They paddled until dark, passing the paddle back and forth as they tired. Pranha guessed they were three miles out, losing the battle to regain Kaua'i. He shrugged and took inventory: three boxes of crackers, a hand of bananas, and a scant gallon of water.

The trades blew all night, and they paddled into them. The good news, at dawn, was that they weren't any farther offshore. The bad news was that they were exhausted. Their hands were blistered and brine-soaked, bleeding.

Mandy squirmed around and knelt in her seat facing Pranha. *What's it take to get through to this hippy hermit?* "We're not going to have sex, are we?"

"Still thinkin' about sex out here? You're not doing so bad." His tired face creased into a smile.

"I don't want to die alone, I guess."

He paddled in silence for several minutes, then braced the paddle and guided them over a roller. He reached from the stern cockpit until they could clasp their swollen, raw hands. "Me neither. I just didn't know that till a coupla minutes ago."

It wasn't easy to talk, but in bits and pieces they told each other about themselves. Mandy shared her grief over Shoshanna, her anger about men and shit jobs and L.A. She told about her four years of love, and yoga, and the crazy, intense woman-sex that just made her hungrier, about no clothes and all the guavas anybody could ever eat. Pranha watched her luminous eyes, her mobile, too-large mouth, as she twisted half toward him in the bow cockpit. When she was through, he talked about his world. "I said sex was too much hassle," he said. "But everything's a hassle. Look," he said after a pause, "if we get outta this . . ."

"If we get to shore," Mandy grinned, "I'm gonna jump your bones. I'm gonna fuck you till you holler. I'm gonna make you hump me like a cocker spaniel. I'm gonna suck your weenie half off just to prove I'm not prejudiced and then I'm gonna stuff your head in my snatch for at least three hours. And then I'm gonna kick your ass. Shut up and pass the paddle. You look like shit."

As he leaned forward, she glimpsed a full erection pushing from the fringe of his shorts. Cock, mouth, fingers: it didn't matter how she got it done. She wanted a beating heart laid against hers. She closed her eyes and let arousal take her, let it invade her exhaustion, grateful to be thrumming like this even in the middle of the fucking goddamn ocean.

The shark came at midday, a fin thirty feet out, circling, then sliding under the waves.

"What'll we do?" Mandy's diaphragm wouldn't let her breath.

"I dunno. It's a mako, I think. If it bumps us, try t'hit it in the nose with the paddle or your fist. They say that makes 'em go away."

"Hit a shark with my fist?!"

Pranha raised a tired arm. "Either that, or it breaks up the boat, maybe, and eats us."

After a few hours it disappeared, and exhaustion hit full force. Mandy slumped in the forward cockpit and went unconscious. She woke later, confused, guilty that she hadn't been paddling. Head on the deck, she stared blankly at the water, only gradually realizing that she was looking into a single small, unblinking eye, inches below the surface. She jolted upright.

"Go easy." It was Pranha, behind her. "It's just hanging out in the shade of the boat. Don't do anything weird."

The shark, an arm's length away, was nearly as long as the kayak. "Hey," she said to Pranha in a small voice, "I'm not thinking about sex anymore." But she was. *Sand under my back. Pranha on top of me, fucking me. No—Shoshanna, and I'm on top. She calls my name. I dig my fingers into the earth to hold us safe.* The shark's unmoving eye made her want to touch herself. To come. To do any fucking thing but be there skewered by that cold gaze.

That second night, under the stars, they could no longer see the shark, and that was worse. Thirst clogged their throats, made it hard to talk.

The wind had slacked off with nightfall. By the time the Southern Cross inched over the horizon, the sea was nearly windless. Past pain, they paddled until their arms would no longer lift from the deck, then traded off. By midnight the island had risen, cutting off more of the northeastern sky. The paddle bit into the phosphorescent water, stroke after stroke. After long hours, the Cross sank behind them and first light grew ahead. The swells lifted, glassy smooth. The *pali* showed detail now: the slash of canyons, pale cliffs, forest.

Three tropic birds flew low over their bow. Mandy wanted to call to them, lovely in the pearly light, but she couldn't speak. Pranha nudged the paddle against her back. She took it and began to stroke.

"Mandy."

She could only paddle, voiceless.

"Mandy. We're gonna make it. Follow the shore. We can put in at Ke'e. Go in close while we can: the wind's gonna come back."

When sun touched the water around them, they were just outside the breakers, under the unbroken rise of the *pali*. They could hear birdsong ashore. The shark circled once, soundless, then sank into the depths. Salt rasped and itched in every fold of their skin.

It took another hour to reach the reef off Ke'e. Pranha found the entrance and they rode a last big swell into the lagoon. The water swirled turquoise under them, darting with fish. *About fucking time,* she thought, tears welling up again. When they beached, their legs wouldn't support them; clutching each other, they fell onto the sand.

The first tourists appeared at midmorning. Pranha sat up. His eyes and lips were salt-rimed, white against his sunburnt skin. "Now who looks like shit?" he said, and she wanted to laugh at him—with him—but her belly muscles were too tired to force out a sound. "C'mon," he said, "I know a place we can sleep."

They staggered together past the cinder-block restrooms, stopping to fill Pranha's jug with water. By the trash cans, some picnicker had dumped a six-pack of soda. Pranha grappled it into the crook of an arm. He led her to a small, fern-fringed clearing. They drank all six sodas and most of the water, then crumpled into each other's arms.

When Mandy woke, late sun was slanting through the leaves of a breadfruit tree, and Pranha was still in her arms. She wanted to caress him, as much for herself as for any pleasure he might find in it, but her hands were unusable, paddles at the ends of leaden arms, stiff with blood and salt.

She looked at Pranha, sun-scalded and raw, sunk in sleep that seemed close to the edge of a coma. Naked herself, she ran her eyes over the male body, clothed only in its disreputable shorts. Awkwardly, she pried the button loose on the shorts and tugged them off him.

Jesus. What am I doing? Every muscle ached. Her long dark hair was stiff and filthy. Two days of sunburn had seared her face, made the breeze unbearable on her tender breasts. *My hands are a mess!* It'd be days before she could use them. But she hungered to touch this man. She wanted his cock. The need to anchor herself in another body was stronger than any anger she still held, stronger than any particular missing.

She bent over him. She licked, and recoiled at the bitter sea grit dissolving on her tongue. She licked again, and found it easier. And again, until she could pull him into her mouth.

He was small and unaroused—beyond arousal, maybe—but it didn't matter. She tongued the convolutions of his cockhead, round and round, finding a rhythm for sore muscles and stiff face. She knelt clumsily, her useless hands palms-up on her knees, bowed over him. She lost herself in sucking.

She began to tug, stretching him out rubbery and thin, searching out the cords and vessels with her tongue. She let her breath spill into his nest of hair and inhaled the smell that came back from him.

With the back of a hand she stroked his chest and lean belly. This brought his first response: he swelled in her mouth and at last became hard. She looked up. He was watching. She bobbed on him, grinning with her eyes. It was evening, and birds were singing again. *Whoo-ee! I'm going to do you, boy!*

He braced an arm under his head, observing. Over a long aimless time as she sucked, he softened, then swelled again. She ran her tongue tip down the bitter-salt midline of his scrotum and it tightened. She sucked harder on his cock, and his hips followed her. His mouth gaped.

After a while his arms canted out as if he were being crucified. His head arched back and the taste of him changed in her mouth. The long muscles in his legs took up a heavy shaking. His body lifted, bridged between his heels and the back of his neck. He hung like that as she devoured him, bent above him as if in prayer. *Follow me, boy. Fly!*

"Wait," he rasped, his voice salt-scalded. "Wait."

"What? What's wrong?" Mandy pulled away.

His voice failed and he could only mouth the words: *Let . . . me.*

He twisted and thrust his face into her sex. She flooded with moisture, her own scent coiling up to her nostrils: brine and musk and exhaustion. His tongue searched her, his blue eyes holding hers from the thicket of her black bush. The furry insistence of his beard made the cords in her thighs ache.

She jammed his shorts under his head for a pillow and fell against his mouth, whispering wordlessly. Braced on her knuckles, oblivious to the pain in her hands and shoulders, she humped. His face rolled and twisted under her, his eyes shut tight now, worshipping. She locked her thighs against his ribs.

Yeah. Her back straightened. She couldn't contain her climax. It ballooned until it was bigger, somehow, than her body, stretching her bones, filling her mouth with a wavering music. *Please!* She rode so high on his face *please fucking please* she was afraid she'd suffocate him *please* but nothing could stop her now, nothing. *Yeah! Yeah!*

Coming was like drowning. *No, like being pitched into the fucking sun. Like burning down around myself.* Something far back in her called, *Shoshanna!* and she fell face-first to the ground.

Long after, she searched out Pranha's face. His pale eyes waited, solemn. She saw loops of semen strung over his chest, already thinning and beginning to run. *A man,* she thought. It didn't matter. She opened her mouth over his. His hand clamped the back of her neck and crushed her closer.

As the swift tropical night flooded through the palm grove, he hobbled to the boat and brought his tarp. They slept.

The third morning he searched out a long-tailed shirt from among his gear, decent enough, they thought, for her to face civilization. The cloth clung alien and imprisoning, harsh from the sea. They hid the kayak in the ferns, limped to the road, and hung out their thumbs. *Shit,* she thought, *I'm back.*

A rattling island car picked them up. After they disappeared toward Hanalei, the narrow road lay empty for a long time. Breakers boomed on the reef. Small waves lapped the coral sand and sighed back into the wide salt of the sea.

First Draft

Andy Quan

It was a lesson I was taught in a sunny classroom with brightly painted concrete walls in a quiet Vancouver neighborhood before most people in the world knew where Vancouver was. To write a report, or a letter, or basically anything important, you would do a first draft, and then a second, and then carefully recopy the whole thing onto clean paper.

I always wondered about the word *draft*. I knew it meant "wind" as well as "forcibly recruit" (I admit to precocity). To write a draft, I imagined, was to write the wind onto a page, have it blown away into a better form, and then disappear altogether.

Foolscap was another intrigue. Within the word was a stupid person and a hat. Said quickly, it was neither, and the syllables could alter to evoke "full," "fuel," "scape," and "cup." So much in a silly rough bit of paper, clearly inferior to proper new lined paper glowing white, showing off three perfect holes.

So, here it is, I'm writing on whatever paper I have found but am imagining it soft and shabby as foolscap, and I'm writing a first draft because really, I barely know you, so how could I draw you into finished form just yet?

This is how we met. I wrote a story. Sent it off. The editor agreed to put it in a book with other stories. You'd done the same. It was your first story published; mine as well.

The publisher had organized a night to promote the anthology where authors of these stories would do a small reading. The event was held in a small bar in Toronto, a bar that was long from back to front, but short from side to side, so when I eventually read, I would have to look far to the right and far to the left to connect with the audience.

I was in a new romance, my first one, and one that remained the most important of my romances for years ahead. Marshall arrived slightly late but managed to catch my whole reading, sitting quietly off to the left-hand side. We barely knew each other, but the quiet support he showed me that night portended well for the relationship.

It was the first time as an adult that I'd read aloud and read in front of an audience something that I'd written. I suppose as a child I had done some sort of reporting in elementary school, but I don't remember standing in front of a podium with a poem or part of a short story. That night, when I finished reading my first poem, the audience clapped. Since they'd not offered the same reception to the previous few readers, my head swelled and glowed. I absorbed their sounds of laughter and their response to my words.

I had read the anthology in the week previous, and without having met you, had decided that your story was my favorite in the book. You read well, but I remember more strongly meeting you afterward. You had a baseball cap on, wrapped around your closely shaven head, and I found myself staring into your eyes after approaching you to tell you that I admired your writing and had liked your story better than the others.

You thanked me and returned the compliment. I wasn't sure if you were sincere. Someone earlier had done the same to me. He'd told me how much he liked my story, and even though I wasn't sure what I thought of his, I felt compelled to say the same. I wondered if you were doing the same as I'd done.

You introduced me immediately to the person you were with, a gesture which I mistakenly took to mean that this was someone significant, a partner or boyfriend or whatever you would have called him. And truthfully, all that I remembered of that meeting was an intense attraction, and that if I met you later in life, I would not know you by the distance between your brow and eyes or the angle between your lips and ears. I would know you by the attraction I felt, your eyes boring into me, at least that's what I had hoped; your thoughts were probably much more innocent.

I apologize that this story is about writers. A writer-friend of mine said if he ever should write a book about writing, he will ask his boyfriend to shoot him. I nodded enthusiastically at the time, but now I'm not so sure. I mean, here I am, re-creating the same crime described. I am telling you of that night, high on accomplishment and the attention, meeting this writer.

If you are not another writer, which you may be, since many readers of short stories are writers of them as well, then I hope that you'll transpose the experience to something more familiar. Like going to a conference and doing a presentation about something you are passionate about. Or joining up with a bunch of hobbyists, though I think that the stamp and coin collectors of yesteryear have mostly been replaced by people who are fans of certain TV shows or who dress up as large fuzzy animals.

But the analogy could be much simpler. Like when you and the kid down the street both got shiny new bicycles at the same time. You rode around, and the other kids in the neighborhood were impressed and jealous. You were happy to share the glory with someone else, the wind whistling past your ears, the smell of childhood at your nostrils.

Between the first time I met you and the next time, seven years later, I had changed from a flirtatious but relatively chaste young lad to an experienced man of the world. This is in the comparative sense. Men get to parade that. If I were a woman, I'd be considered loose and sluttish. As a man: a Romeo, Casanova, stud? Well, not really: as a gay man, similar terms apply as to women, but I'll wear them loudly like a Hawaiian holiday shirt. The words *promiscuity* and *slut* along with *been around the block* and *sex pig* instead of tropical birds and flowers.

When I see you again, I do look at your eyes, but quickly scan downward at the more physical, and more carnal. I like what I see: a strong gym-built body, curves in all the right places. I also see that you dress as carefully as I, but probably carry it off better. I can still be a bit lazy with ironing and sometimes mix two genres without getting the right blend. You dress as hip young urban gay men do: the cut of your short-sleeve shirts is flattering but not skin tight, and the trousers are slightly baggy, a pair of knee-length shorts which a colleague of mine likes as he can see your strong calves below the fabric.

Since they've been pointed out to me, I consider them as well. They're strange things, the muscles of the calves. Round humps pushing out from the backs of our lower legs, poised solidly but awkwardly above the ankles. They point out how thin our ankles really are and the strange way our weight above balances on so little below. Some calves are barely noticeable, like a thin vase of a nondescript color. Others are hard and muscular and showy. After meeting you again, and admiring the slope and curve of your calf muscles, I start to notice them on other men. I am suddenly aware of a body part that I've never really noticed.

Another thing I found amusing about your calves is that their shapes are echoed at the top of your head. Not exactly the same curve really, but my same desire to reach over and stroke them. Your legs. Your head, closely shaven. Your hair dark but light in weight and texture, so your crown was shiny and smooth, a strong form that accentuated your handsome features.

I, on the other hand, had gone blond. It was something that I'd considered for a long time, but was detracted by the fact that I'd seen so many Asian men with odd glowing shades of orange on their heads and blond that wasn't really blond. The story, my hairdresser had revealed, was that they dyed their hair at home. A professional job, bleached carefully with an expensive toner, would result in what I wanted.

It did, a gesture which I found radically improved my sex life. The incongruity of an Asian with blond hair caused people to look at me a little more closely, and getting handsome men to look at me was certainly an advantage if I wanted to look at them.

So we stood next to each other, a dyed blond and a shaved head, and I thought to myself that there was quite a bit of similarity in that. We were both writers (who had stories and poems published in similar books and magazines), and I was fashioning in my mind the hopes of twinned desire, that you were attracted to me as much as I was to you. But the real twinned desire was evidenced by our hair, or lack of it. A desire to be noticed by others.

I've left it behind, poetry, to write this. The sculpted form, careful placement, snappy one-liners. Instead I fall into the tumbleweeds of prose, my thoughts jammed up against each other like tenement houses. I dare to be sloppy, sloppier than poems at least.

I read your latest poems and during any stanza about the body or sex, I imagined making love with you. The poems were variable. Like me, you could slip into describing sentiment rather than evoking it. That, and a tendency to overwrite, to use a phrase too literary or pretty for the image behind it. This we share in common. "Some of the poems are very old," you'd said, handing your chapbook to me.

Unlike me, you hold back. You can tell stories in few words that allude to larger histories. Your short brushstrokes make do for a painting. When it works, it's compact and haunting. You leave the poem alone, even if you might want to stay. I explain too much. You know this already.

When I read your poems, I can't always analyze them, though I know that you've hit your mark. Sometimes I want more narrative though, more connections between the poems themselves. I want to read twenty short prose poems about your last boyfriend and a dozen couplets about your current one. I want to insinuate myself into your skin so that you write one about me.

We have met again at a conference. It's impossible not to meet people at conferences, but sometimes surprising when you've met them before in different lives. The first time I'd met you, I was studying political science, and you medicine. Years later, we are both working with AIDS, the virus that confuses and confounds us and mutates with each replication. It is not strange that we've both been drawn into the same arena.

"Are you seeing anyone?" I ask, more interested in your personal than your professional life. I ask you about the man you were with the first time we met, and realize with some embarrassment that I have revealed my desire too early.

"No, he was just a friend, never a boyfriend. I am seeing someone now. We live together." You explain that he is a schoolteacher and is kind and is called Mark.

Later, I am still asking you about your personal life. "Do you have an open relationship?"

When I came out in my early twenties and during travels to Europe soon after, I would never have asked this question. I asked instead, "Do you have a partner?" If the answer was yes, no matter how close they sat next to me, or stared intently into my eyes, I was breezy and amiable but gave no encouragement, nor understood that some may have been given. Monogamy was the only model I'd heard about and if someone was attached, it meant they weren't available to me.

Actually, I might have asked, "Do you have diplomatic immunity?" A joke that I pretend I made up but probably got from someone else, and which, after a beat of incomprehension, is always met with a slight laugh. *D.I.,* as I call it, is different than an open relationship, because it only happens when one or the other partner is off traveling or at a conference or otherwise out of the city.

My questions are usually meant to be straightforward.

You replied, "Well. Kind of."

"Kind of? What does that mean?! You've either got it or you don't." I try to sound jovial so I seem as if I'm gently prodding rather than needling you.

You look thoughtful but unperturbed, and change the subject.

Our meetings that week are not worth reporting. We see each other between sessions, ask how our presentations went, and manage to have a meal together a few times.

I am fascinated by the layer of hair on your forearms, surprisingly dark, and a dusting of it on your calves (again, revealed below your knee-high shorts). Even with this evidence of hair, I'm thinking that you are quite smooth, perhaps a thin line between your groin and belly, or a patch between your pectoral muscles, reeds peeking up from soil after winter.

I like a smooth body the best, I have to admit, the hand or tongue traveling unobstructed over hard surfaces. Clean like the skin of beluga whales or dolphins or even a pillowcase, my head pressed into it, the weight of a lover on my back, a pulsing, grinding rhythm.

I have brushed up against your body at times, and I think your torso is smooth. I know that your body is strong, and the weights in the gym have left the right kind of evidence that I, a faux detective, must examine closely.

Thank goodness the tension breaks regularly. When you speak, I'm jarred into a lesser fantasy. In my travels, I've managed to de-eroticize the Canadian accent. Its round, open, and earnest softness does little to make me hard. Its musical lilts are too familiar. They're like someone in indecision or maybe like elevator music, not the swinging joke of a Glaswegian brogue or the low xylophone tones of a Caribbean parlance. It's friendly and comforting and calms me. It reminds me of friends but does not excite me. I'm glad that there's something in you that I find lacking.

Still, you don't need to talk during sex.

I'm happy to discover that you like foreplay as well. And after-play too, but we can get to that later. Some guys come in about as quick a time as I'm *thinking* of warming up. It's not that I'm a slow starter. It's that I like the tension to build. So, no clothes ripped off, zippers and snaps burning your skin in their rush to flee you. This is about restraint: martini glasses filled with white chocolate mousse, and no one is around anywhere. You could dip your finger in and smooth over the indentation. Would anyone notice? *Hold it in, hold it in, don't spoil your supper.*

My mouth is watering as if I'm already swallowing you and I'm soiling your clothes with saliva, stains of wet at your nipple (if you were a woman, you could be lactating), at your crotch (like a teenager who fantasized too much, too quickly), at the hemline of your shorts (as if you were wading in the ocean). The small of your knee is wet; it echoes your salivating mouth.

Articles of clothing get taken off one at a time, and generally we take turns. I remove your shoe. Then another shoe. You remove my shirt. The process is interrupted because you cannot believe the size of my nipples, and have to check with your tongue to know if they are really that large and round. You suck on them, and a space just behind my temples starts to be drawn into the same suction. I unbutton your shorts. And then the buttons at your groin. We do not allow the other to undress himself. Certain procedures must be followed.

Finally, both of us naked, it is like being born again. If we stopped to think about it. Which we do not do since we're occupied with each other's senses and movements, textures beneath our hands. You suck cock as well as you write, and I try to show you my talents too. I put my tongue up your ass, milky white, hard and soft, a marble Italian statue come to life and writhing above my mouth. I have a weakness for strength, and you have it. There are so many muscles in your back, thighs, and shoulders. They shift constantly under my hands, as if I am the wooden bridge to Noah's Ark and all manner of beasts—light, heavy, round, horned—are shifting over my walkway. While my mind tries to take in these various sensations, you add to the difficulty and press into me with human hands, tongue, arms, breath, cock.

I have always fantasized about getting good at being fucked. So why not with you? There was something political about my objections in my early sexual career. I had a thing for older men; but just because I was with older and sometimes bigger men was not an excuse, I thought, for me to be penetrated and vulnerable.

The various techniques of coercion also left me feeling that I didn't really want it. "Please please fuck me," said one lover, on the night we were breaking up. When I grabbed the lubricant and condoms, he said, "No, I'd rather fuck you." I straddled his stomach, jerked off in his face, and left the room. Others: "Oh, you'll *really* like it"; "It's easy, you just have to relax"; "I bet you've been waiting for it."

With other lovers, who I felt more comfortable with, I tried. I mean, I really tried. We would foreplay endlessly, I would be rimmed like I was a Chevy going through an automatic carwash, I had fingers up me like a Dutch dam in need of constant repair. But the moment of truth, when it came, the first time, and most of the next times: *Ow!* "You'll get used to it." *Ow!*

One lover told me, "It hurt a lot at first, but when I got used to it, it became my favorite position. I can't get enough of it. I sometimes can't come if I'm not being fucked."

Hmm, this sounded good. "And how long did it take to get used to it?"

"Well, it kind of hurt for the first two years, and then it was okay."

Two years!?

Of course, other friends had no problems at all. "I'd been putting things up there as long as I can remember. Candles. Carrots. Lots of C things. It's never hurt at all. Maybe try it on your side." "Practice with a dildo," recommended another, who was giving advice from personal experience. The most helpful advice was from my gay doctor, who, asked for a general sexual history in order to figure out my risks for various infections. "Do you get fucked?" I liked that he used the slang rather than something more clinical like "penetrated."

"Not really," I said. "I find that it kind of hurts."

Later, his finger up my ass, checking for warts, lesions, and whatever, he commanded, "Squeeze." He inserted his finger farther and repeated his command. "You need to ask your lover to do this so that your sphincter muscle is exhausted and gets completely relaxed. If you do this, it should be fine, shouldn't hurt." Businesslike, he removed his glove and turned away, and I have no doubt that he was giving no more than helpful professional advice with a useful demonstration.

I have been fucked since then, on various occasions, sometimes more painful, sometimes more pleasurable. But always with a little discomfort and never for very long. What would it be like to be like one of those famed bottoms in porno movies, leaning over (or standing up, or on their back, or on their head, or basically any which way), saying, "Give it to me"?

So. Give it to me. We haven't discussed this either. But I want this. I'm gagging for it. My anus is puckering like a kiss, and I'm thinking that you're the one. This is it. You inside of me, and me feeling better than I've ever felt before.

Poppers give me a headache, and god, they smell bad but they *work*. Dizzy. Heart beating faster. Sometimes a headache the next day. To avoid that, I take an empty small brown bottle and run it over your skin, capturing your sweat and spit in it, the remains of your day, until I have my own personalized vapor. There's cologne in there too, musky and sweet. I think it's going to have a Japanese name, but you say, No, it's something that's hard to get. But I've got it now, and as I close one nostril with my finger, put the bottle to the other, and inhale deeply, there's a chemical effect that burns my skin. My head is pounding. I want you in, in, in.

Your cock is long, not particularly thick, beautifully proportioned and slick with moisture. We smother it in the finest oils and grab a condom, one of the new-technology ones that don't need water-based lube. It makes a strange crinkly sound, but that's okay, it's so thin that it's like a layer of skin, like a spray of water that you use to revive yourself from exhaustion. Your cock glows. From what, I don't know. Heat? Light? My desire? No matter. Fuck me: with all your might.

You knock at my door. When you enter, there is a moment of sharp pain, sweet rather than sour. It is replaced immediately by a pleasure that storms my thoughts and senses and suddenly my sphincter is exhausted and relaxed, so relaxed that it is lying back at the poolside with a tropical cocktail. With a tiny floral-patterned paper umbrella in it. Served by a Norwegian waiter named Olav. Who is naked. The hair on his arms lit up in the sun like a cornfield. Cheekbones like curved fists. A dick of wonder. The drink makes me giddy and I spill it and laugh and laugh.

You take me through rhythms all night long, a dance party where you lose track of time, the DJ slows and speeds the music, sometimes there are voices, a chorus, sometimes only beats, and then this big diva voice brings you up and over and spinning around the room. Sometimes you press into me gently like leaning into the wind, and sometimes you are pounding me like an animal, like television violence. I can feel you up to my stomach, shivering through my legs, to the top of my cock and all through the center of my body. My insides pulse and expand and contract as you slide in and out of me.

We've come to the point of orgasm repeatedly, and pulled back with deep breaths, tugs on the scrotum, and sudden changes of pace. But now, they are rumbling up like premonitions, like the nerves of animals before a thunderstorm, or the iron figures of lions in China that wait for centuries and finally, when an earthquake is approaching, metal balls hidden in the animals' skulls are jarred loose and fall into their mouths. You see them, their mouths full, and you know the moment has arrived.

Though our eyes have closed and opened, our vision has sometimes clouded, now we look at each other clearly. My cock bobs and sways like a conductor's baton. You hips are tired. Exhaustion ripples through the xylophone bars of your stomach, and up through the striations in your chest. My come shoots into your chest, wet syllables of laughter, and yours into the condom inside of me. We ejaculate simultaneously at the exact moment that dawn breaks.

Whatever happened to Liquid Paper? I remember a tiny bottle with a black-and-white label. If you left the cap off too long, or the product was too old, it would brush onto the page in a thick paste, unsuitable for writing over.

A classmate, Al Kershaw, who had a fascination with Nazism and the gym (a frightening combination, I thought), shocked all of us by painting swastikas on his tongue and sticking it out at us. Those were the days.

Now, writing takes such different forms. The paper moves onto a screen, ink from pens moves to printer cartridges. We still have use for paper, erasers, carbon paper, Liquid Paper, and foolscap, but not as often. For me at least, and millions more, we constantly revise, and when we print out a clean copy, you cannot tell what has gone on beforehand.

This is goodbye: the conference is over. We both have late flights. The night before, you came out dancing with friends. We flirted with each other, and I knew that you had some attraction for me. You wore a short-sleeve shirt and left the buttons undone. Your torso appeared through that curtain and the definition and contours were more beautiful than I had expected.

Music, celebration, goodbyes. Friends and colleagues all around. A distracting atmosphere. When I looked for you next, you had disappeared, and emerged much later, a Brazilian man with you who hung back at the last minute.

I'm struck again at how handsome your eyes are.

I expect to leave you at the nightclub with your new friend, but when we're about to leave, you ask if you can get a ride with us. We leave you at your hotel and arrange to meet the next evening for dinner.

The week has reminded me most of high school sexual tension, and I'm giddy with it. Sex is easy as water these days; the fact that this has not been easy makes it all the more exciting. I recall complicated teenage years, where thoughts and worries and words got in the way of anything physical that might have happened. I was not one of those who are called early bloomers.

Rather than my newfound confidence asking "My place or yours?" I search for signals in our conversation, shared glances, and body language.

When I knock on your hotel room door, you are in the middle of a phone conversation and ask me to meet you downstairs in the bar. Over a cheap gin and tonic, I plot the night out. I could survive if nothing happens. I have much desire but no expectation. But I'd much rather have something happen. I figure dinner, get a bit sloppy over drinks, and then back to your hotel room for hanky-panky.

This is the conversation you recount:

He had asked what you'd been up to. You'd told him about the conference and about dancing last night. He'd asked if you'd met anyone and you'd told him about the Brazilian. But nothing happened, you explained. You had only kissed him in the corner, a short giddy drunken kiss, and that was all. Boys will be boys.

"And what are you doing tonight?" he demanded.

"Dinner with a friend." Your tone sheepish in response to his jealousy.

"And the friend's name is?"

"Joseph."

"And are you going to have sex with Joseph tonight too?"

I look at him but he doesn't quite look at me. Still, it's like looking through a camera lens and you can't get the framing right. There's something in the way: a camera strap, your finger, a tree.

And of course, like you, I know it's not going to happen. Even if you didn't have sex with Mr. São Paulo and even if you "kind of" have an open relationship, there is no way that you, or I, can escape the direct question that your boyfriend has asked.

We find a restaurant around the corner, Indian food. It has elegant white tablecloths and glassware, but is too open and bright to be intimate. Still, I spill my confessions.

"Well, and yes, I would, in another circumstance, certainly want to." You can't quite get the words out right. I'm not convinced that you would throw yourself at me at another time, but I think if you were boyfriendless and I threw myself at you, you'd take me up on it.

We talk about the week, and about work, and have a long conversation on writing. You'd like to take some time off. You wonder if you could make it as a writer by giving yourself time to do it. I, on the other hand, never imagine supporting myself through mere words. I write when I can, and have managed to have more success at it than you.

I can't resist dessert, and order *gulab jamun*. You pass on it, but taste mine. "Too sweet." But the rosewater syrup trickles down my throat and the two round balls (of what substance I've never known) are too obvious a metaphor.

"You're not, after a week of sexual tension and mixed messages, going to leave me without anything, after I've jerked off all week thinking about you."

"So it is sexual!"

Of course it's sexual, as well as emotional, intellectual, psychological, historical, and spiritual. Literary most of all, but yes, of course, it's sexual. Did I make it sound otherwise, that I was after a passionate sexless extramarital encounter abroad with a man I'd eroticized for seven years?

"I want to say goodbye to you in your room. The two of us. I won't try anything."

I do, of course. I turn off the lights, and an oddly weak street lamp pushes bits of white light into the room. My heartbeat quickened, I face you, and you are leaning against the wall. I pull you toward me in an embrace, a chaste embrace to start with, like a friend or a brother, my arms sinking around your shoulders and V-shaped back; the contact between us is at the top of our shoulders. The fingers of my right hand reach up to stroke your bald head. Then I relax, breathe deeply, and let our torsos press against each other. We hold each other in the most chaste and the most sexual hug possible, the words of your boyfriend ringing in our ears. A long time passes. This is as much as I'll get.

Suddenly, I press my lips to yours. Our tongues begin to dance. You taste as good as expected, better; the Indian meal is a memory, but the rosewater trickles in at the edges of our mouths. I rip your T-shirt upward and lean down, my lips, mouth, and teeth sinking into your chest, your perfect chest, the edge of a round cumulus cloud, a freshly printed topographical map to explore. Your torso is unmarred; not a single hair breaks its surface. Your left nipple is small and round, the tip of it hard. I don't bother looking at your right nipple, I'm sure it is the same. Delicious.

"Joseph." You, slightly breathless. "Joseph."

I put each of my hands to your biceps and press myself up.

"I'm sorry," I say.

A tenderness in your gaze.

But I'm not.

I should probably end here. I mean, why *dénoue* when I could just leave it at that, pre-cum staining my underpants, and I suspect, yours as well?

I'd love to make love to you one day. From the way you write about sex, I think you'd be quite hot. The foreplay has certainly been amazing, and I can thank you for a number of particularly hot nights stroking myself while stroking you. And there are, after all, the stories we could write after we've done it. First drafts, revisions, and final or not-so-final copies. I'll eat your words until I come.

It's not like this narrative demands a particular order—I've lost it anyway, and worst of all have completely stopped pretending that I write about people other than myself.

Of course it's me. My desire on the page.

I learned the word *sublimation* at an early age.

Hollywood Christmas

Thomas S. Roche

It's not exactly our first date; we already went out for coffee once. But that was during the day, and this is at night—a hot night right before Christmas, pulsing with all the energy of West Holly-wood when it's eighty degrees here and snowing in the rest of the world. There's a Christmas party up on Mulholland, at the big house of a friend you met when you were dancing, some closeted movie-industry semi-big-shot. Jacob is his name, but you won't tell me his last name because you're quite sure I'd recognize it. "He's very secretive," you tell me conspiratorially, brushing your long bottle-blond hair and putting on your bright-red lipstick while you careen through Mulholland's curves, driving with your knees. "You have to be, when you work in Hollywood."

I dread the thought of going to the movies right before Christ-mas, and a dinner out wouldn't quite be celebratory enough for us, so I'm relieved you suggest the party.

From the moment we park the car, I can see the house is packed with young queer guys. As I get out of the car, three of them come up to you, their eyes lazing over me. They shriek your name, hug you, kiss you, let their eyes linger on me.

You introduce him as Aaron, tell Aaron my name as the other guys kiss you and drift away.

"Who's the hunk?" Aaron asks. "Does he play for our team?

We can always use another pitcher with perfect biceps." He reaches out and squeezes mine.

"He's mine," you growl in a sudden show of feminine territoriality. You and Aaron kiss again, this time on the lips. He says something in French to me and drifts off with his friends.

"You don't mind, do you?" you say as we mount the stairs toward the throbbing music.

"Looked like a platonic kiss to me," I say.

"No, no," you tell me. "I mean you don't have a problem with guys flirting with you, do you?"

I shrug. "Did David have a problem with Michelangelo?"

You giggle. "Not a great metaphor, isn't that what your last review said?"

I jab you in the stomach and you giggle more. I go on tickling you all the way up the stairs, a convenient excuse for us to press our bodies together. I wonder if it seems like I'm trying to look straight. I don't care, because the feeling of your body against mine is making my dick hard in my jeans, and I'm more afraid you'll notice that than that my attempts to surreptitiously grope you will seem like conspicuous heterosexuality. By the time we make it in the door, my hand is around your waist and my fingertips tucked just under your waistband on that magnificent curve of your hip. You've got one finger hooked in my belt loop.

We walk past some guys barbecuing on the front porch. Big, thick sausages sizzle on the grill, phallic delights that look pasty gray and smell vegan. One of the guys, a bald, goateed guy, looks at me, then the sausages, then me again. He winks.

"Hungry?" he asks.

"Not yet," I deadpan. "Maybe later."

You introduce me around, subjecting me to a whirlwind of faces and names that I don't take note of and won't remember. There are a few women, two of them in the dozen people you introduce me to. At least one of them clearly didn't start her life that way, and the other makes it quite clear that she's at least as interested in you as I am. You can't find your friend to say hello, so, "I'm parched," you say, and drag me toward the punch bowl.

The punch bowls are marked "Magic" and "Not Magic." You pour us each a cup of the mundane kind. From the saucered eyes shimmering wildly in the sweating press of male bodies in the enormous living room, which has been cleared of furniture to better facilitate the surge and seethe of flesh to the loud house music, it appears that the other kind is dangerously magical.

"Ugh," you say as you take a drink. "I hate vodka." Then you finish the punch in one gulp like you're slamming down shots. Over the punch bowl, you press your lips to mine like my tongue's a lime to complement your tequila. I taste thirty-dollar-a-bottle vodka and one-dollar-a-gallon fruit punch. Your tongue has a post through it. You're a damn good kisser.

You pour yourself another cup of punch, and I daintily sip mine as I realize with puzzlement that the pulsating music is a techno version of "The Little Drummer Boy." It bleeds into grinding happy-hardcore "Carol of the Bells" with the sounds of men orgasming mingled conspicuously with about 180 beats per minute.

"Fuck the fruit punch. Let's dance," you say. I shoot my punch and wince, then follow you obediently out to the dance floor, your finger still hooked in my belt loop, this time one right in front, dangerously close to my zipper. I feel my cock swell at your touch. We have to practically wedge ourselves in among the dancers, bodies pressing us so tight that we're almost in full contact as we grind and squirm. I reach back and move my wallet to my front pocket. You put your arms around my neck and pull my face close to yours. I kiss you and let my hands curve around your waist. You're wearing one of those trendy, slutty shirts that shows off your belly, and as I let my hands creep back I feel the top of your thong showing over your low-slung jeans, which I noticed a long time ago. It makes me want to slide your pants off of you. Instead, I just tuck my fingers into your waistband, letting them squeeze between the very top of your buttocks and the stretched fabric of your jeans. If I had still had any doubt about whether you were going to fuck me, which I didn't, it would be dispelled by the way you react to my touch on your ass. Pushing back, squirming against my hands, the jaunty cock of your body bringing your tits into contact with my upper body while you kiss me deeply, your pierced tongue working into my mouth as your nipples harden against my chest and your ass grinds into my hands. I'm so hard I know you can feel it, smell it, taste it, even though your body isn't pressing against me that low. But a moment later, your hands are, your fingers working the bulge in my pants as you pull back and look into my eyes.

I lean over, speaking into your ear. "You call this dancing?" I ask.

Your lips brush my ear, and you say it low, husky, a hungry invitation.

"No. I call this foreplay."

Then you kiss me on the lips again and massage my cock, grinding your ass back into my hands. Your pants are so tight that as I wedge my hands in, I feel one button of your fly go popping open. That only makes you kiss me harder, stroke my cock harder. I don't even bother looking around to see if guys are watching us. I can feel their bodies pressed against us, smell their arousal. I can feel the whole dancing mass grinding together in a way that spells sex, and I'm sure more hands than just ours are wandering. If the guys aren't watching, it's because most of them are too blasted or too busy. But the tightly pressed bodies do provide a perfect cover.

Everything goes black in an instant.

A disappointed sound goes up from the crowd, mingled with shrieks and laughter. It's just a blown circuit breaker, but you take your cue and in a single fluid motion, you've slid your glorious ass out of my grasp. You're down on your knees in front of me.

I've never had a woman get my pants open so fast; but then you hang out with fags, so perhaps you get pointers. Before I know what's happening, your mouth is around my cock, gliding up and down, the back of your throat embracing my cockhead. The bodies keep grinding even though there's no music, and my hands rest gently on the top of your head as you bob up and down on my cock.

When the lights go on a moment later, you're not the only one down on your knees. A few of the guys right around us see you and start to applaud and cheer. You come up for air and daintily shove my cock back into my pants. You don't bother to zip; instead, you just button the top button and put your arms around me.

"I'm sorry," you say. "When the lights went out, I just couldn't resist."

"No wonder the circuit breakers blew."

"Come upstairs with me," you say. "I know where there's an empty bedroom."

Half of me wants to button my pants, but the rest of me doesn't care. You lead me by the hand up a winding staircase to a long hall with hardwood floors. Guys are lip-locked in line for the bathroom. You push past them, fish in your skintight jeans, and take out a key. You open one of the doors and a guy in line—one of the few without another guy feeling him up—says bitchily, "Is there another bathroom in there?"

"Afraid not," you say, and drag me in.

It's totally dark in the room beyond. You lock the door behind us and shove me against it, dropping to your knees again. My cock is in your mouth even faster this time, and when I throw back my head and moan, you stand up quickly and kiss me. I can taste my own cock on your mouth. You guide me around as if you know the room intimately, and when you push me back I go tumbling onto a big, soft bed.

You're on top of me, kissing me, voracious. I reach up under your top and peel it off of you, discovering what I already knew—you're not wearing a bra. I press my mouth to your nipples and gently caress your tits while you writhe and moan on top of me. Just a few more strokes of your mouth and I'll come, but I don't want to come yet. Still sucking your tits, I push you onto your back and unbutton your jeans.

They're so tight that it takes some doing to get them peeled down your legs. They're damp, and so's your thong. My eyes are starting to adjust to the darkness, and I can see as I kiss my way up your legs that your pussy is shaved smooth. Not that I wouldn't have found out a moment later, anyway, as my tongue glides be-tween your soft lips and strokes your clit. You're pierced there, too, and in a row down each cunt lip, three or perhaps four rings through each side of your shaved pussy.

Obviously, you know your rich queer friend from the Holly-wood Boulevard side of Mulholland—he must like to slum. Girls in the hills never wear more than five or six piercings under their Prada skirts.

You're on the huge bed edge-to-edge, instead of head-to-foot, so it's easy for me to drop to my knees and get a better angle at your hungry cunt. You lift your ass off the bed, moaning as I press hard into you.

My fingers slide into you easily, telling me just how wet you are—as if your soaked jeans and thong hadn't already told me. You're naked now, writhing on my tongue, your thighs spread wide and your pussy open for me. My eyes are finally opened to the semidarkness. When I look up I see your glorious body stretched out before me, white in the moonlight from a nearby window, tits gathered in one hand, the other gently caressing the top of my head. You're looking down at me, your mouth hanging open and glistening moist like your eyes. Your blond hair is swept in big messy strands around your face, neck, and tits. You're gorgeous, and I can see just how close you are to coming.

I can also see the guy standing in the nearby doorway. Beyond, it looks like there's a bathroom, lit only by candlelight. But with the moonlight, and my eyes adjusted, I can see him pretty clearly—he's older, suit-clad, silver-haired, and I do recognize him. He's a screenwriter and actor, British, famously unmarried, famously eccentric. Everyone knows he's queer, except, of course, for everyone.

Jacob is watching us intently.

"Oh, don't stop on my account," he says. "After all, the door *was* locked, you naughty kids."

"I'm sorry, we—" I begin.

You're so close to coming that it takes you a moment to regis-ter the voice. Your head twists around and you look back at him.

"Jacob," you say hoarsely. "I didn't see you."

"Hello there, Suzanne. Having a good night, I hope?"

You start to slide out from under me, but he puts up his hands.

"Please, don't stop. As long as you don't mind me here, you're welcome to use the bed. That doesn't bother you, does it?"

You look down at me, guiltily, scared, like you're expecting me to run screaming. From downstairs, I can just hear the pounding rhythm of "Oh Hanukkah."

"Not even a little bit," I say. "Watch away."

Jacob laughs. "Must be another actor," he says. "She needs very badly to come. You can see it in her eyes. You must be really quite good with that tongue of yours. Isn't that right, Suzanne?"

"He's great," you say, your voice breathy.

"Then by all means. Give the poor girl what she wants. We've been friends far too long for me to stand in her way."

My cock is throbbing hard against the edge of the bed, and I'm still hungry for your pussy. I lower my face and press my tongue between your lips again, and you gasp and claw at the bed as I begin to lick in earnest.

Jacob watches, fascinated, as you hover on the edge of orgasm. I lick faster and you moan, your back arching—it only takes a moment to drive you over the edge. My two fingers inside you feel the tightening as you get close, and when I try to slide three in there I discover that Hollywood girls do their Kegels. You almost squeeze my fingers out when you come, and you all but box my ears as you shudder all over and your thighs quiver tight, closed against my head. Your ass is lifted so high off the bed I have to tuck my arm under you to keep my mouth on your clit. Nothing like a little Hollywood Fitness to keep a girl limber.

"Very, very good," says Jacob. "You're really quite adept at that. Isn't he, Suzanne?"

"Fuck me," you gasp, sitting up fast and pushing my head out from between your legs. "Please. Fuck me?"

I want to fuck you more than I've ever wanted to do anything in my life. I look up at Jacob and he says, "By all means. She's certainly earned it."

I'm on you in an instant, your hands hungrily stripping my shirt off and pulling my jeans down over my ass. Your nails dig into me as I enter you, and you come again just as I start to thrust. I kiss you hard and feel your tongue, still tasting of my cock, still urging me forward. I fuck you harder, lifting your legs over my shoulders, bent at the knees, giving myself just the angle I like. I reach down and touch your clit as I drive into you, and you come a third time before I let myself go inside you. I've pushed you back across the bed, so intent on fucking you that I didn't realize you're hanging halfway over the edge, only your ass supporting you. As my spent cock slides out of you, we both go tumbling onto the floor. We would both giggle if we weren't still breathing too hard.

I lay there, sprawled on the floor, limbs tangled with yours. Jacob walks over and politely kneels down next to us; you look up at him, your face a mixture of embarrassment and excitement—with a good deal of post-orgasmic dullness mixed in.

Jacob leans down and kisses you on the lips, gently, not a sexual kiss—paternal, friendly, kind, affectionate. He strokes your sweaty, tangled blond hair and says, "Well done, my dear. It's good to see you dating again."

Then, without asking, he leans over you and kisses me, once, on the lips, at first equally paternal, equally kind. I don't stop him, but I do notice his tongue grazing my lower lip in the instant before he pulls away.

Then he strokes my hair a little.

"You are an actor, aren't you?" he asks. "Suzanne does tend to favor actors."

"Screenwriter, actually," I tell him. "Well, novelist. But working on a screenplay."

His business card is already in his hand.

"I'd love to read it," he tells me, and gives me his card.

Then he leans down and gives you another kiss, this one slightly less paternal—and more, you might say, friendly.

"Thanks for bringing your new boyfriend over," he says. "Hope you enjoy the party."

He stands up, brushes himself off, smiles down at you, and blows me a kiss.

He vanishes into what I assume is the bathroom, and I hear his footsteps across the floor on the other side.

We don't say a word as we dress and make our way down through the grinding male bodies and the opulent front yard. I open the passenger door for you and go to get in my side. You stop me and put your hand at the base of my neck, your body tentatively close to mine—barely touching this time, not close like before.

"Are you mad?" you ask.

I smile. "Do you know how hard it is to get someone to read your screenplay in this town?"

"I'll read it," you say meekly.

I lean forward and kiss you—gently at first, then harder, tasting your tongue.

"I'd like that," I tell you, and walk around to the driver's side as the pulsing strains of "Rudolph the Red-Nosed Reindeer" throb temptingly up the long Mercedes-packed driveway.

All in a Day's Work

Mistress Morgana Session Notes

Mistress Morgana

John
DOB: 5/9/42
10/25/01; 3 hrs; dungeon. Business suit and stilettos.
LIMITS: no nudity on my part; no strap-ons; no men in scene.
John asked to videotape our session during our initial phone conversation, classic executrix-interrogation fantasy, sexy strong woman in business suit that shows just a little too much thigh, that sort of thing. I made it clear I would not appear in the tapes, but that I'd be happy to videotape his predicament. He came to the door with a huge case (not very discreet), and proceeded to set up two digital video cams and a digital audio recorder, which he immediately turned on, thinking I didn't notice. Had to remind him repeatedly that I would not allow him to record my participation in our session. In his fantasy, I was an Executive Director at the ACLU and John was my secretary who is secretly surveilled going through my in-office panty drawer. Heavy verbal interrogation about how I had caught him on tape and had irrefutable evidence of his misbehavior. Put him on the bondage rack in locking leather wrist, ankle, and thigh restraints, stretched to level 4, stuffed his mouth with the inflatable gag.

Told him we had been working in secret with Castro for years on perfecting our interrogation techniques, and that if electro-genital torture was good enough for the Cuban government, it was good enough for us. CBT with electrodes and clamps; light cock whipping (he assured me he was a masochist, but he can't take any real pain); sensual teasing; light breath play by smothering with breasts (inside blouse). Just lies there like a piece of plank wood, no energy exchange. When I went to turn the cameras on to begin filming him in bondage they were already rolling (surprise!), so I had to take a moment to erase each tape before resuming filming (this took about fifteen minutes, during which time the electro unit was on level 28 balls and 34 cock, a bit too much for him but at this point I was so annoyed I didn't really care). No SR, only became visibly aroused when I repeated certain key words and phrases (*surveillance; security; teach the enemy a lesson*). Pushy, constantly tests boundaries, responsive as a tin of Spam, looks like every other client on earth.

Martha
DOB: 8/3/41
6/3/03; 1.5 hrs; boudoir. Sheer floral-print slip dress, rubber apron.
LIMITS: no heavy pain, no lesbian rape role play.
Gold Star client! Pretty middle-aged blonde with lots of great fantasies of the cathartic-release-without-pain variety. Wanted to work through her fear of inescapable captivity. Spread out a tarp on the boudoir floor, then sensually stripped her, laid her down, and bound her wrists and ankles with latex Therabands. Used silk remnant from cross-dressing wardrobe as blindfold; drizzled chocolate sauce, honey, tapioca pudding, and crème fraîche all over her body, mashing it around with my bare feet to create an emulsion while repeating, "You're a very messy little girl!" while she moaned and giggled. Full-body cling-wrap mummification over the big goopy mess we made, light tickle torture on soles of feet, GS over the cling wrap, keeping it off her face. After about forty-five minutes, when she was warm to the touch but not too

hot, cut her out of the cocoon and had her shower, then into the dungeon for toy show. Nipples the size of plums. Tipped twice the session fee, but I'd do her for free.

Larry
DOB: 11/19/33
9/30/98; 3 hrs; dungeon. Leather skirt and corset, open-toed stilettos.

LIMITS: no heavy pain, blood, piercing. No blindfolds.

Not terribly submissive or responsive, has the belittling habit of telling you what to do in the form of a question ("Don't you want to whip my ass? Don't you want to hit it harder? You want to piss in my mouth, don't you?") On the phone he asked for medium CBT; NT with fingers, clamps, and weights; spanking; strapping and caning. When he came in, I decided we'd play mostly with gags. Resistant to any form of bondage, but I kept his suspenders in plain view and had to repeatedly threaten to tie his wrists if he didn't keep his grabby little hands to himself (note for future sessions: he's an ass grabber, don't see unless you have the energy to fight him off). Refused to use safewords but said "ow" and "stop it" a lot. Likes being positioned in front of mirrors so he can watch himself being tortured (and grabbing your ass). Rope and leather CBT, whipped clothespins off cock and tits, gagged him after twenty minutes, and kept a steady rotation of gags in his mouth for the rest of the session (inflatable, ball, rubber bridle bit, stainless dental, o-ring). Finished him off on the floor under the toilet chair with a piss gag and funnel, ingested GS while SR. Don't see again for longer than one hour. Smelled like cheese.

Rick
DOB: 5/10/58
4/20/03; 1 hr; dungeon. Leopard minidress with furry ears and tail.

LIMITS: no religious iconography, no CD.

Goofball from PA by way of DC. High-energy session, heavy slut training and verbal fantasy. On the phone, he asked if I could wear a puppy costume or something like a football mascot outfit; I told him sexy kitten was the best I could do. No real bondage or torture, just lots of talking about all the cock he wanted to suck and all the different positions in which he'd be fucked by my über-macho gay male friends. He's a classic case of homosexual ideation that just can't translate into reality: he can't suck a dildo to save his life and could barely take my index finger, let alone a strap-on. Throughout the scene, he kept whimpering, "If I don't do this well for you, Mistress, are you going to force me to serve your homosexual friends?" and "Homos have bigger penises, don't they, Mistress?" There was an uncomfortable five minutes in which he started talking about how he wanted to fellate my Rottweiler (didn't want to break his heart and tell him I own a Boston terrier; then felt strangely protective of my dog). SR on his knees slobbering on my strap-on while shouting, "I want to be your nasty homo slut bitch." Refuses to wear a condom. Nice enough guy with some serious repression issues, just needs to blow off steam.

Orrin
DOB: 3/22/34
1/26/02; 1 hr; parlor. Business suit over latex teddy.
LIMITS: none that I could find, nice heavy player.
Kind of stodgy older guy, cross-dressing role-play fantasy in which he was my secretary and I was his sexually harassing corporate lesbian boss. Put him in white Frederick's crotchless lace teddy (cheesy as hell, but it strangely suited him), white lace stockings, red stilettos (women's size 13), and the red and blue skirt and jacket combo. I called him into my office to let him know that his typing was not up to par, and that if he wanted to keep his job he would have to find a way to be more useful around the office. Lots of manhandling, face slapping, spitting. Had him crawl around under the desk looking for lost files while I repeatedly kicked his white flabby ass with the pointy toe of my leather pump. Takes a heavy spanking, strapping, caning, whipping, marks okay (pale, pasty skin, he marks easily). No limit to

the amount of pain he can take on his tits, everything I did left him sweetly whimpering for more. After thirty minutes of smacking him around the office and berating him, I dragged him into the dungeon ("our corporate retraining center") and bent him over the bondage horse. I figured I'd do a little light strap-on play to teach him his real place on the corporate ladder, but much to my surprise he ended up taking my fist to within an inch of my elbow. Says he's been playing for about thirty years, has the distended nipples and anal flexibility to prove it. Thanked me profusely after the session, huge tip.

Trent
DOB: 10/9/41
12/2/02; 1.5 hrs; boudoir.
LIMITS: no marks.
Average-looking middle-aged guy with a weird smile and a vague frat-boy quality, came in requesting traditional OTK role play. I was his young aunt, he was living with me while attending a prestigious Southern university. He disobeyed the house rules, and as a result had to submit himself to a thorough spanking or I would call the dean of his school and have him expelled. Started out as a fairly talented role player, but not great in the personal hygiene department. Had the annoying habit of grinding around on my lap while I spanked him: his masturbatory wiggling was so out of hand I finally incorporated it into the role play and told him he would receive the birch for his pelvic inappropriateness. At this point, he dropped to his knees and begged, "Please don't tell your big black boyfriend about this, please don't let your huge black lover come in here and punish me." After several minutes of this sort of ridiculous mumbling, I finally signed on and told him that my boyfriend wouldn't hesitate to take his big black hand to Trent's wormy little white bare bottom if he didn't do exactly as he was told. The rest of the session was spent trying to administer discipline (wooden frat paddle, leather strap, cane) while listening to an increasingly sexual stream of negrophilic fantasies from a man who I can only suspect burns crosses in his

free time. I made him SR while singing "We Shall Overcome." Creepy energy and nasty hidden racial agenda. Alert local hate-crimes groups and don't invite him back.

Kofi
DOB: 4/8/38
12/10/01; 2 hrs; dungeon.
LIMITS: no military or other uniforms, no humiliation.
K is quiet, very respectful. Classic "I've got too much responsibility in my daily life, everyone looks to me for leadership, and I just want to give it all up" scenario. Really nice energy; long slow meditative full-body rope bondage to St. Andrew's Cross; rhythmic flogging on back and butt (brought in his own music: Ravel's *Bolero*); medium to heavy OTK spanking (he can take a lot with a good warmup, lovely smooth skin, doesn't mark easily). Suspension sling and sensory deprivation hood (he got dizzy, we unzipped the eye vents); swung him around the room and let him feel weightless for a good half hour. Excellent "Mistress' choice" session, spent the last half of the session with him kneeling at my feet, stroking his neck and holding him while he had a nice long cry while telling me he just needed a place he could go to be safe and not have to make any decisions. Beautiful hands.

GLOSSARY OF SM TERMS (from www.mistressmorgana.com)
CBT = cock and ball torture
CD = cross-dressing
GS = golden shower
OTK = over-the-knee spanking
NT = nipple torture
SO = strap-on play
SR = self-release (masturbation)
Toy show = masturbation show

From *Good Faith*

Jane Smiley

The leaves fell off the trees, and Hank went to the University of Arizona for a land-use conference. Jason went to Virginia to visit Clark in college, and I was feeling flush. The townhouses in Phase Four were closing one after another like slamming doors, and another friend of the Davids had bought two places in Deacon, a large house and an even larger warehouse. He was a costumer in New York, and rental space for keeping the costumes had gotten too expensive in his West Side location. I had found him an old cold-storage facility that would be easy to convert to the perfect temperature and humidity for silks, brocades, satins, and chiffons, not to mention veils, crowns, scepters, swords, scabbards, and golden goblets. The collection, according to the Davids, was worth millions. Anyway, it was the Friday before Thanksgiving. I picked Felicity up at her place, and she threw her bag into the backseat and got into the car with the happy air of someone whose tracks are covered.

My car had a bench seat, so she scooted right over next to me and we began kissing at once, secure in the knowledge that no one ever came down her road. I have to say she was as uninhibitedly ardent right in front of her own dwelling, with the garden hose hanging over the railing of the front porch and a light in a second-floor window, as she was in the most anonymous empty house. As we drove away, Felicity locked under my right arm, I said, "Why doesn't it get old?"

"The sex?"

"Yeah."

"Because I never get tired of it."

The weather was damp and overcast—umber and ochre November. The hillsides were dark with the tangled net of bare tree branches; closer to the road, we could see their trunks rooted in a thick bed of wet leaves. Felicity leaned against me and gazed out the window. From time to time, she kissed me on the shoulder or the cheek. At one point, she took my right hand off the steering wheel, turned my palm upward, kissed it, and then put it back.

The snow began about an hour outside of New York. It wasn't an unusual snow at all, at first. Each flake landed on the windshield with a tiny splat and was swept away by the wipers. The road was wet but not slippery. The roadside turf turned gray and then white, but the snow was fluffy and appealing. Felicity said, "I looked at the weather last night. It didn't say anything about snow."

"Very attractive snow, if you ask me," I said.

"I wonder if it's snowing at home. I suppose it will look very suspicious if the driveway is unshoveled by Monday."

"Don't you have friends in New York?"

"That woman from college I was out with the night I picked you up."

"Yeah. Just the sort of person to talk you into a trip to the city at the last moment."

"Absolutely. But I'll have to remember her name between now and then."

"Anyway," I said, "I'm sure it's not snowing at home."

"No, you're right."

The car was so warm and the company was so comfortable and I was so happy that it took a very long time for me to comprehend that the snow cover on the cars coming toward us in the southbound lanes had anything to do with us. Every time we came to a dead stop, we kissed until the car in front of us started moving again. At one point, for some undefined length of time, she spread her skirt across my lap and then flung her leg over mine underneath it. Then she hiked up the back of her skirt and pressed herself against my pant leg. She sighed and closed her eyes, rocking against me. After a moment, she murmured, "Have you ever gotten a blow job in a moving vehicle?"

"Not in a traffic jam."

"But on the highway?"

"Well, we pulled over."

"We didn't."

"That was very daring of you."

"It was daring of him."

"Hank?"

"Oh my God, no. My college cheating boyfriend. Driving around having oral sex was about all we did. He was a good driver, but he didn't have much to say otherwise ... *mmm*." She continued to move against me while she was talking; it was very exciting. We approached the tunnel. Traffic intensified, with honking and jostling for position, but still I floated along on a sea of patience and only once thought of what this trip would have been like with Sherry—a prolonged exercise, for me, in calming her rotating pattern of annoyance, anxiety, fear, and boredom. Felicity removed her leg, turned around, and lay down on the seat with her head in my lap. Her deep-set and very dark eyes were peaceful, even sleepy. I felt a little discomfort—self-consciousness, I suppose—rise, take hold, and then subside. After that, her regard got to be a fact, a function of our situation together in the car. I looked down at her when I could, looked up at the traffic when I had to, stroked her face lightly with my thumb and the tips of my fingers.

The Hilton was bustling with happy conversation about the snow. In the lobby, though it wasn't especially cold outside, people were bundling or unbundling into or out of brightly colored down-filled coats and knitted hats and mittens and boots, as if they were just going out into, or just coming back from, long treks down snowy roads to crossroads grocery stores where the only remaining provisions were wholesome items like bread and milk and oranges. We got to the desk. The clerk acted delighted to see us, Mr. and Mrs. Joseph Stratford, who had made it at last. Adding to the festive atmosphere were the early Christmas decorations in the lobby—a tall tree decked out in silver and gold ornaments and clusters of poinsettia and holly. I kept my arm around Felicity, who yawned from time to time. "Long trip?" asked the clerk.

"Longest ever in my whole life," said Felicity.

Our room was small but comfortable, and while I was in the bathroom Felicity turned down the bedspread, took off her clothes, and climbed between the sheets. When I came back into the room, she was nestled into the pillows, yawning and stretching. She said, "This time yesterday I was busy with laundry and making veal broth for my mother and talking to Leslie on the phone and in general doing three things at once, and now I can't imagine doing one thing at once. Oh, your skin is cold. It's very refreshing." Her skin was warm and peachy-looking and I got as close to it as I could, putting my arms and legs around her and nestling my face into her neck and the curtain of her hair. "Oh," she murmured, "this is very nice. It's like being tossed around in the surf. I might as well give up and go under." She stretched against me for a few moments and then softened all over. I felt her sleepiness seep into me like the slow swirling of a drop of ink into clear water, and then, even though I had been planning in the bathroom to make love to her, I fell asleep.

It was twilight when I woke up. As I rose to awareness, I noticed that the window light was pearly and bright as well as bluish, and I lay there for a long moment, warmed by Felicity's embrace and simply appreciative of the unusual color of the light. It would be wrong to say that this was a fleeting moment, since everything about it impressed itself upon me—the color and the brightness of the window, the way the pinkness of the room's décor took on a kind of silvery sheen, Felicity's fragrance and quietness, the softness of her breathing, my own molasses heaviness.

Just then she turned away from me, and I got up and looked out the window. The glass was cool against my cheek, and there it was, Fifty-fourth Street, at least three feet deep in snow, lit by streetlamps that were just beginning to come on and completely deserted. The snow was still falling—very thickly—in patterned gusts around the lamps and in a rich cold particulate fog everywhere else. As best I could, I looked upward. The undersides of the clouds were pinked by the reflection of the city lights, and the snow poured out of them in a deadening cascade that was very reassuring. I went back to bed.

Felicity turned toward me and, without waking up, I thought, put her hand on my cock, which instantly hardened. She smiled, though she didn't open her eyes, and rolled over and presented her beautiful round buttocks to me, and I entered her at once, and her hand went immediately between her legs and she stroked herself while I grasped her hip bones and pulled myself more deeply inside of her. In the twilight, I could see her buttocks press against me and then taper gracefully into the contours of her back muscles, which fanned into her shoulders. That was what I looked at while I felt her vaginal muscles pulsating around my cock, which was moving into and out of her. Here's what it was: The perfect relaxation of our whole bodies had concentrated at this one amazing spot and come together, and the effect then reversed itself, and the electricity of that spot gathered and spread out through the rest in hot waves and finally emerged in sound—the sound of Felicity singing out and me groaning, and then Felicity laughing and saying, "Oh, Joey, feel my hair. This is so amazing that my hair is getting hot." We sighed simultaneously. She said, "It's dark."

"Look out the window."

"Snowy?"

"Look."

She got up naked and walked across the room—that was what I'd been aiming for—and pressed her forehead against the windowpane. She said, "Thank God we're stranded. Let's order room service before they run out of food."

Seduction

Cecilia Tan

She knows what seduction is, because until the night she lost her virginity—a night she had waited for a long time after many near misses, several broken dates and a few broken hearts—she had thought what most people think, that seduction is something dishonest and dangerous, sultry and tawdry, slow and cautious, but really it's none of those things, for as she learned, the most important part of seduction is the removal of fear—that instinctual safeguard without which one feels perfectly secure, safe as a hatchling nested deep in downy feathers, for that is exactly how she felt when he—he who is only significant by the fact that it was he who seduced her, finally, that night in the hotel bar where she sat waiting for someone she didn't know would be him—pulled her hand gently until she was near enough to feel his warmth, and he pressed the backs of her fingertips to his fly as if to show her it was nothing dangerous, the way they let small children touch snakes in a zoo, with a care and deliberation that says it is safe, and it did seem so, it seemed hungry to her, but not in a predatory way, rather more like a pet needing to be cared for, harmless and within human control, and so it was that she was seduced, not slow, but quick and sure, so that the panic, the fear, that had driven her from all the others was entirely absent, and she embraced him like he was a big, dependable dog ready for an afternoon walk, but of course they went straight to his room and stripped out of their clothes, quickly, to keep ahead of the fear in case it should return; that is why she was the one who grabbed him by the shoulders and pressed him down, and pressed herself upon him as she looked into his face flushed with thrill and surprise, engulfing him, because she was not afraid in that moment, and now knowing what she did, would not ever be again.

The Magician's Assistant

Cecilia Tan

The magician's assistant is looking at herself in the mirror, trying to attach a sequin to just the right spot on her face. The makeup mirror shows the tiny wrinkles beginning to appear as she squints and turns her head from side to side, the white Vegas feather-plume wig rustling against her bare shoulders as she looks at the curve of her cheeks, the dimple of her chin. The damn sparkle needs to be placed just so or it'll look like a crystalline cancer on her face instead of a little bit of magic. The plastic gem poised on her index finger, a tiny dab of spirit gum glistening, she points her hand at her reflection, reflecting. He was going to put her in chains tonight, and then plunge her into a glass-sided tank filled with cold water, and then a bunch of other mumbo jumbo, the result of which always was she emerged elsewhere miraculously freed, but also soaked to the bone in her see-through dress, nipples erect . . . it's Vegas, after all.

She waves the sequin in the mirror and thinks . . . hmm. She pulls the clingy white fabric away from her breast and plants the sequin onto her nipple. She gets another from the tray on her makeup table and makes the other nipple match. She poises a third, but hesitates. This magician isn't really much fun. He's married and is putting two kids through college and she doesn't really see very much of him beyond a few lame rehearsals and the show itself. She's had bosses before who appreciated the situation a bit more, shall we say. Who could find the rabbit under her dress. Who sawed her in half after hours.

What the hell, she thinks, so he'll never know. She hikes up the glittering Elizabeth-Taylor-as-Cleopatra dress and slides down in the chair. Her knees fall open and her hand hovers under the makeup table. Her face is ringed by soft white bulbs all the way around as her unseen finger places the last jewel in one place no one is likely to see it tonight. She presses it into place and gasps, transfixed by her own reflection, at the half-lidded look of longing on her face. Maybe tonight the dress will tear in the water, under the chains. Maybe tonight she will shine.

To the Marrow

Sharon Wachsler

When your life is at stake, everyone starts to look good, or, at least, doable. Sex becomes a means of survival. Everything does: vitamins, acupuncture, walking the dogs. You do it, and you know it's at least half as important as the amputations and radiation. I fuck, therefore I am.

I met Jessica at my support group. We were the only two not married with a pack of kids. I figured that upped our survival chances right there. Those mothers looked haggard as a lifestyle. I bet the cancer just dug in deeper with them.

At the first meeting Jessica looked across at me and leered. She ran her tongue over her lips, smirking, while the woman next to her said how she'd lost her hostess job because her appearance made the diners nervous.

Jessica was vintage punk: a safety pin through her ear, a red velvet blouse with lace at the cuffs, pale jeans she'd probably ripped herself. She was all jagged lines and ruffles. On our first date we dyed her sparse hair hot pink. It stood out in little tufts and patches, so the color contrast was excellent. She looked like a lollipop—bright and sticky. I wanted to lick her.

Wearing my steel-toe boots, muscle shirts, and black jeans with the key chain on my belt, I looked like a skinhead. Even after my hair came back in, I shaved it off. That's where the no tits comes in handy. I freak, therefore I am.

The sex was not the best I've had—it always felt like something was slipping out of place—but it served its purpose. Sex as an affirmation of being alive. Sex as accounting what we've still got. Cunts and fingers and minds.

For Jessica it went deeper. It was in her bones. Her marrow, in fact. The first time we did it, she puked after. Right in the bed. She'd finished her first round of chemo. "It's all right," I told her, stripping off the sheets like a pro. "I like the idea I fucked your guts out." She screamed like I was the funniest dyke on the block, then covered her mouth and ran to the bathroom. I heard her retching while I put on a CD.

I was in remission, but I had a stash of pain pills from when I should have used them and didn't. I wanted to be awake during it all. And I wanted a way out, later, if I needed it. I even tried to bully the docs into letting me have the surgery without general. I think it made them squeamish, the idea of me being awake while they sliced off my breasts like two bloody custards. The nurses seemed less barbaric. One of them let me flirt with her, even though I could see her ring when she adjusted my morphine drip. I let it drip. At home I took just enough dope to keep on.

When Jessica came back from the bathroom she flopped down on the bed, wiped her pale hand across her face. I was afraid she might fall asleep, so I kissed her. Her mouth still tasted like puke, even though she'd brushed her teeth. That was a nice gesture, because during chemo everything smells twenty decibels higher than it did before. Mint toothpaste stinks about as loud as you can get. I wanted to say something but it all seemed too corny. So I slid my tongue down her chin, across her chest and belly, and into her cunt. She tasted surprisingly sweet. Like a hummingbird, I lapped at her, my heart beating like hell to keep me there.

I wished she had her period. I knew it was in her blood, her danger. Mine had been removed—slice and sew and the problem is gone. But you can't empty a person of blood and then refill them, like changing the oil in a car. I could get under her hood all I wanted and still not see the problem. I wanted to taste it.

After she came, we took some of my pills. I let her fuck me for a while. It felt distant, like my cunt was a thousand years away, but her face was right up close. She only had a few eyelashes. I liked her eyelids then, bare and swollen, and kissed them. I liked her nose, her ears, her forehead; I stared at them while her fingers fluttered inside me. When the drugs really kicked in we just lay side by side, sleeping on and off, drooling, like the dogs draped across our legs.

I came to before Jessica and found *King Kong* on cable. I could see where he was coming from. I felt like I could hold all of Jessica in one hand. Like my mere presence could make her swoon—with fear, with love, with pain pills, sometimes. Later, of course, I *could* have held her in one hand. Well, only theoretically, since the family wouldn't let me near the urn. They thought I was sick. The laugh was on them because I had beat it, but for some people it's not about the cancer. When I met her family at the funeral, I understood why Jessica had stayed a punk so long.

Her friends threw her a real memorial, with people talking about Jessica's art and drinking tequila and wearing slutty black stuff from secondhand stores. It made me wish Jessica were still there. She would have loved it. We would have dished everyone afterwards, in bed, harshed on their haircuts.

On my way home from the memorial I bought three marrow soup bones. I gave one apiece to the dogs and kept the third. I watched how each dog held its bone between its paws and licked out the middle, like an ice cream cone. I got down on the floor with them. Sprawled on the cool kitchen linoleum I sucked out the marrow, imagining Jessica open before me, tasting blood on my tongue.

Genuflection

Lana Gail Taylor

The sun gets in my eyes when I step out of the porn shop. Anyone living on East Colfax knows the sun never burns out here. Even when the sun goes down, we got the heat inside us. The gringos explain our heat as hostility: that's what they think. Maybe they think right—in some cases—but building a baseball field and coffee shop chains deeper into the east, that's just like gringos to think a baseball field covers brown with green, and cappuccinos smother the stench of drugs and drunks, gunshot and blood, the smell of come in backseats.

I don't hate gringos; I'm half gringo, half white, even if I don't look it. Back in the trailer park, the gringos—let's face it, they were crackers—didn't know what to make of me, so they just kicked my ass. Mom was silkworm white; she had blue eyes and scarlet lips. She was a whore; she was also a traitor. Mom fucked men so brown they looked Indian, and if there's anything gringos hate, it's beautiful gringas fucking spics—then giving birth to kids that can't pass.

My daddy, Mom said, was real beautiful, real brown. Her dad, of course, tried beating the Mexican's identity out of her. When she wouldn't give him up, her dad said, "You're losing that kid." Mom told him, "No way," and he said to his brothers, "Hold her still," before he punched her in the stomach; she counted eight blows. I think it's a miracle he didn't kill her. I think it's a miracle the blood she gave up blew through her lips and not from be-tween her legs.

Two months later, when her dad's beating proved a failure, he threw most of Mom's shit, which wasn't much, in the back of a neighbor's truck with directions to leave her at the Creek Side Trailer Park where the creek was dried up. He threw enough money at her to last her a month and said, "So you're going to hell? So what?" Trailer parks, if you haven't seen any lately, are where white retards and rejects live; the working-class poor; drunks who keep hold of their minimum wage jobs; and what-ever else is left over from white society's wet dreams.

"You ain't no bastard out of the trailer park," Mom said to me, but I was a bastard, all right.

Mom wasn't always *La Puta Merengue*. She didn't always shop at the Goodwill, eat cold chili out of the can, or sleep all day on the couch in a terry-cloth robe, then rise after sundown to prepare for her tricks. Before I left, or before Mom kicked me out—you could see it both ways—she was horribly thin and crusty-eyed. The Cracker stood in the door to the trailer with a sawed-off shotgun, threatening the Mexicans. José Lopez stood his ground for ten minutes. He called to Mom in Spanish. I didn't know him, except for his name, except he came to see Mom three times a week, and José was probably the reason Mom managed to keep the trailer. Mom told José to go away.

The hog-bellied Cracker took over; it was all shit from there. Maybe our life wasn't perfect before that sack of shit showed up, but at least Mom and me didn't wear matching black eyes. Fuck-ing Cracker knocked her around every damn day and was con-stantly fucking her, fucking her in front of me, whacking off in her face, and I don't know why, but she was hooked.

One night, I went to Mom's bedroom and found the pictures of Kari Carpenter, who once bought silk underwear at Victoria's Secret in the Cherry Creek Mall. Good girl, good grades, Kari was the most popular girl in her high school. Mom told me about her: how Kari's friends wanted to be her because she was pretty and sang in the glee club. Kari's first boyfriend, Toby Ellis, drove a Toyota Camry and drove Kari bored out of her skull, Mom laughed, and straight to her knees in the backseats of East Colfax.

East Colfax—a mixture of the last places to buy vinyl, tattoo parlors, diners, pool halls, and porn shops—this is my home now. The buildings are often ugly and the streets usually smell like what bums leave in the gutters: sometimes a bum takes a shit on the sidewalk, and it's like saying, "I was here." Sometimes the junkies piss their own pants. I let Willy use the broom closet in the porn shop to clean up. After his second time using the closet, he told me, "Manny, I been on the junk so long my dick is dead." He tried to revive it, stayed put in one of the booths an hour, looped reel playing, and him behind the curtain grunting. I imagined Willy's eyes squinting at the sunny slice of the twelve-by-twelve screen, knees pressed together, shoulders hunched, and his fist yanking violently—the same intensity you might use to clobber a wad loose from a choking victim—and I willed his cock back to life. When Willy pushed back the curtain, he just shook his head. His poor dick was a shoestring that wilts when you try to lace it through a hole.

"Sorry, Willy." I was really sorry for him; whacking off kept me from impaling myself on a fence post in back of the trailer after the Cracker took over.

On East Colfax, you get exactly what you'd imagine: me; Willy; runaways clogging the alleys; high school truants crowding into the pool halls; thugs and gangbangers patrolling the main drag; dealers hunkering down on the side streets; pimps parking their Thunderbirds in front of Church's Chicken; and the hookers and hustlers holding all corners.

The junkies get to me the most, like Willy: would you believe he's lovely to me? Thin, pale, and trembling, sour and musty, his face (probably no older than thirty) rubbed out and soiled, but his eyes like scrubbed flint in the sun. His memories are like scattered ash after the phoenix rose and didn't take him with it. I listen, sometimes for an hour or two, to Willy's fragmented stories: his mother's dead, she isn't; he was once in the military, he was a college professor; he's never been in love, he falls in love every day.

I listened to Hank, Willy's friend, too. Hank says the Almighty exists in a plastic baggie packed inside a dealer's cheek and plays hard to get. When I see what Hank and Willy and the rest of the junkies give up for a piece of celestial bliss—crumpled dollar bills, their assholes—I believe that nothing sublime exists long on this Earth.

I leave the porn shop at three every afternoon. My trip down the avenue feels like getting thrown around in a boat sometimes, except I haven't been on a boat lately, so it's more like the bus, how people cough and someone's elbow hits my ribs, and I just try to breathe. On the bus, I lean my head to a window smeared by god-knows-what and imagine Kari Carpenter rebelling against her upper-middle-class white upbringing. She was a girl in a car full of girls; anticipation hung above the seats like perfume, and every girl with a butt stuck to the leather seats wanted to do something Daddy wouldn't approve of, and besides: some truth was being withheld from them, and Kari was the most eager to take it.

She told the girl driving, "Cross the bridge over I-25 onto Colfax, then drive east." The other girls giggled. Kari applied lipstick, then stuck her head out the window, tasting cool freedom, opening her mouth to the danger and heat from the street. When Kari pulled her head back into the car, the breeze rushed through the opened windows, pushing tendrils of her corn-colored hair against her lips, turning them darker.

The car full of girls got as far as Chubbys before the driver braked a little too late and collided with a low rider's chrome bumper. The brown boys circled the other car before peering inside; smiles opened their faces. Kari stepped out of the car and coolly studied both bumpers. Then she announced, "No harm done."

Were the brown boys' advances just for kicks? A *fuck you* to white suburbia? Pure lust? Well, who knew? But Mom told me,

"Toby was sloppy and stupid. But this brown boy: he made my body feel born again."

So I'm going to blame Kari Carpenter for letting passion get the best of her? I wrap my arms around my chest and hear myself breathing; I'm alive.

The Mexican gangbangers named me my first day on the avenue. They called me "Manny" because it's funny to them, but also a way to keep from kicking my ass. I might look brown, but I'm *jotito,* a "little faggot," so when the Mexicans taunt me, "Get it up the *chiquito* today, Manny?" they're letting me pass. They don't kill me.

Three o'clock, and I leave the porn shop. I feel the sun on my back like a dry tongue. The avenue rushes past me. I blink up and down the sidewalk in both directions, hold a hand to one hip, let the toe of one dirty shoe scuff the ground. Willy and Hank sit side by side on the bench bolted to the sidewalk, so I go over to check on them. They're "not feeling well today." Hank trembles and pulls his collar up against the sun. I sit beside Willy and hold his hand, see the veins through the skin of the other man's wrist, pulsing ropes.

"Willy," I whisper, "you look tore up."

"Manny," he croaks. "Jesus Christ is a black transvestite, saw her with my two eyes last night."

He saw Black Tina. Rocket-high on dope, anyone might mistake her for Jesus Christ. She's something of a ghetto-bound messiah, picking out the new arrivals and giving them Church's Chicken (her favorite) while warning the junkies away from bad dealers, keeping the thugs in line after a gringo ran his SUV over a "Fucking spic, get out of the way!" or robbed a hooker of her pimp's money. Black Tina knows who all the undercover cops are; hell, she bangs the undercover cops. She told me where to score a good soup line, too; I had beef stew and corn bread that night.

Black Tina is like Tyra Banks in a purple tube top and green pants. She wears orange lipstick and blue-metal eye shadow. She also packs an Adam's apple that's like a bird while she belts out a tune. Her favorites are "You Turn Me Right Round (Like a Record)" and "Love Shack." The gringos trolling by in their Camrys check her out with eyes that let you know what they're thinking: she might have been Diana Ross if she wasn't a whacked-out whore. Black Tina told me the gringos like her to sing while they try ramming their cocks to her vocal cords.

I pat Willy's wrist. "You saw Black Tina."

Willy mumbles something. "I know what I saw." Then, "Got something, Manny, make me well?"

"You know I don't pack, Willy."

"And if you did, I'd hate you."

Next to him, Hank shivers and moans; a bum wanders next to the bench; his cardboard sign reads: *Am sik nede mony God blis.*

"Hey, man. Stay here." I jog back into the porn shop, then return with a pen to fix his spelling. I tell the bum to hit the corner of Glenwood and Colfax, next to the Gentlemen's Cabaret, where suits come out after a martini-and-stripper deluxe lunch and have to wait for a valet to bring their cars. "Holds them up," I clue the guy in. "They got to give you some change."

The bum starts walking. I watch him blur into the heat. I slide the pen in my pocket and Willy asks, "What would you want, if someone gave you the time of day?" His teeth rattle together.

I almost say, "Mom back," but bite down on that wish. I had her as long as I could; now I had to want for something else. "The truth, Willy?"

"Give it to me straight."

"A brown boy who loves me."

"Well, I knew that about you." Willy closes his eyes. "Next time I see Jesus Christ, I'll tell her that's what you want." He falls against Hank and the two of them hold each other.

Before the Cracker put a stop to it, Mom sang to me, "This little light of mine, I'm gonna let it shine." That was love; Mom and me put our heads together, and she sang, and the look the

Cracker gave her was nothing like the glare he gave me. I wanted the fucker chained to a peg stuck in the ground behind the trailer. I could have watched his mayo-white flab turn to nothing but flaps in the breeze. But I didn't have the guts, *comprende?* If I had, Mom wouldn't have had to push me out the window to save me. Maybe, I would have saved her.

Four blocks from the porn shop is Chubbys. I heard it got written up in the newspaper for having the city's best green chili. (You never see the gringos lingering in the parking lot after dark though.) At Chubby's, the Mexican gangbangers park their Novas, soft-top Mustangs, and low-riding Chevys. On the benches outside the restaurant, somebody leaves a half-eaten burrito lying in an inch of already gelling green chili, maybe a few french fries.

I count used condoms while crossing the parking lot. If I don't watch my step, I get one in love with my shoe and then the Mexicans tease me: "*Jotito* thinks he can put his foot up someone's ass because his cock is too small."

I play it cool. Except while sniffing for leftover menudo, I admire the Mexicans, muscles like reeds running elbow to shoulder, brown as an Indian summer, and pants belted low on the hips. Soon enough, the papayas show up, and the Mexicans wipe their chins like they've just eaten pussy. The papayas don't do much for me, but the Mexicans start posturing, jockeying for position.

The Papaya Parade breaks just short of the curb—I'm standing at one of the benches with my fingers in leftover chili—and then the *Mexicanas* scramble over the seats and tumble out doors; purple mouths crack gum and each girl poses harder than the last. One *Mexicana* yells, "*¡Anda con otra!*"

I finish the chili—my stomach still feeling empty.

The bell rings every time a customer comes into the porn shop. The customers' faces all show the same bored detachment, the same quiet loneliness. The guys are regulars—hardly ever strangers—and usually gringos. The first day I got behind the counter, the guys hit on me with an intensity that was unnerving. They said they suffered "Latino lust." They eyeballed me as if through a scope. I gave them breaks anyway: free lube, extra time in the booths, and turning my head when they sucked each other off in the aisles. What I understood about these gringos was that the porn shop was a kind of trailer park on the avenue for white trash that needed to feel comfortable in an uncomfortable place because they didn't feel comfortable anyplace else.

The sun comes in one window where I sit at the register, but I shiver because the manager insists you got to keep the air conditioner high so it forces the smell of armpits and jizz up to the ceiling. I stare at the light through the window and imagine it getting closer to me; it's wrapping me up like a warm kiss, a man's arms—a brown one who loves me.

Then I catch something in my nose: a scent of peppery sugar and a muskrat smell. I come out of my zone. I never saw this Mexican before. He walks like a panther, or your imagination walking tracks in the carpet at the foot of your bed: you can't hold him for long. He's a hustler but not smudged or bruised like the ones I've seen on the streets. His brown shines like the surface of a dark soda. A rope of black hair swings across his back, and he flips it over a bare shoulder.

The hustler stops at the register and cracks the counter light with his knuckles. He wears a gold band on his right hand, little finger. "Hey," he says, and his breath breathes clove.

"Hey," I say back.

The Mexican's mouth is blood dark. His eyes are velvet pincushions hemmed with inky lashes. A small scar edges the corner of his left eye; another runs from the corner of his mouth, and when he smiles, the scar disappears in the crease. His teeth are as bright as the white on a chessboard, but something sticks to his front tooth, a piece of tobacco.

The hustler moves away from the register and his narrow hips twitch; the tight loaves of his ass are wrapped in leather pants, and the skin running out the sleeves of his white T-shirt pulls taut across slim, solid bones.

He stops at the condom display and grabs: grooved, lubed, and magnum, shoving individual packages in his front pockets. He's already packing: I mean, between the hipbones, barely constrained by his zipper.

I start to sweat beneath the air conditioner.

The hustler returns to the register and holds a finger to his mouth and then pats his pocket. I think he lets his fingers pass across his zipper on purpose. He flicks a hip against the counter, leaning forward so I can see his arm tightening just below the shoulder. Then he places his hand on mine before flipping my hand over and jabbing at my palm with his finger.

"Bueno," he says. And his cushion eyes pin me.

"What?"

"Good. You got a good line," he says. "All the lines in your hand, long and solid. You'll live to fuck a long time. Or fuck so much you'll live a long time."

"Are you trying to hustle me?" This is pretty unlikely; he'd have to be stupid or desperate to think I could afford him.

I calculate ways to skim the register.

The hustler's hand encloses mine, and the pressing heat makes me think of the pressure of two chests against each other, the push and pull, the friction of two bodies embracing, wrestling, fucking.

The hustler's black eyes are ringed by gold. The scar has a pulse. "I haven't seen you before."

I shrug.

"Got any friends?"

Is his finger rubbing my knuckle? "Hmm, yeah." With my other hand, I swipe at my forehead.

The hustler looks amused. "Like who?"

"Hmm. W-W-Willy. Black T-Tina." I suck in my breath.

"What you need, *chico,*" the hustler says, "is someone looking after your ass." And he laughs.

Did I just gulp over the loudspeaker, piss my pants? "W-what? You offering?"

The hustler lets go of my hand, and I feel the air-conditioned air rush for the warmth in my palm, so I close it.

"Well, hey. It ain't a big deal." He knocks on the counter again, then stands straight. "What d'you go by?"

"M-Manny."

"You got one of those s-s-stuttering problems, Manny?" Then he punches me soft in the shoulder. "Just kidding."

I recover fast enough to give him the bird. "Just kidding, too."

The guy blows me a kiss.

HE. IS. ON. MY. MIND. Yeah. Feels like the guy is a hot one through the veins; pincushion eyes and shining skin and a blood spot for a mouth and those sexy facial scars; and let's not forget—yeah, yeah, breathe—the twitching hips, that scent of muskrat, and the kiss that went from the air to my face to my chest to my toes and then zipped straight to my dick. Charged blood. Erect the whole damn rest of the day. I beat off five times, and each time: He. Is. On. My. Mind.

When I come out of the porn shop at three o'clock, I barely miss walking on Hank, who pounds a vein in his elbow and barks, "See here? Still got a good one!" Then I trip over Willy, who says, "Hey, Manny, I scored!" And I mumble hello and take another step before hesitating and looking up and down the sidewalk like it's race day.

"Hey, Willy, hey." I rush my friend and engulf him in a hug.

Willy pats my shoulder. "Manny scored too, huh?"

I laugh and wave good-bye to Willy, heading toward Chubbys, turning my face into the sun as if snuggling the crook of the hustler's arm. I serenade the crowd, "This little light of mine; I'm gonna let it shine." I'm wearing my girl's narrow T-shirt that says *Porn Star* and punch out my chest, hear catcalls. After discovering an unwanted beef taco and an almost cold soda outside Chubby's, I holler, "¡Hola, chicos!" to the Mexican gangbangers, then keep walking, singing, "This light of mine; I'm gonna let it shine; all right!"

Black Tina stands on a corner facing the traffic. I'm dancing, then spinning. The bird in her throat dips when she chuckles. Then she cuffs my hair lightly. "What's the matter with you? You high?" She's teasing.

"Don't mess with the do." I smooth down the strands. Then, "No drugs." And I jig.

Black Tina stoops to catch if the gringo in the SUV is signaling her, then studies my tight jeans and T-shirt. "Don't tell me. You're a working faggot now." Black Tina eyeballs me under metallic-blue lids. "You keep your ass behind the counter. I'm in no mood to worry about you."

I stand on tiptoe and land a wet one on her shiny black cheek. "Don't need to worry about me. I got me someone who's watching my ass." I grin, doing more jigs.

Black Tina wipes her face, but she's smiling. "So Manny has a sugar daddy."

I shake my head.

"Good. That's a surefire way to end up right here." Black Tina stamps the corner with her heel, then ducks to see if the gringo in the Cutlass is signaling her. When he drives on, she swears under her breath.

"What I got," I quip, "is pure perfection." Then I drop my voice an octave as if we're in church. "Hey. You must have seen him somewhere. He's real beautiful, real brown. He's got these scars on his face." I touch a finger to the corner of my eye, then my mouth.

Black Tina shakes her head. "Oh hell, that one's trouble, Manny."

"Tell me. Who is he?" I feel the heat again, like a lighter hovers close to my wrist, heating the pulse underneath.

Black Tina stares down the block. "Carlos has no loyalty," she says. She looks sad.

I look down the block and watch the hustlers. Some of the brown boys paint their eyes and pucker their lips at the traffic. Some grease their hair and sport enormous muscles. A few look scrappy and nervous.

"Look at all the lovely faggots," Black Tina murmurs. "Want my advice?"

I shrug.

"Stay clear of Carlos and the rest of those boys. Misery loves company."

"I'm not miserable." I show teeth as evidence. Then I fidget, searching the next block for the one Black Tina calls Carlos.

"Keep it that way," she says.

A long car slows at the curb. A window rolls down revealing a gringo's face. Black Tina leans in to negotiate.

I take this as my exit and head straight for the next block. Some of the working boys snicker at me. Some of the hustlers hang in groups studying their nails, bitching about tricks, about lockjaw, and a lot of them brag about the size of their tips. I spot the beautiful hustler on the southeast corner, in front of the record shop: real records, slick vinyl, rare. Carlos holds his corner alone. I watch him watch the traffic. "This little light of mine . . . I'm gonna let it shine. . ." Next to the record shop is a Pete's Kitchen, serving runny eggs and buttermilk biscuits with lard gravy. Next to Pete's is Rita's Flowers: a dozen roses for seven ninety-five. I wonder about them roses.

Carlos has one hip bent toward the traffic. A finger nudges the inside of a pocket. A teenage gringo sticks his head out the window of a sports car and spits. Carlos shows him the finger. Other cars go by; the gringos size Carlos up; he acknowledges the attention by patting his crotch. I back into the wall of the record store and stuff my hands down my pockets. I've got a boner. But I'm there for a while before Carlos notices me.

"Hey. You're the *chico* from the porn shop."

"Yeah."

"Good lifeline."

I shrug, half smiling.

His lips curve. The scar beside his mouth disappears. "Real good. You didn't rat me out about the condoms."

I nod.

Carlos props a shoulder against the wall next to me. "Owe you one, eh?"

"It's nothing," I say, but it's hard to talk. My boner hurts.

Looking me up and down, Carlos notices the tightness in my pants. "What's that?" His eyes zero in; he's smiling.

"You know." And I blush.

"Tell me," he says.

I try to laugh. "My dick's hard, all right?"

Carlos scoots closer. Our arms touch. "Why?" Bangs flop over his eyes and his breath blows against my neck. With a finger he tugs on my belt loop. "Tell me, M-M-Manny." His breath is as hot as spiked punch.

"Shit," I say. Sweat noses its way down my spine. Carlos touches the bone that rises out of my collar with his lips. "Porn star, huh? What would you do to me?"

I move my elbow a little, to touch him.

Carlos chuckles.

"I'd fuck you," I tell him in a determined voice.

After a minute, Carlos cups my crotch with his hand. I hold his wrist and push his hand harder against me. "I want you, okay?"

"Nice, *chico*." In one quick motion, his hand lowers my zipper and the fly falls open. He grips my cock tightly but tenderly. I moan, unable to help it. "That's nice, too." And he gives me a squeeze before letting me go.

Carlos steps back to the curb, watching the traffic. I zip up hurriedly and follow him. "What's going on?"

He squints at the traffic. "I kind of got to work now." After several minutes and me not budging, Carlos looks at me. "You need some *dinero*? I mean real money, none of that minimum wage shit?" He waits. The traffic seems to move faster, a blur. The other hustlers laugh loudly.

I scratch my neck, my arms.

"You anxious about something?"

"No."

Carlos nods for me to come closer. I do.

"I got this trick, *sí*? He wants to watch me with an amigo."

I don't answer.

"You my amigo?"

One scrappy-looking hustler stands apart from the rest. The boys don't talk to him. I imagine he charges ten for a blow job, anything to get them to stop.

"Hey." Carlos knocks on my head with his knuckles. "You cool with this?"

"Sure, I'm cool."

A Ford Taurus pulls up. Carlos leans in the window; the trick is a gringo, older, like forty, and he seems nervous, craning his neck to get a look at me out the window. He doesn't seem impressed. Carlos laughs, which says to the trick: easy does it, this is good, let's try it out, and then I'm in the backseat. Carlos relaxes in front next to the trick.

In the motel room, I just want this trick to scram. His hair is buzz-cut; his jaw is rough with whiskers; he smells like a TV dinner; and his pale eyes dart around the room before landing on me.

"Well?"

I look at Carlos, who nods and begins removing his clothes. His body is slim, taut, and dark. His cock isn't erect but nestled like a brown dove in a nest of thread-like hair. I want to push my nose there and breathe. I undress slowly, shivering. Carlos smiles and nods me over. I go to him. He lowers his head and lets his mouth trail across my shoulder. I shudder, teeth rattling.

The trick moves to the bed, yanks the covers off, then asks real polite for us to get on the bed. Carlos lies with his head on a pillow, hair back from his face, arms stretched above his head.

"Get him hard," the trick says.

I crawl my way to Carlos. Leaning over him, I kiss his face. Carlos says, "Nice." He licks my lips, licks my chin, smiles. I kiss his throat.

"Nice, baby."

I push my face in his hair, laying tiny kisses on his temple.

Carlos breathes into my collarbone. My cock hangs heavy and throbbing between us. I touch him with my hands. I'm not worth a shit; I'm too anxious. I want this too much. I want the trick to get lost.

"Carlos?"

"Yeah?" He smiles up at my face.

I melt on top of him, relax, let it go, and hold him. His hands reach around my waist, rubbing my back. I feel his cock pressing into my stomach.

"Suck me off," he whispers in my ear.

I nod, my face still in his hair. But I just want to touch him, take my time, make it last, make it count. I start slow, rubbing his chest, then his stomach.

"Come on, faggot. Make him come." It's the trick behind us, slouched in a chair, watching.

I lift my head and glare at him.

He glares back. "You're out of your fricking mind if you think I'm wasting money on this."

I bite down on my tongue, losing my hard-on.

"Well?" the trick demands.

I want to tell him to fuck off. The trick springs from his chair. "This is bullshit!"

Carlos pushes me off him. He smiles real easy at the trick. "It's okay, amigo, it's just the *niño,* you know, he's new at this, nervous." Carlos pats my back. "Get dressed, Manny."

I shake my head. "What? No."

He nods for me to do it, then looks at the trick. "You and me have fun, *sí?*"

"Get the fuck out of here," the trick says to me.

Carlos says, "Hey, easy does it, he's going." He nods to me again. "Go on, Manny. I'll hook up with you later."

I hesitate. "Promise?"

The trick curses.

"Yeah," Carlos tells me, and the scar near his eye ticks. "I promise." I hardly hear him.

Mom told me, "Go. You have to leave, baby."

I tripped over stuff moving through the yard. It was dark. I got a pain in my stomach. So I started to run. The faster I went, the better I felt, like layers were falling off, and I ran as far as I could without stopping. When I reached Colfax Avenue, the porn shop manager made a deal with me: if I watched the register, and swept the floor after each shift, wiped come off the seats between customers, I could crash in the broom closet for free.

In that closet there's a window. If I stand on the ladder, I can push my nose to the screen. I spit in my hand and hold my cock, short and wide in my grip. As my cock grows and tightens, I'm stronger for those moments before I think of him and lifeblood come spills through the cracks between my fingers. My body sags in the corner of the closet. That's how I drift in and out of what's sleep every night since the last time I saw Carlos. My arms fall over my legs pulled to my chest, my cock nestled between them. Mostly what sleep brings is an instant replay.

The trick in the Ford Taurus is nervous. I can tell it, and Carlos can, too. We don't go.

The trick is cool and we go to the motel and toast with champagne, and then we make love—me and Carlos—and the trick cries because we're so fucking beautiful together.

The trick freaks out in the motel room and Carlos says to forget it, then says, "We're getting the hell out of here," and we hightail it back to Colfax swearing and laughing at the close call. Carlos buys me breakfast at Pete's Kitchen, eggs with soft yolk bleeding over the white, and tells me that we need to stick together.

No matter what, I don't wind up lost because I don't know exactly where this motel is, and that bunch of crackers doesn't shove me face-first in the concrete while one takes a leak on the back of my neck. I don't stumble down streets and end up in a head shop lifting a pack of "all natural" cigarettes and getting hauled off to jail. I don't stay the night in a cell where I think I see the trick in the Taurus as a moon face glaring through the hole of a window. I don't scream until the guard promises to knock me out cold.

There's a tiny headline in the back of the newspaper about a hustler that got cut up in a motel room off Colfax. I put fifty cents in every newspaper stand I can find on the avenue and carry as many papers as I can back to the closet. The air smells like newsprint. Willy waves at me as I'm walking between the newsstands and the porn shop. The junkie's arm trembles. He looks like fucking hell, and I tell him so.

"Thanks, friend." Willy's eyes are foggy.

Black Tina grabs me on my third trip with the newspapers.

"Okay, this isn't doing you a lick of good." The whore knocks the papers out of my arms and I lunge for them, screaming.

"Okay, Manny," she says, still steady, calm. "A friend of mine will load you up so you can sleep this shit off."

"Fuck you," I say. The sun hasn't shone in three days. The air is biting and cold and inky.

Black Tina grabs my arm. She studies my face, and when she breathes on me, the air is sour with vodka. Her mascara is running. "I know where this heads, Manny. I know what you're after."

Yeah, she would know what I want, the whore who carries a knife in her purse.

I clean up and buy a pair of boots just like his. I take up the southeast corner and hold it. The other hustlers avoid me; they think I'm insane. Eventually, a car slows down at the curb: a trick, the first one. He isn't the one I'm waiting for, but that's going to take time, and so this one will do. I got the heat inside me, and it's exactly what the trick thinks it is, and so he sizes me up warily. I show him the smile. The trick relaxes. I climb into his car, coiled tight on the seat.

The gringo tells me to bend over so he can see my cherry ass. The trick swabs the cherry with spit on his finger. Then the trick gasps, "Motherfuckinggodohgodthatfeelsgood."

But it's only this for me: bile washing over my tongue, payback in my heart, and oh, I got the guts, *comprende*?

CONTRIBUTORS

Steve Almond's latest book is *Candyfreak: A Journey Through the Chocolate Underbelly of America.* He is also the author of the story collection *My Life in Heavy Metal.* For more information on his various perversions, check out www.stevenalmond.com.

Greta Christina is the editor of *Paying for It: A Guide by Sex Workers for Their Customers.* Her writing has appeared in both *Ms.* and *Penthouse* magazines and several anthologies. Her erotic novella, "Bending," is part of a trio called *Three Kinds of Asking for It* coming out in June 2005.

Mary Gaitskill is the author of the novel *Two Girls, Fat and Thin* as well as the story collections *Bad Behavior* and *Because They Wanted To,* which was nominated for the PEN/Faulkner in 1998. Her story "Secretary" was the basis for the feature film of the same name. She has taught creative writing at the University of California, the University of Houston, New York University, Brown University, and Syracuse University. Her stories and essays have appeared in *The New Yorker, Harper's, Esquire, Best American Short Stories 1993,* and *The O. Henry Prize Stories 1998.* In 2002 she was awarded a Guggenheim Fellowship for fiction.

Martha Garvey's writing has appeared in *Best American Erotica 2000* and *Exhibitions,* under the name Nell Carberry. She lives in the New York area with her beloved husband and their remarkable dog. She welcomes your comments at mgarveynyc@yahoo.com.

Nelson George is the author of novels, nonfiction, and screenplays. His latest novel, *The Accidental Hunter,* is coming out this year. His last nonfiction work was *Post-Soul Nation,* which is now available in paperback. He executive-produced the critically acclaimed HBO film *Everyday People.* He lives in Brooklyn, New York.

Alicia Gifford has been writing short fiction since the fall of 2000, when she took her first class at UCLA Extension's Writers Program. In addition to appearing in *The Barcelona Review,* her work appears or is upcoming in *NFG Magazine, The Mississippi Review, The Paumanok Review, Pig Iron Malt,* and a one-sentence story in www.thephonebook.com. "Only the beginning," you'll hear her sing on a good day. She lives and loves near Los Angeles.

Robert Glück is the author of nine books of poetry and fiction, including the three novels *Denny Smith, Margery Kempe,* and *Jack the Modernist.* He's an editor of *Narrativity,* a web site on narrative theory, at www.sfsu.edu/~poetry/narrativity/issueone.html.

Bert Hart, age 61 and married, lives in Madison, Wisconsin. This is his first published work. He is now at work on a longer story, an alternate history in which Anne Frank survives the war.

P. S. Haven was raised on comic books, *Star Wars,* and his dad's *Playboy* collection, all of which he still enjoys to this day. His work has been published at www.scarletletters.com, www.cleansheets.com, and www.peacockblue.com, as well as in *Taboo: Forbidden Fantasies for Couples,* edited by Violet Blue. Please visit www.pshaven.com.

Maria Dahvana Headley's plays have been developed at venues including the Sundance Playwright's Lab and The Kennedy Center. In an effort to wring profit from her expensive New York University education, she's currently thigh deep in a screenplay, a novel, and a short story collection. "Brontitis" is her first piece of erotica. She lives in Seattle.

Shu-Huei Henrickson's writing has appeared in *Standards, American Voices, Fourth Genre, Mind in Motion, Fiction International, Spectacle, Earth's Daughters, Out of Line, Towers, Seven Seas Magazine,* and

Drexel Online Journal. An essay is forthcoming in *Under the Sun*. Her work also appears in the anthology *Toddler: Real-Life Stories of Those Fickle, Irrational, Urgent, Tiny People We Love.*

Karl Iagnemma's writing has appeared in *Playboy, The Best American Short Stories, The Pushcart Prize Anthology,* and *The Journal of Autonomous Robots*. His first book of short stories, *On the Nature of Human Romantic Interaction,* was published in 2003.

Bernice L. McFadden is a Brooklyn native and resident. She is the mother of one daughter, R'yane Azsa, and the author of the novels *Camillia's Roses, Loving Donovan, Sugar, The Warmest December,* and *This Bitter Earth*. Visit her at www.pageturner.net/bernicemcfadden/.

Lisa Montanarelli is coauthor of two nonfiction books, *The First Year—Hepatitis C* and *Forgotten Faces*. She has written for *Agence France-Presse, The San Francisco Bay Guardian, Art and Antiques Magazine, Playboy,* and more than a dozen fiction anthologies. She's delighted to be in the *Best American Erotica* series for the second year in a row. Visit her at www.lisamontanarelli.com.

Mistress Morgana Maye is a professional dominant and BDSM educator who lives and works in San Francisco. While she's delighted to theorize on the fetishes of the powerful and famous, in real life she would never violate the confidences of the men and women who visit her for sessions. To learn more, visit www.mistressmorgana.com.

Bill Noble is a writer and activist in Northern California. He is the longtime fiction editor of the online magazine *Clean Sheets* and a volunteer with the Human Awareness Institute. His erotic chapbook, *May Touch Redeem Us,* is at www.slowtrains.com. This is his third appearance in the *Best American Erotica* series.

Canadian-born **Andy Quan** has lived in Sydney, Australia since 1999. He is the author of the fiction collection *Calendar Boy* and a book of poetry, *Slant*. His smut has been published in five of the *Best Gay Erotica* series, three *Quickies,* and numerous other anthologies. Visit www.andyquan.com.

Carol Queen has a doctorate in sexology. She is an award-winning erotic author and essayist. She is the author of *The Leather Daddy and the Femme, Exhibitionism for the Shy,* and *Real Live Nude Girl.* She is the author of several excellent erotic anthologies including the collection from which her *Best American Erotica 2005* story is taken, *Five Minute Erotica.* She lives in San Francisco and works at/co-owns Good Vibrations. Visit her at www.carolqueen.com.

Thomas Roche is the author or editor of ten published books in the fantasy, horror, crime-noir, and erotica fields. In recent years he has worked his mojo on the Web, showcasing his noir and fetish photography. His new web sites are www.crime-and-punishment.net, www.smarttarts.com, www.noirotica.net, and www.skidroche.com. He maintains a web log at www.thomasroche.livejournal.com, and hundreds of his stories and erotic comics are indexed at www.skidroche.com. He is currently working on his next anthology, *Naughty Detective Stories from A to Z,* a graphic novel, and a perpetually unfinished crime trilogy.

Simon Sheppard is the author of *Kinkorama: Dispatches from the Front Lines of Perversion, Sex Parties 101,* and the short-story collections *In Deep* and *Hotter Than Hell.* His work has appeared in well over one hundred anthologies, including four previous editions of *The Best American Erotica* and nine of *Best Gay Erotica.* He also writes the columns "Perv," at www.gay.com, and "Sex Talk," which is syndicated in queer newspapers and online. Visit him at www.simonsheppard.com.

Jane Smiley is the author of many novels, including *A Thousand Acres,* which won the Pulitzer Prize. In 2001, she was inducted into the American Academy of Arts and Letters. Excerpts from her novels *Good Faith* and *Horse Heaven* were featured in the *Best American Erotica* series. She lives in Northern California.

Cecilia Tan has been writing erotica since she was a teenager, but didn't get around to publishing any until about ten years later. Now firmly in her late thirties, Tan's work has appeared just about everywhere erotica can be, including *Ms., Asimov's, Penthouse,* Nerve.com, and many other places. She also edits anthologies of erotic fiction for Circlet Press. The story "The Magician's Assistant" was written for Penn Gillette. Read more at www.ceciliatan.com.

Lana Gail Taylor is a pseudonym for Alana Noël Voth, a single mom and M.F.A. student at the University of Oregon. Her writing has appeared in *Best Women's Erotica 2004; Best Gay Erotica 2004; Best Lesbian Love Stories 2004; Best Bisexual Women's Erotica; Ripe Fruit: Erotica for Well Seasoned Lovers; Bedroom Eyes: Lesbians in the Boudoir; Slow Trains Literary Journal; Element Magazine;* and *Blithe House Quarterly.*

Sharon Wachsler has published over one hundred poems, essays, stories, and cartoons in dozens of books and periodicals, including *Best American Erotica 2004, On Our Backs, Harrington Lesbian Fiction Quarterly,* and *Best Lesbian Erotica 2003.* Sharon edits *Breath & Shadow,* the disability literature and culture journal. To read her humor columns or learn more about Sharon, visit www.sharonwachsler.com or www.abilitymaine.org/breath.

CREDITS

READER SURVEY

Please return this survey, or any other BAE correspondence, to Susie Bright, BAE-Feedback, P. O. Box 8377, Santa Cruz, CA 95061. Or e-mail your reply to BAE@susiebright.com.

1. What are your favorite stories in this year's collection?

   _____

   _____

2. Have you read previous years' editions of *The Best American Erotica*?

   _____

3. Do you have any favorite stories or authors from those previous collections?

   _____

   _____

4. Do you have any recommendations for next year's *The Best American Erotica 2006*? (Nominated stories must have been published in North America, in any form—book, periodical, Internet—between March 1, 2005, and March 1, 2006.)

   _____

   _____

5. How old are you? _____

6. Male or female? _____

7. Where do you live? _____

8. Any other suggestions for the series?

   _____

   _____

Thanks so much; your comments are truly appreciated. If you send me your e-mail address, I will reply to you when I receive your feedback.